"YOU WANNA DO SOMETHING FOR NANCY, GET HER REVENGE? DO IT HOT, DO IT NOW."

Drover turned and looked at the man in the wheelchair. "I give you the edge on Slim," Tony Rolls said. "What do you say, Jimmy?"

A long time ago, before Johno, there had been Nancy. Before the lady in the gray suit standing on a knoll in a cemetery, there had been a girl in a bright yellow dress and a bright smile. Nancy had love in her then. It was clean then.

"What about Slim Dingo?" Drover said.

"He bleeds, Jimmy," Tony Rolls said, and smiled. The smile was the ugliest thing Drover had ever seen. "Bleeds," Tony Rolls repeated, seeing the blood.

Worse, Drover could see it too.

Drover

BILL GRANGER

AVON BOOKS ◆ NEW YORK

AVON BOOKS
A division of
The Hearst Corporation
1350 Avenue of the Americas
New York, New York 10019

Copyright © 1991 by Granger and Granger, Inc.
Published by arrangement with the author
Library of Congress Catalog Card Number: 90-49661
ISBN: 0-380-71210-5

Published in hardcover by William Morrow and Company, Inc.; for information address Permissions Department, William Morrow and Company, Inc., 1350 Avenue of the Americas, New York, New York 10019.

First Avon Books Printing: May 1992

AVON TRADEMARK REG. U.S. PAT. OFF. AND IN OTHER COUNTRIES, MARCA REGISTRADA, HECHO EN U.S.A.

Printed in the U.S.A.

RA   10   9   8   7   6   5   4   3   2   1

ACKNOWLEDGMENTS

The author wishes to thank Richard Martins, Jean Anderson Williams of Next Door, Brian Wolfgang Huebner, John Kelly, Polly Kelly of the mermaids, Jim Agnew, and others too shy to be named for explaining some of the arcana of sports gambling, commodities trading, and aiding in research. If I got it right, any of it, they get credit; if not, put the blame on me. Thanks is also given to Dusty Sanders of the *Rocky Mountain News* for telling me about his town, buying me a drink at the Press Club, and to the Denver Press Club members who let me join their gallant band one spring day. Thanks as well to the distinguished faculty of Maguire University, founded in 1963 in a Forest Park, Illinois saloon, who let me join the faculty for the purpose of researching a number of important football and basketball games, including the Super Bowl and the Final Four.

PRINCIPAL CHARACTERS

Jimmy Drover—ex-sportswriter banned from journalism for knowing "known criminals," who is as straight as he can be given the people he knows. He lives on a pier in Santa Cruz and works the world of sports and gambling.

Black Kelly—his buddy and an ex-Chicago fire fighter who devotes his life to lotteries and cooking firehouse pot roast on the pier at Santa Cruz amidst the quiche eaters.

Nancy Harrington—whose first bad break in life was Johno and who keeps seeing trouble.

Tony Rolls—a Chicago mobster on the retired side who has more cousins in Vegas than in Palermo.

Tommy Sain—who has a disease called gambling he thinks he can cure with more of the same.

Bart Brixton—commodities trader who wants to hit the big one by fixing an NFL game.

Lenny Gascon—a twenty-six-year-old ego wrapped in a Cajun body who happens to throw footballs better than anyone.

Lori Gibbons—Len's main squeeze who doesn't do drugs and doesn't do men who do.

Frances Downes—size 4 model who would put her life in the toilet for a line of cocaine.

Slim Dingo—Texas sleaze who figures he can own women when not playing cards for the mob—and the G.

CHAPTER 1

JIMMY DROVER TOOK the phone from across the bar. Black Kelly watched him listen. When it was over, Drover said, "I'll be there."

He handed the phone back to Kelly who hung it on the hook under the mahogany. Cardboard letters hanging on the back bar mirror wished everyone Merry Christmas though it was October in northern California. Some things never got thrown away in Kelly's life.

"Bad news." Kelly wasn't asking.

"No. When you get a call at two in the morning, it's always good news."

"Who is she?"

"Nancy Harrington."

"Girlfriend."

"I used to think so."

"Down on her luck?"

"Ran out yesterday morning."

"You want another?"

"Definitely."

This time Kelly put the bottle of Red Label on the bar after he poured off a portion. Kelly poured himself V.O. and soda. "A child's portion." He had the habit of saying that too many times but no one seemed to count.

The fog was snug along the night shoreline, filling in the blanks, hiding the tops of the rides on the boardwalk

1

along the beach. Santa Cruz was one hundred miles and a world south of San Francisco. It was the last small city in California where people walked to work. Kelly's was in the middle of the long pier that poked from the beach into the Pacific. There was, as the song has it, no one in the place except you and me.

"Nancy Payton. Sang in the saloons in Vegas. Then she met a highroller named Johno Harrington and she liked him better than anything."

"Better than you?"

"Better than me."

"And she married him."

"Nancy was that way. The marrying kind. A blonde, she had a voice halfway to Billie Holiday but half only counts when you bet the first two quarters."

"So what about her luck?"

"Johno just killed himself. In their bathroom. He put a gun under his chin and guessed he'd hit the target. Asshole."

"You knew him?"

"Vegas loves guys like Johno. They stitch 'Loser' on their foreheads. He had good jobs, he worked construction, contractor or something, he could hustle enough. They lived in Anaheim, wall-to-wall building going on. But he was a big shot, he played poker with people like Slim Dingo."

"And lost."

"His shirt and more. Nancy said Slim was on him about what he owed. Funny. I never heard of Slim extending anyone credit." Drover stared at his brown drink and thought about it and the tone of Nancy's voice. There wasn't pain in it, just exhaustion. She recited what had happened the way a railroad dispatcher reads you a timetable. This happened and then this happened. All aboard and have a nice day.

"What does she want?"

"My shoulder. I'm driving down. Borrow the bus?"

"You leaving now?"

"Now. Get through L.A. before gridlock."

"Need anything?"

"Nancy."

Kelly looked at him.

"But that was over a long time ago," Drover added.

CHAPTER 2

SUICIDES ARE NEVER easy to bury. There are papers and police inquiries and more papers. The funeral director fretted openly about makeup on the corpse. It was a closed coffin wake, who cared how much lipstick Johno wore?

Nancy shivered when Drover put his arms around her and hugged. The hug was what she had needed most. And then he had taken care of some details and she realized she had needed that as well. Nancy was still as pretty as a songbird can be. She knew how to hold a stage and fend off drunks and make magic when the room held four people but she didn't know how to believe that her Johno had blown his brains out.

The second night, she talked it out with Drover.

He was staying at the Hi-De-Ho Lodge near Knott's Berry Farm. He had one gym bag's worth of underwear, polo shirts, and an electric shaver kit. Nancy had asked him to stay in the house with her and he had wanted to, really wanted to, but there was too much temptation for that.

They buried Johno at noon. Actually, the burial had to be taken on faith because they had left the casket resting on metal rods above the open earth which was covered with Astroturf. In the modern funeral, you don't say good-bye to the deceased; it is more in the nature of "see you later." He wasn't buried in the Catholic cemetery or out of the Catholic Church because suicide is against Catholic tradition—nothing is ever bad enough to kill yourself over because it can always get worse.

After the funeral, Nancy sat in her kitchen. She sat with a see-through in her hand. The ice cubes in the glass numbed her. She stared at the martini and talked to it, not to Drover, but Drover was on the other side of the kitchen table and he overheard.

"Johno was in bad to Slim Dingo. Worse than I must have known but I knew he had troubles. I knew Slim in Vegas, he was a shit, I wouldn't touch him."

"I never met him."

"You did yourself a favor." The blonde hair was frosted ashen. The eyes were pale pools of quicksand. Nancy always sucked you in by the way she looked. At least, Drover had always thought so. "I wish I would have . . ." she began.

"What?"

"He wanted me. Slim Dingo. He said that when Johno was down in San Diego on a job, he said I should come out to his ranch and he would knock off the juice loan to Johno for. . . ."

Drover saw.

Her eyes were wet. "I did it."

"You did it for Johno."

"I loved him. He made me laugh. Then he'd get this crazy thing come over him, he had to throw his money away. I could keep some of it but he was crazy when he was like that."

"Slim Dingo. I should meet him."

"Why?"

"I don't know. Maybe to see a living shit."

"I did it too. I went to his ranch and we. . . . I did it too. And then he said he was going to suck in Johno so

we could do it again real soon. He said I was better than
a four-hundred-dollar-a-night whore and he told me that.''

''Nancy.''

''I'm putting this on you because I can't believe it. I've
got to get it out of my head so I can see it. People make
their own misery, don't they? They can't let well enough
alone. They've got to do something to make God forgive
them, don't they?''

''Nobody needs forgiving. You loved Johno, that's all.''
Why the hell was he reassuring her about that? Why didn't
he say that he had loved her more than Johno ever did, the
way she looked in the spotlight, singing Gershwin as
though she and George had put the song together themselves? But she hurt and he smeared her with balm. There,
there, the way monkeys groom each other and mothers
silence children's tears.

She shook her head and took his hand across the table.
''I'm sorry, Jim. I'm sorry I called you. I had to call someone, I was in this house and I had to call someone. You
helped me.''

''I told you once I loved you.''

''And I told you once I loved Johno.''

Silence.

''God, I loved Johno, he didn't have to kill himself.''

Silence again.

She started to cry.

He understood enough to hold her hands across the
kitchen table and not to say anything.

CHAPTER 3

MORNING FOG OBLITERATED Santa Cruz. The fog made Drover feel good, always had. Fog made him the invisible man, the way he liked to be as a kid back in Chicago, spying on the old neighborhood from the rooftop of the Shakespeare movie theater. He could lie on the roof and watch his mom call him from the gray-painted back porch of the six-flat and watch the beat cop Reilly sneak into the side door of Deuce's Tap for a freebie morning shot and watch the world from the place where it couldn't hide its secrets. That's what the California coast fog did for him; made him a kid again.

He had the morning press folded in his hand. Six days after Johno and Nancy. He carried the papers inside the wider pages of *The Wall Street Journal*. The papers were about games and gambling on games. The sports in the *Journal,* for instance, were usually done by Fred Klein, a nice guy from Chicago, and the rest of the games were done by business and political writers. Everything in the paper was about gambling in the long run and he had explained this to Kelly and Kelly had nodded and explained the secrets of the lottery to him.

He was in sports and gambling activities and people seriously in the games depend on knowing a lot of things. That's why he held all these papers in his hand.

He was thinking about Nancy again when he noticed the van. GMC. Gray. Customized by Geneva Vans.

Illinois plates.

Illinois goddamned plates.

He was parallel with the van and saw the handicapped card in the window. The plates didn't register but now they might as well have carried the owner's name on them.

A guy came from around the back of the van. He stared at Drover. He wore a short-sleeve white shirt with its square tail hanging out over the pants, scarcely concealing the little bulge in his belt line. The guy's pale face was not at all like California. You acquired that shade of pale by sleeping days. Night-shift pale.

Drover was dead still.

"Inside," the guy said. There weren't a lot of extra words, because he was one of those guys who starts life with a roll full of words and doesn't want to run out before they put two dimes on his eyes. He had big arms. He nodded at the van, in case Drover missed the point.

The sliding door with darkened windows slid open.

"Hullo, Jimmy."

Drover didn't speak. The burden of the press in his left hand was bleeding black news onto his palm.

"Come on," he said. The speaker sat at a Formica-topped table in a wheelchair. A second man was seated in a captain's chair. The second man was pouring a cup of coffee.

"Your mother never told you come in outta the rain?"

"It never rains in California," Drover said.

"They got you brainwashed, Jimmy," the wheelchair man said. He was squat but not soft. His neck was thick. Muscles lay unused beneath the first layer of self-indulgent flesh. Drover remembered Tony Rolls always ate Oreo cookies. His hands were big enough to choke a horse. There was a story in Chicago that Tony Rolls had done just that forty years ago when sheer muscle still proved something and there was a horse around to prove it on.

Drover put his free hand on the ledge of the van's roof at the opening and stuck his head inside. Nothing was neat but it never is in a custom van from the moment it's driven out of the showroom. A twenty-inch Zenith and a VCR were shelved in one corner, along with a library of videocassettes. The Mr. Coffee was plugged into one of a series of ivory-plated outlets around the crushed gray velour interior.

"Surprised to see me?" the man said. His voice still rumbled like an elevated train above a narrow city block. "Tell me. I bet you're surprised."

Drover pulled his head back to look at the lines of the van. "You get good mileage?"

"Seven, eight, who knows? You gotta count, you can't afford one." The old man smiled. Those horse-choking fingers settled around a red ceramic cup and drew it to his lips. "Good coffee, Jimmy. Not with an egg, that's too messy, but pretty good. You wanna doughnut?"

"Tony Rolls still thinks the world is flat," Drover said. He stared at the old man who was waiting for a smile. Drover's face was not made for smiles. When one slipped through, it came out sardonic.

"I know it's round but that don't make me a dime," Tony Rolls said.

"So Tony Rolls still don't fly."

"I coulda gone to a shrink to talk myself out of it, but what the hell," Tony Rolls said. He shrugged. He was used to the way Drover talked about him in the third person. It put them both outside the man in the wheelchair where they both could look at the act, look at the way it went down with the two companions in their white shirts, sunglasses, and waistline bulges that were not caused by fat.

"I know shrinks. My Mae Tina went to a shrink when she was in school. Shrink tells her she's got sexual suppression. Imagine telling that to a fourteen-year-old girl."

"What happened to the shrink?"

"He ain't in business I heard," Tony Rolls said. He shrugged at the thought. "Shrink'll tell you you can't fly because your second grade teacher wouldn't let you go wee-wee during spelling test. Or something. I want silly talk, I listen to Don Rickles at the Trop, it's a lot more fun, am I right? I don't need to ask something from someone who don't know what the hell he's talking about."

"Yeah. What the hell," Drover said.

"You in or out?" said the guy standing next to him, wasting four more words off the roll. He bumped Drover. Drover bumped back and felt the bruise of the hidden pistol in the guy's belt.

"This a game?" Drover asked Tony Rolls. "If you're hustling morning action, get a better shill than Gonzo. He'll scare off the marks."

Tony Rolls made a small smile. "Nah. No game. Just a talk. Vin, get the elevator, get me down. I wanna see the ocean with the man. Walk in the rain."

The second man crawled out of the van and worked the electric lift. Tony Rolls wheeled himself onto the platform that lowered his bulk to the sidewalk. Drover took a step back and watched.

"You wanna push me? I like to save on my batteries," Tony Rolls said.

"You carry my papers," Drover said, dropping them on his lap.

"What're ya reading *The Wall Street Journal* for?"

"Same reason I read the *Racing Form* and *The National*," Drover said.

"Yeah. I guess it's all the same."

"You're in a no-parking zone, Tony. You might get a ticket."

"Jesus Christ, I don't wanna break the law," Tony Rolls said. "Vin. You and Thomas find a place to park this thing while I go singing in the rain with Jimmy."

"I should go with you," Vin said. Thomas didn't feel the need to open his roll again.

"Whaddaya think? Jimmy's gonna shove me in the ocean?" The A train voice rumbled past in good humor—it had to be the voice because there wasn't an elevated train in California. "Go on, Vin. Come by for me in a half hour. It'll take me a half hour. A half hour long enough?" The last went to Drover.

"Ten seconds is enough," Drover said. "The answer is no."

"Maybe you didn't hear the question the right way the first time."

Vin and Thomas gave Drover the look. The look came out of the rehearsal halls in all the West Side Chicago bars, trattorias, and gaming rooms they had trained in. The look was the same on Taylor Street as it was in River Forest, even if the clothes might be different. Drover gave as much thought to the look as he did to the owners of them. All he knew was that Tony Rolls had spoiled the perfect solitude of the foggy morning. It was time to climb down from the roof of the Shakespeare Theater.

The wheels bumped over the uneven planking of the pier. Ocean surged against the pilings. The stink of fish and ocean air mingled. The fog-muted morning life began stirring on the pier. The pier was lined with restaurants and bait shops and boutiques. A hundred years ago, Santa Cruz decided a big pier was what it needed to become a first-class port. It wasn't.

"I called you because I needed you," Tony Rolls said. He stared straight ahead. The newspapers rested on his lap with one horse-choker holding them down. Gulls squealed at the fog, to find each other.

"I don't play in your league," Drover said.

"Everybody plays in our league," Tony Rolls said. "You're different, I appreciate that even if some people don't. You keep yourself to yourself and you don't bother me." Like an exterminator giving a pass to a bug. "But this thing that's come up, well, it's something you can do. Something you gotta do."

"Not for you."

"For the good of humanity, then," Tony Rolls said.

"That's the key word all right, Tony. Humanity. Say humanity to me and I start waving the flag."

"All right, all right, I'll cut the bullshit. The good of our . . . league and the good of the game," Tony Rolls said. "The goose has been laying golden eggs and we don't want to ace it because golden eggs don't come along every day."

"I never thought of pro football as a goose. You should have been a poet or a farmer."

"Oregon. Figure a John Square place like Oregon got into the parley card business for a lottery. Figure it. Ten years, there'll be parleys in every state. You think that bothers me? It just opens up the game, Jimmy. You know how many people out there would like to bet on football but don't know how it works? They don't know a spread or beating the spot. Sure, you don't believe me but it's true. I was in New York once, I ask this guy why they got those pipes on the street the steam comes up. I wanna know where the steam comes from, I mean, I never seen that in any other town in my life. What's going on? So I ask this guy and he's grown up in Brooklyn, for Christ's sake, and he says he don't know. That's the way it is with everyone: No one asks. I like Oregon, they're running a remedial course on parlay betting and it'll be good for everyone's business. If we had the only house in Vegas, you think that'd make me happy? You need a town full of houses. A state full. A country full.''

"The government should put you on a literacy task force,'' Drover said.

"I don't get it.''

"You want everybody to learn.''

"Oh. Yeah. I see what you mean.''

Drover stopped pushing. He had found his favorite bench, the one he used on Monday mornings to run down the Sunday scores in the *Los Angeles Times*.

He sat down and looked at Tony Rolls on the same level. He let his hands rest on each other and his elbows rested on his knees. He waited.

"Jimmy, Jimmy,'' Tony Rolls said. He shook his head. "I drive out to Vegas every spring, see my cousins.''

"I hope everyone is well.''

"I see, I party, I listen. I'm an old man, they got respect, they tell me things. Sometimes, I think I can help them out. I think about you out here in California. I look at a map. I'm in Vegas, California is just over here. I didn't know there was so many mountains but I make the trip, I come to you after you turn me down the first time—''

"Tony Rolls being sincere,'' Drover said, putting the third person out there again even though the two drivers were out hunting a parking place. "You got balls. I ought to push you in the ocean except it would turn out your chair floats and has a secret outboard motor on it. You don't get it when I say no. Nobody ever got into trouble saying no, unless you count Thomas More and he was pretending it was yes all along. That's what got him into trouble. I'm straightforward. No is no.''

"I saw the movie,'' Tony Rolls said. "Since I got handicapped, I seen every movie ever made. Thomas More,

you know what I think? I think he was a schmuck, Jimmy.
The main guy, the king guy, wants him to say yes. So he
says yes, so what? The king is gonna do what the king
wants to do, It don't matter if Thomas More says diddly-
squat. So he says yes, so what? He goes to confession,
gets off. He ought to know his own religion, what's the
big thing? People today get divorced all the time, even
Catholics, my cousin Sally's gone through two legit wives,
I ain't even talking about what he drags out on Friday
nights. No means no if it was what you think it was but it
ain't.''

"That's a nice speech, Tony. I wish I had a tape re-
corder.''

"I don't need wires around me.''

"Free enterprise, Tony. That's what this is, the one thing
the Outfit is always against if it means competing with
anyone. Some guys on the Chicago Board of Trade are
trading in sports-gambling futures.''

"That's what I told you when I called.''

"So what's the harm, Tone? They stealing from you
guys or what?''

"Stealing is stealing,'' Tony Rolls said.

"So make them pay a street tax. You got guys for that.''

"This is not about that. It doesn't amount to that much
except . . . well, it amounts to something.''

"What is this about really?'' Drover said.

"These guys on the CBOT. They work in two ways.
For three, four years, they put up a . . . what they call
. . . a basket of games. Maybe twenty games over the
whole season. They work it like a futures trade. Maybe
thirty, forty maybe fifty guys. They buy and sell the
games against each other before the fucking season starts
and then they can middle their bets the rest of the season
by selling individual games to their own chumps. So you

got fifty inside guys and maybe a couple of thousand outside guys. That's a lot of guys.''

"And you guys spill that much action with morning coffee,'' Drover said.

"We don't want the game on the commodities exchange. That's chicken feed. But what's behind it? I mean, these trades are always looking for an edge and it ain't ten percent. The guys that set up the basket of games in the first place—I mean, why those twenty games and not others? I mean, we're talking over six hundred games in the regular season and playoffs, so why those twenty? And the traders, they lay off their bets with their regular bookies and that begins to bother some people. They ain't playing by rules nobody understands. How the fuck you bet on a game ain't gonna be played for eight weeks?''

"They're betting on other things. Injuries. Weather. It's a game. So they bet a few hundred thou, so what, Tony? They like to bet on things. It's what they do for a living.''

"If it was just chump money, I wouldn't care. But there's more,'' Tony Rolls said, letting his El-train voice rumble in his gut.

"Is that the word on the streets?'' Drover gave the last four words the solid sound of a cliché.

"I wanna know what the word is, not hear my own questions,'' Tony Rolls said. "You're gonna be my outside audit.''

"That isn't me, Tone.''

"Not even for trade?''

"You got nothing I want.''

"Because you don't want nothing, right?''

"Nothing you got.''

"I got a houseguest in three weeks. Comin' out to Chicago.''

"How nice for you.''

"Something you want."

Drover waited. The teasing could go on a long time if you didn't shut it up.

Tony Rolls stared at his thick fingers, turned his wrists, checked out the fingers in profile. "How's Nancy? You went to see her after Johno killed himself?"

Drover said nothing.

"Now you say, 'Nancy who?' or something, make it look like it doesn't mean nothing."

"I know lots of Nancys."

"This is the only widow you know by that name," Tony Rolls said.

"What do you want, Tone?"

"I want you to do me a favor. Legit."

"What about Nancy?"

"You want to do the right thing for her. The right thing is to do something for Johno. Doing something for Johno involves my houseguest."

Drover thought the fog was all ruined, like the morning. He was up on the roof of the old movie house but now everyone could see him and they were watching him. His mom and the old cop had paused and were staring straight at him. Tony Rolls had joined them.

"Slim Dingo. He comes to pay his respects to me every year. He gets his California tan on an airplane and comes out to Chicago in the fall and he pays respect, comes to play some poker. And to take my money. We play a little friendly game. It used to be friendlier. Slim Dingo is so full of himself he forgets where he is. He's in my house, he's my guest. He does that cowboy cool bullshit and he plays for blood every time. He's getting to be a pain in the ass but I can't not invite him just for face. For the respect he shows me because by cousin Theo wanted him to come out once a year, show his crippled old cousin a good time, show him what he's missing not living in

Vegas. Last year, Slim Dingo took enough to retire but he ain't the retiring kind.''

"Not like you.''

"Not like me. What'd I need to learn to fly for? I got time. I got a nice van. I see the country. I see what's going on. People ain't got time got to learn to fly. I gave up on that part.''

"Slim is going to play cards at your house.''

"Nice game. Used to be nicer. A few pals come around. You could come around, do what you gotta do with Slim.''

"I can get Slim anyplace. If I want to get Slim. You aren't doing me any favors.''

Tony Rolls made a face that might have been a portrait of a man lost in thought. Except Tony was an actor and he was never lost.

"You know why I don't fly? Twenty years ago, I was in Detroit doing business with some friends in the union. I got a commuter plane in, I was getting the plane out. A twin-engine Cessna. Zip, Zip, in and out, nobody spends the night in Detroit unless he's unlucky or black, which is the same thing. I do my business and get the limo to the airport. Except, this is the God's truth, the car gets a flat. A flat on a thirty-thousand stretch Caddy, as thirty thousand was in those days. A fucking tire. Well, to make a story shorter, we get to the airport and the plane is gone.''

Drover got up from the bench. He went over to Tony and picked up the papers on his lap. He carried the papers to the ancient piling jutting up from the water. He looked into the fog.

"The plane went down in Lake Michigan. A bomb,'' Tony Rolls said.

"Sell the story to Amtrak,'' Drover said over his shoulder.

"There's a point.''

Both men were silent a moment.

"Slim Dingo is a buttoned-up man. He was on *Wide World of Sports* once, showing why he's such a great poker hustler. It was all bullshit, full of cowboy hats and these guys in their cowboy shirts and those skinny strings around their necks. All bullshit, like television is. But even if it wasn't bullshit, even if Mike Wallace was asking questions, it wouldn't have mattered. Slim made himself up a long time ago. If he was in *Who's Who*, it'd be fiction. But you got to get under his skin to make an edge. I don't mean nothing but you can't beat him flat out, Jimmy. You ain't in his league."

"Who said I wanted to?"

"You can't fog me, kid," Tony Rolls said. He was down there in the alley with the cop, staring up at him on the theater roof. His mom was shaking her head, knowing he would come to no good.

"You wanna do something for Nancy, get her revenge? You do it wrong because you ain't got the blood. You want to do it hot, you wanna do it now."

" 'Revenge is a dish best eaten cold,' " Drover remembered.

"There. You didn't forget everything. So how do you get under Slim Dingo, give yourself the edge?"

"And you know."

"And I know," Tony Rolls said. "It's like me and the airplanes. I know my weakness and that don't make it any easier. If you was to force me to get on a plane, I know the odds are it ain't gonna crash but knowing and feeling is two different things. Slim knows what his problem is but that don't make it better if it comes up."

"You're gonna tell me."

Dull, without any tone. Drover turned and looked at the man in the wheelchair.

"And invite you to my house," Tony Rolls said. "Don't forget that."

"A great honor," Drover said.

"Hey, fuck you. I don't have to be nice. But I like you. I even liked Johno, even if he was a fuckup."

"Talk nice, Tone. You're in California, not on the West Side."

"I forgot. It was the fog. Yeah." He paused. "I give you the edge on Slim."

"Why?"

"Because then you got to listen to me about the other thing."

"That's small-time," Drover said. "You don't care if Oregon steals a corner of the chump market, why do you care about a futures exchange on football betting?"

"Why do you think?"

"Socrates time."

Tony shook his head again. "Why do you think?"

Drover said, "Because it's gonna hurt you more than Oregon."

"That's it. Part. And there's more, stuff you can use legit."

"That's twice you used that word, three times counting your cousin's wives. One more and your turn into the tooth fairy."

"What do you say, Jimmy?"

A long time ago, before Johno, there had been Nancy. Before the lady in the gray suit standing on a knoll in a cemetery, there had been a girl in a bright yellow dress and a bright smile. Nancy had love in her then. It was clean then. He had known her when she could laugh. When she could cry on the outside if it came down to it, not inside, the way she did now.

"What about Slim Dingo?" Drover said.

"He bleeds, Jimmy," Tony Rolls said, and smiled. The smile was the ugliest thing Drover had ever seen. "Bleeds," Tony Rolls repeated, seeing the blood.

Worse, Drover could see it too.

CHAPTER 4

"HOW MUCH ARE you out?"

Drover was packed for travel. He wore jeans, sneakers, and a green pullover two-button shirt. The case on the bar was brown vinyl and held his tan summer suit, two white shirts, underclothes, and thirty thousand in one-hundred-dollar bills, wrapped in packets of fifty with red rubber bands.

He looked at Kelly and nodded at his drink glass. A trip of over three hours required two glasses of Johnny Walker Red Label with just enough ice to chill the smoke.

Kelly made the drink while he waited for the answer. They both had forgotten he had already asked the question once before that morning.

"You don't want to say?"

The September morning was made for postcards. The restaurants along the pier were just opening up. Sunlight danced on the perfect sand. The girls had already settled on the beaches for their tanning sessions and the boardwalk was filling up with the usual collection of tourists, hustlers, and drug pushers. The game room at the end of the boardwalk was crowded with noise from half a hundred games that destroyed the universe, downtown Cleveland, or race cars on video screens. The only thing the games had in common were quarter slots and total destruction of something somewhere.

Kelly and Drover had found each other by accident in this far land five years earlier. Black Kelly took almost a year to know as many people in California as he had known in his past life in Chicago. He attributed that to middle-age slowness. Now, he treated the state like his old neighborhood and Santa Cruz like his old block. Drover had been going through Cruz on his way to somewhere when he had stopped for the night. It turned out to be a long night and he never moved on. Cruz suited him as well as the next place as long as he didn't know where he really wanted to go. And Kelly suited him most of the time, except when he did his big brother act. Like now.

"May the road rise up to meet you," Black Kelly said with a phony brogue, lifting his own glass to his own lips. His thirst was constant but containable—some thought he was called Black Kelly because of his fondness for Black Label. (He wasn't. His drink was V.O.) He had a fire department pension from his previous existence when he broke his back on a 4-11, and the ability to forswear strong drink for twenty-four hours out of every seventy-two. When he was on watch—twenty-four hours on and then forty-eight off—he never touched the stuff. The watch continued now, even if the fire house days were over. Drover understood; everyone needed a schedule, especially people like him and Kelly who led unstructured lives. It was the way he needed that morning walk into town to get the papers every day.

"You didn't say how much you sent Nancy Harrington," Kelly said.

"That's perceptive," Drover said. The place was half full of late-morning people, some of whom wanted to eat. Sitting in the middle of the pier in the midst of the Pacific Ocean, Kelly's place had a formula: It only served red meat dishes. It was a success because it was so contrary.

"It's none of my business."

"That never stops you."

"The smarter thing would have been to wait to see what you could pick off Slim Dingo before you did your Lady Bountiful act for Nancy."

"This gives me an incentive," Drover said. He ran his hand through his hair. His hair was brown and stiff and cut short, all against the fashion. Somehow, it went well with the deep tan and the thin, sharp face and bright brown eyes.

"I could fix up something for Nancy down here," Kelly said.

"Nancy doesn't want charity right now."

"So what was that you gave her?"

"A loan."

"And she took it."

"She didn't have a choice."

"You pull a gun on her?"

"I pulled rank. Friends can do that."

"You told her what you're gonna try to do with Dingo?"

"No."

"You gonna tell her if it goes off?"

"That's part of it."

"You think she wants revenge?"

"Yes."

"Why?"

"It's enough that I know." It was more than enough. Slim Dingo had worked Johno because of Nancy. He had seen Nancy in the poker parlor in Southern California the first night Johno got in too deep. Johno was a fool but he was her fool and Dingo had just looked at her with those lizard eyes and figured out what he would do because he knew Nancy would do anything to save Johno. Johno went pretty far out on the string before Slim Dingo let her know what he wanted. Just a weekend with all the trimmings.

And she had done it because Johno was so far gone that if she hadn't done it, Slim would have let him drown.

It had all come out before the funeral and the trip to the cemetery where they left Johno's casket on brass and steel rods perched above an open grave covered with Astroturf so that the sight of an open hole wouldn't make tears. The gravediggers needn't have worried. Nancy was beyond crying by then. She had cried enough across a kitchen table.

She had told him in a flat, hard voice all about it. Even when he didn't want to hear. She had told it for herself, the way a drunk on a hangover turns over all the bad things he has done the night before. Slim Dingo had used her up and sent her back to Johno. And a week later, he had pulled the string anyway and Johno had drowned, his mouth full of his own blood caused by the .45 he had put under it.

Slim had sent his regrets right away and suggested a week with him at his ranch in Amarillo, just as if it hadn't mattered to him at all. Nancy had made her confession but had not waited for absolution. Only Drover understood how deep the hurt was and how it wasn't ever going to stop.

That's when Jimmy Drover had given her the money, ten grand. It had taken Kelly near six weeks to find out about it and another two to ask about it. Time was running out. The 2:15 P.M. United for Chicago was three hours away.

"Why do you trust Tony Rolls?" Kelly tried.

"He wants something."

"You don't want to fool with those guys that close," Kelly said. Suddenly serious. His eyes were clown blue sometimes when he wanted them to be and he was acting the mine host role, sipping at his V.O. and soda with one hand and explaining the universe with the other for the wonderment of customers. And sometimes they were as full of bad streets as a telephone book, with all the mean pages turned down at the corners.

"Tony wants something and I can't get him off my back until I find out what it is," Drover said. "and he knows what I want, which puts him one up already. He also knows it ain't enough, so he must know something more, something that might interest Mr. Vernon. I don't like that but I still want it." Vernon was Fox Vernon, the Las Vegas sports book and line maker and Drover had a working relationship with him. As as investigator.

"Marked cards?"

"Black, you shock me. Is that the way the Irish do it?"

"Of course. Cheating in a good cause is worthy," Kelly said. "If we had tried to pray the English out of Ireland, we'd still be on our knees."

"Not in Tony Rolls's house. This is his house. Besides, there's nothing subtle about cheating."

"You can't take Slim Dingo any other way. You ain't that good. Slim is a good watcher."

"People get distracted."

"Not Slim Dingo and not people like him."

"Maybe he's afraid of flying," Drover said. "Or something."

"You gonna play on an airplane or in that Guinea's house?"

"Might be the same thing."

"Cards, boy. You know how people cheat, that's how you can make what you call a living. That and gambling on the side. But gambling—playing poker—is all Slim does."

"It's still cards, Black. Never draw to an inside straight and never eat Cheetos because you grease the cards."

"Yeah, you're ready for Hoyledom. He gave you an

edge. Tony Rolls gave you an edge or you think it's an edge and you think it's enough to get Slim.''

"You're a good guesser."

"What's the edge?"

"It isn't an edge if everyone knows."

"What if nothing turns out right?"

"I'll be back Friday morning. If not, drag the Chicago river.''

"You think it's funny?"

"You think someone is going to hit me for a Texas card-sharp? They save that stuff for important things, like the Central States Pension Fund.''

"I'll light a candle for you."

"You don't have to. I know the way."

"Kid," Black Kelly said. He was six years older than Drover. "Kid, just take it easy."

"Nancy'll be all right. She hates herself for it but she's a survivor. She'll find another loser to adopt along the way," Drover said.

"She should have adopted you a long time ago."

"She can't stand success," Drover said. The words were too hard and they came out of some place inside him that he didn't want to open up; he didn't mean it to sound so hard. He looked at Kelly and Kelly looked away, as if he hadn't heard. That's what friends were for, to pretend to look away when you didn't want them to see you too closely.

Drover put down the empty glass. "Where's the bus?" he said.

They climbed into Kelly's Lincoln Town Car outside the restaurant. The smell of cooking hamburgers from the vents mingled with the fresh ocean smells of fish and salt. The sun was hanging flat against the blue and everyone wore sunglasses.

Kelly turned on the ignition and listened for the faint

sound of the motor. "If it don't work, don't panic. You can get him some other time."

"It'll work," Drover said.

"You don't want to tell me where your safe-deposit box is or anything? In case?"

"I'm leaving everything to the Vegetarian League to set up an eternal picket line outside your restaurant," Drover said. "Instead of Mass cards."

"That'll improve business," Kelly said.

"Anything for a friend."

"That's the kind of shit that gets you in trouble in the first place," Kelly said, and let the car roll into Drive. He didn't say another word, though he had a few thousand in mind.

CHAPTER 5

JOE CAMP WAS hot. It was the second night of the game, around that time of the morning when everyone is a little mesmerized by the cards and the succession of deals. Joe Camp had followed Tony Rolls's wheelchair into the kitchen. The kitchen was big and white with every kind of stove and freezer and rotisserie.

"Where'd you get this geek?" Joe Camp said. He had said it before.

"Which one?" as though he didn't know.

Tony Rolls picked up one of the Italian sausage sandwiches and took a bite. It was a small sandwich as these things go, smothered with *giardiniera*. He bit and chewed. The *giardiniera* was nice and hot and full of olive oil.

"The geek in the tan suit."

"I told you: He was in from the Coast. He knows my cousin Theo."

"Your cousin knows geeks."

"Electronics in California. The kind of silicone you don't put in tit implants."

"The guy wouldn't know a tit from pistachio ice cream," Joe Camp said. "He throws my game off. He throws everyone off. He's taking pills and sniffing and wiping his nose all the time. And he coughs."

"He's got a cold, what can I tell you."

"Nobody gets a cold like that and keeps walking

around,'' Joe Camp said. He looked at the hors d'oeuvres on a silver tray. Tiny meatballs on toothpicks, tiny sausage and Italian beef sandwiches, fish eggs on brittle toast. It was an eclectic mix.

"No pizzas?" said Joe Camp.

"You and your fucking pizzas," Tony Rolls said. "You sell that shit in Kansas City, not here.

"I got good pizza."

"You got shit. Two for one. And you put those little Al Capone dolls in the middle of them. What kind of image is that? You think that's funny, making fun of your own kind? Capone woulda hung you on a hook you try to serve him pizza like you sell."

"It sells," Joe Camp said. He used to be Campabella. Tony Rolls was Tony Rolls because in the old days he carried rolls of quarters in his pockets and used them to fatten his fists. There was a difference in names; Tony hadn't changed his but had it done for him because of what he did. Joe Camp had wanted to sound downtown.

The game was at a round table covered in green felt, illuminated by a single overhead Tiffany lamp in the dining room. The house on the knoll was immense and dark; Tony lived alone now that his wife was dead. Except for the two guys who watched him. One was asleep and the other was in the dining room, keeping the bank and watching the game.

Degnan, the construction Mick, was playing, along with the geek named Drover and Slim Dingo. They were passing the time of the break with a few hands of five-card showdown. The pots were in chips and Vin, the bodyguard, kept the cash in an open metal box. The chips were red, white, and blue and a big pile of blue chips sat in front of Dingo. He had done all right both nights. Very all right, especially at Joe Camp's expense.

The night was warm and close. The grounds around the

big house were dark. Twelve miles straight east, Chicago soared on the lakefront.

"He looks at Slim alla time," Joe Camp said. "He working something with Slim? In your own house?"

"He don't know Slim Dingo from shit," Tony Rolls said. "I tol' you. The guy wired the Vegas house, a friend of my cousin."

"Slim is winning," Joe Camp said, explaining himself.

"Slim wins alla time," Tony said, finishing the dainty sandwich and grabbing another.

"Then why do you invite him to your house to rob you? To rob me?"

"This is my house, nobody gets robbed," Tony said. "You gotta mouth, Joe, you ought to watch it."

"Slim Dingo wins too much."

"Tell me."

"So why you invite him alla time?"

"It's a tradition, like Christmas. I get tired of Christmas too but you don't stop Christmas just because you get tired of it. It's a favor to me, shows some respect to me, from my cousin in Vegas."

"You got more cousins in Vegas than you got in Palermo."

Tony Rolls smiled at that. He was feeling good. He was watching the show and Drover was putting on a show. He hadn't moved at all in the first game the first night but Tony Rolls had a feeling now the second act was going to be better. He liked the way Drover was setting it up. He liked the cough a lot. And the pills were a nice touch.

"Come on, let's go out and play cards. Nobody wants to eat," Tony said.

"They'd eat pizza, you shoulda had pizza," Joe Camp said.

"Pizza I'll get from the West Side, not from you. You

ashamed of pizza or what? You make pizza like you was making peanut butter sandwiches.''

''I got two hundred and ten places.''

''So what. McDonald's sells a trillion hamburgers and they still don't prove nothing to me except a lot of people don't know nothing about eating hamburgers,'' Tony Rolls said. His chair motor whirred. He propelled himself through the swinging white doors into the dark, cool dining room. The air-conditioner filtered everything in the house, including Slim Dingo's cigarillo smoke. A box of Sherman's all-natural smokes was on the table next to his pot.

Slim's small eyes watched the last card fall and he shrugged at the small loss. His toothpick rolled from one side of his thin mouth to the other. It glittered in the Tiffany lamp's light. Some people thought it was gold; *Wide World of Sports* thought it was gold.

Drover knew it was glitter on wood. He knew a lot of things. He coughed again and wiped his lips and this time he let them see the blood.

Only a thin speckle of blood on linen but it was there.

Slim stared at him and at the blood.

Drover made sure he caught it and then shoved the handkerchief in his pants pocket. His suit coat was on the back of the captain's chair. Everyone had a captain's chair but nobody slouched. Except for Tony Rolls's wheelchair and Tony's way of slumping back against the canvas.

''Whaddaya wanna play, you guys?'' Tony said. ''Last night for our guest. Whaddaya say?''

''Cards,'' Joe Camp said, sitting down. ''Just deal, Tone.''

''Okay. Draw, jacks,'' Tony said, taking the deck. Everyone anted a fifty-dollar white chip into the pot. Tony shoved out a blue worth two hundred.

"Let's go," he explained. "Make 'em bleed. Real money."

Everyone followed.

The cards went down all around. Slim never touched his cards until the deal was finished. He played poker the way some people play chess and others play solitaire. He was the only man in the room as far as he was concerned. His lizard eyes looked from one player to another. He had them all figured. Well, maybe the blood spot on the linen had thrown him off a little. He knew the coughers but he never had seen blood on anyone else. He wiped at his neck with the tips of his fingers before picking up the cards. He couldn't get it out of his mind.

He looked up at Drover. "You got bleeding," he said. His voice was softened by a drawl but was the color of ice water anyway.

"Just something," Drover said.

"Cold," said Joe Camp.

Drover smiled. Thin and quick. "Little worse than that."

Joe Camp didn't want to hear if the guy had pneumonia. He looked at his cards one by one as the deal came down. He made a face. It was one he had learned and he thought it disguised everything.

"Worse," Slim Dingo said, still not touching his cards.

"Nothing catching," Drover said.

"It ain't AIDS," Degnan said. He was a little drunk and his face was flushed. Degnan was only forty-seven but he had made all his money and time was on his hands. If he wasn't playing cards tonight, he would have been passed out on the sofa in his den at home in Oak Brook or sprawled on his mistress's bed in the Condo on Elm Street downtown. Time was something he thought he had too much of.

"Open," Slim said.

He pushed a blue chip into the pot.

Drover coughed again, a really long one and fished out the handkerchief from his slacks. He wiped at his mouth carefully when it was over and examined the handkerchief. Everyone watched him.

"And raise you," Drover said, shoving three chips onto the table.

"So who's got all the good cards?" Degnan said. He was puzzled by the two queens staring at him. One guy opens, the next guy triples. Was this a pinochle deck?

"Okay," Degnan said, and met the bet. Camp did the same, just to stay in the action. Tony Rolls followed.

Slim said, "Two and raise you four dollars."

The two-chip bet was met with two more.

The mood of the game was all different suddenly. It came from the spooky dark house and the silence all around them. Nothing in the world existed except for this table, these cards, these chips that might be money. They had felt it first with Tony Rolls's raise at ante.

"I guess," Drover started. "Jesus," he added, coughing again.

They waited.

Drover's face was all white under the tan when he finished. Slim stared at the handkerchief. Drover let him see it before he put it away.

"I guess I gotta make up or go home busted," Drover said. He tried a smile to show it didn't mean anything. But he put two more chips in than required.

"I don't get it," Degnan said. He blinked, saw his queens, tried to figure it out. Maybe he had missed something. "Nobody's seen anything but their openers. What the hell are we all betting on?"

"To make it interesting, Degnan," Tony Rolls said. "What are you beefing about?"

"I ain't beefing. I just didn't want to miss something."

Slim put his cards facedown on the table as though they didn't interest him. It wasn't a ploy. He was staring at Drover. "You cough like you got TB."

"I do?"

"Yeah," Slim said, sliding the toothpick along his lips.

"That a guess or you betting on it?"

"It don't matter to me," Slim said. He picked up the cards again and frowned. Slim never frowned. Stoneface Slim, said *Wide World of Sports.*

Drover caught the frown and caught Tony Rolls looking at him.

When the bets were laid, Slim wanted two cards. Drover took one. Degnan took three and Joe Camp took two. Rolls took three.

"A dime," Slim said. He pushed five blue chips into the center of the table.

Drover smiled. "One and raise two," he said.

Degnan stared at three queens. He looked at Drover and his own hand. He followed the bet.

Joe Camp folded and got up. "I'm gonna get something to eat," he said, and left the room.

Tony Rolls stayed.

"Meet two and raise five," Slim Dingo said.

Degnan's three queens winked at him and he folded the hand before Drover spoke.

Drover coughed again, a good long hacking cough this time. He reached for his handkerchief.

Dingo snapped his gold toothpick in two.

Only Drover heard it. He stared at Slim for a moment. Then he said, "Five and five."

"What are you, in a hurry to get broke?" Tony Rolls said.

"In a hurry," Drover repeated.

Slim sniffed. He had a reputation and it was usually good enough to keep him calm, even when he didn't feel like being calm. He had written a book about playing poker and revealed little about the game while adding to his legend; it was usually the point of such books. He had won three big tourneys in Southern California in the early 1980s and made network TV. Poker was even duller than chess to watch or read about and Slim had put a spin of glamour on it with his down-home looks and cowboy legend. He was a cowboy playing poker like Wild Bill Hickock or something. But it was all failing at the moment. He looked in Drover's wan face and saw exactly what he wanted to see. He touched his throat and cleared it. He looked at the cards. Aces and eights. Dead man's hand.

He counted the cards drawn and discarded in his mind. He kept his eyes on Drover.

He played into the raise and matched it. A lot of blue chips filled the center of the table.

"Call," Slim said.

"Diamonds," Drover said. The straight flush started at eight and went down from there.

Slim put his cards facedown.

Drover scooped the pot across the table.

Degnan shook his head.

Gambling and sports seemed to go the same way. On a turn or a break, the luck shifted. Skill went along for the ride in sports and maybe it did in cards but when the luck shifted, it could break nerves. That's what Slim Dingo usually had in reserve. Now, for a moment, he wasn't sure. He hesitated like the quarterback on the better team who suddenly sees a free safety crossing his line of flight a moment after he releases the ball. It shouldn't happen; it hasn't happened before; but there's an interception and the mood of the game undergoes a sea change. Slim removed the broken remains of the toothpick and tried another.

It was his deal. He shuffled a long time. "What ails you?" he said to Drover.

"Nothing," Drover said.

"Cough like that you hear in sanitariums," Slim said.

"You got cancer?" Joe Camp said.

"Just a touch of something," Drover said.

"What?"

Drover looked up. "I told you. Nothing catching."

"How do you know?"

"They wouldn't let me out if I could give it to anyone," Drover said.

"Who?"

"Tuberculosis sanitarium," he said.

"You got TB?"

"Yeah," Drover said. "Deal."

"TB?" Degnan said. "Nobody gets TB."

"That's what I thought," Drover said. "Let it go a long time."

Slim made another noise in his throat and broke his second toothpick. Everyone looked at him.

"Something wrong?" Tony Rolls said.

"Nothing," Slim Dingo said.

Drover watched him through the deal and he saw it in the lizard eyes. He tried to remember how he wanted to hurt this lizard bad enough to make it last, bad enough to make Nancy feel better. Bad enough to make talking to Tony Rolls again worth it.

"You know about TB?" Drover said to Slim.

"I dunno nothing," Slim said. His eyes turned to the cards as though they were turning away from something unpleasant.

Six hands later, the tide was running silent and fast, washing everyone's chips into Drover's pile. Drover still hacked and coughed but he kept winning and the money was getting heavy at his side of the table.

The grandfather clock in the entry hall did sixteen notes of Westminster before tolling five. Dawn was edging up pink beyond the windows and the birds were awake. A cardinal attacked the bay window in the dining room as it always did and stared inside at the players.

"I love that bird," Tony Rolls said. "Stupid. Sees a red reflection in the window and goes to attack the other cardinal, except it's seeing itself. It's the way the sun comes up. Does it all spring, summer, fall. Never learns."

Drover almost smiled.

Tony Rolls shook his head. "See yourself and attack yourself."

"I'm beat up," Degnan said, yawning. "Got to make an honest living, boys."

"You wouldn't know how," Joe Camp said. He was out twenty dimes.

"A helluva lot more honest than selling those matzo crackers with tomato catsup on 'em," Degnan said. It would be the perfect end to an evening, getting into a fight.

"Hey, not in my house," Tony Rolls said, and Vin, ever alert at the cash box, gave the Irishman a Taylor Street Number Two look.

Slim said nothing. He looked at Drover and the pile. He let his fingers crawl on his neck again. He cleared his throat again. He did a lot of things again he hadn't done the first night. He was studying Drover and he couldn't get through it.

"One more, Slim?" Drover said.

"Sure," Slim said.

"What d'you want?"

"Whatever you want."

"I want to win," Drover said. Tony smiled.

"So do I. Except you have a substantial part of my money."

"So what do you want?"

"Chance to win it back," Slim said, very easy and cool.

"How much you got?"

Slim looked at his chips and understood. He shoved them into the center of the table. Then he began to stack them into tens. There were thirty thousand dollars worth of stacks when he finished.

Slowly, Drover did the same.

The other three men watched. Joe Camp let his mouth fall open.

Drover looked at Tony. "You want part of this?"

"Nah. That's crazy betting," Tony said.

"You're right," Drover said. "Sometimes you got to be crazy. Right, Slim?"

"If you say so."

"I got bad luck the last year, got TB, got treated, got to go back for treatment, what the hell does it matter to me?"

"Is that right?" Slim said.

Joe Camp glared.

Drover picked up the deck and began to shuffle.

"You ever get a run of bad luck, Slim?" Drover said.

"Not like you got, boy," Slim said.

"Naw. You're lucky. So am I tonight. Tomorrow I got to take my chances again."

"You gonna die?" Degnan said. Death was usually on his mind when the sun came up, no matter where he found himself.

"Yeah," Drover said. He passed the cards to Slim for cutting.

He dealt. The clock sounded the first four notes of the chime for the quarter hour.

"How many?"

"Two," Slim said.

"I'll take two."

They stared at the final cards for a long moment. Then Slim reached into his shirt pocket and pulled out the money clip. There were only ten bills on the clip and they didn't make much of a wad.

"Gimme ten dimes' worth, Vin," Slim said to the money changer.

Vin studied the bills like a border guard. He nodded to Tony Rolls and put the bills in the box.

"Raise you ten," Slim said to Drover.

Drover looked at the chips and then at his cards. "I figured the first pot was enough."

"Did you." Not a question.

"Shit," Drover said.

Tony Rolls bit his lip.

Drover took out his handkerchief and coughed into it. They could all see the bloody spot on the linen. Drover smiled and there was blood on his teeth. He stared at Slim Dingo.

"And raise twenty."

"Aw, come on, you guys," Degnan said. It was getting scary.

Slim watched Drover put all his chips onto the table and then watched him reach into his hip pocket. He had a very fat wad because twenty thousand dollars in hundreds is nearly an inch thick unfolded. He started to hand the money to Vin and then stopped.

"What the hell, last pot. It's only money," Drover said.

Joe Camp sucked in his breath.

Slim saw the stack of bills in the middle of the chips. Real money on the table changed the smell of the game. Even when you know what chips are for, real money makes it real.

"Call," Drover said.

"Four kings."

Drover let him wait.

Joe Camp turned to him. "Well?"

"Aces," Drover said, letting the cards drop.

Everyone thought the same thing in the same moment. Even Vin understood and patted the pistol under his coat. Four aces beat four kings in movies, not in real life. It was too neat and everyone felt the edge of it, like picking through a junkie's pockets trying not to get stuck by the needle. It was one thing for one player in one game to pick up four kings; it was impossible for the second player in the same game to pick up four aces. It just didn't happen, not ever. Except just now.

Slim waited, the famous pause of the toothpick man. He shifted the pick.

"I guess it's your lucky night," Slim said.

"Yeah," Drover said without interest. He started for the stack. Joe Camp started to say something and turned to Tony Rolls who gave him Taylor Street Number One. Joe Camp swallowed it.

Vin counted all the chips and doled out all the money. There was a lot of money in front of Drover.

"Whaddaya gonna carry it with?"

"You got a paper bag?" he asked Tony Rolls.

Tony Rolls smiled at that. "For that, I got a real bag. Vin, go up to the bedroom closet and get out one of the little brown bags."

"You keep little brown bags?"

"I pick 'em up all the time. I like luggage, you know?"

"Luggage?" Joe Camp said, staring at the piles of money. He was trying to figure out how much it was.

Slim just sat there, for the first time letting his backbone rest full on the rest of the captain's chair.

The thought was settling in over them like morning streaking through the windows.

"Lucky hand," Tony Rolls said at last, to give some words to the edge of the thought.

"Yeah," Drover said.

"Tony," Slim spoke at last.

"What is it?"

"I gotta go, Tony. I hate to run, but I gotta plane to catch—"

"Are you crazy? Lemme get you some breakfast—"

"I gotta go," Slim said. He pushed himself up from the table suddenly. He was different. He didn't want to look at the money but he stared at Drover. He knew, Drover thought. He knew it right down to the heels of his rattlesnake boots. Drover smiled and it was a bloody smile.

"What sanitarium you were in?" Slim asked.

"Harrington," Drover said.

Johno Harrington.

"I hope you get better," Slim said, biting every word.

"Like the guy won a million-dollar negligence suit against the Archdiocese of New York," Drover said. "They knew he was faking but when he won, the cardinal's lawyer said in court, 'We're gonna watch you and if you ever get outta that wheelchair, we're gonna get you. So what are you gonna do with all that money?' And the guy said, 'Take a trip to Lourdes. And pray for a miracle.' "

Joe Camp blinked.

Degnan said, "Did he get cured?"

Slim just stood there. "Maybe we'll get a chance to play again," he said in the soft drawl.

"Yeah," Drover said. "Stranger things have happened."

"Four aces is strange," Joe Camp said. It was on everybody's mind and nobody could top it. Everyone knew the deal was funny but you didn't laugh unless Tony Rolls did.

CHAPTER 6

VIN SAID, "You don't make yourself hard to find."

"I didn't know I was supposed to."

"You got a lot of money. You made some people sore. Everyone knows you're staying at the Drake."

"Hard work and being thrifty," Drover said. "It always attracts the envy of the idle."

Vin drove with one hand, as though he owned the car. The streets were slick with rain and the traffic was picking itself up, fitting together the coming morning gridlock with the demented drive of players in a jigsaw puzzle tournament.

"I can't figure what Mr. Rolls wants with you," Vin said. Said sly, as sly as Vin could ever get.

"He's trying to get in my pants," Drover said. "It's been a long time since the missus died."

Vin went from sallow to red in a second. "You watch your mouth."

"No. But Tony does," Drover said. He didn't usually take candy from babies to hear them cry but Vin had caught him at a bad moment, coming off one trick and heading for another with no breathing space in between.

The Caddy slid to the canopy entrance of the Drake Hotel on the Walton Street side. A picket line of thunderclouds on the lake had started banging a half hour ago and turned the pink September morning gray and lonesome.

"Don't forget your bag," Vin said, looking at Tony Rolls's leather grip.

"I'll treasure it."

"Mr. Rolls wants to see you for lunch."

"I know, Vin. You told me four times. I would have written it down the first time if I thought it would have done any good."

"You're an asshole," Vin said.

"And I was going to give you a tip. Thanks, Vin." Drover opened the door and swung the bag out. He smiled at Vin and closed the door. The big doorman in his burgundy coat was just a moment late. Drover looked around. He saw the black Buick parked across the street in front of the Knickerbocker. Ahead, three cabs filled the line waiting for someone to go to the airport. It wasn't a comfortable moment; nothing had been comfortable after he played a hand full of aces on the green felt cloth of Tony Rolls's dining room table. It was part of the gotcha for Slim Dingo and it had been necessary to do a gotcha all around. A winning hand like that over a losing hand like that would have gotten you a small .22 in your skull in any self-respecting back room in this town or in Vegas. Maybe the .22 was still in transit.

Drover crossed the sidewalk and went through the revolving door and up the grand staircase to the lobby. He went to the cashier and checked out. Then he went up to his room. The elevator operator was wearing perfume that seemed too strong. He might have put that on the checklist if he was a hotel inspector but she was pretty enough to make him forget the demerit. He rested on the upholstered bench on the way up and stared at her legs because they were the only interesting things in the cage.

His room had a phony bookcase decoration on either side of a twenty-seven-inch television set. You wanted books, bring them yourself. The plastic book spines

imbedded in wood included sixteen *Huckleberry Finn* titles, two dozen *By Love Possessed,* and a smattering of
other great books. The titles weren't made to be examined, just appreciated for the effect the bookshelves gave
the room. He dropped all his clothes in a pile by the bed
and took a long shower. The shower was for thinking. It
was ten minutes after seven and he had been thinking too
hard for too long. The shower had the same effect as a
double Johnny Walker on the rocks and was better for him.
At least it made him clean. He closed his eyes under the
spray and saw Slim Dingo's lizard eyes pour hate on him.
That made him feel warmer than the water. Only when he
thought of the other three men did the warmth fade. There
were things to figure out about the next step and about the
Buick parked downstairs.

He thought he had it figured out in part by the time he
dried.

Ten minutes later, he went out under the street canopy
again. He wore jeans and his pullover short-sleeve shirt
and sneakers. He carried the small leather bag. The same
doorman with the lantern jaw and haunted eyes started to
whistle a cab but Drover tapped his shoulder. "They're
waiting for me over there," he said.

He crossed the street and the big Buick came alive.
Headlights went on in the rainy gloom and the car crept
forward. The passenger window rolled down.

"You saw us," the passenger said.

"You stood out like a black Buick."

"Get in," he said.

"United terminal and step on it."

"Very funny."

"For seven-twenty in the morning, it's not bad."

He climbed in the backseat and closed the door. Everyone wore white shirts and sport coats. He knew the style.

"You gonna take the expressway?"

"Shut up," the passenger in the front seat said.

Nobody said a word until the car slid into the basement parking level of a tall, anonymous building that dominated a corner in the south end of the Loop. Drover sighed; he knew the building. Then the word was "out." Same speaker.

The office was on the sixteenth floor and the name on the door said "United States Interior Survey Division." Drover smiled at that; it was the first smile without malice that day and it made him feel as good as the shower.

Window walls revealed fog from the lake, rain, and the tops of buildings falling away like a man-made hillside toward the neighborhoods farther west. There was a single gunmetal-gray desk, two government-brown lamps, and some chairs shoved in as an afterthought.

The man behind the desk had an overnight's growth of beard above his shirt. The shirt was white but tieless, to go with the Federal Casual look. Everyone was dressed halfway between FBI Courtroom Gray and DEA Beer Bar Country. He wore wire-rimmed glasses and his hair was the same material.

"My name is Jose Jiminez," he said without an accent. "Before you do Steve Allen, let's cut the crap and tell me what you and Tony Rolls like to talk about until all hours."

"His fear of flying. I'm counseling him."

"Fritz. Get the bag."

Fritz turned out to be the passenger. Fritz opened Tony Rolls's gift leather bag and dumped it on the desk. A wrinkled tan suit, wrinkled shirts, and wrinkled underclothes fell out, along with a Dopp kit. Fritz opened the Dopp kit and found a razor, a toothbrush, and a tube of Crest. Also a bottle of Mennen Skin Bracer.

"Mennen Skin Bracer. What a sport. You must swing in a lot of places," Fritz said.

"You'd need more than that to smell nice," Drover said.

The driver of the Buick hit him then very hard in the stomach. Drover had expected it but not the force of it. He doubled over and decided to retch on Jose Jiminez's desk.

"You asshole," Jose said to the driver. "Get some paper towels. And keep your fucking hands to yourself."

"I'm a bleeder too," Drover said, still feeling sick enough to hold his belly in both hands.

"Is that right?"

"Ask anyone, Jose."

"Where's your money?"

"Money?"

"You won some money at the game."

"Did I? What game is that?"

Fritz said, "I could hurt him without him throwing up."

"Don't bet on it, Fritz. I'm very sensitive all over," Drover said.

"Let's start again."

"Okay. You Jose Jiminez. I'm Steve Allen. Fritz can be Gordon Hathaway. He looks like Gordon Hathaway, there's that swish when he walks."

Fritz held it in.

"Money. Where's the money?"

"Maybe it's in my hotel room."

"Is it?"

"No."

"Then where is it?"

"Why is there supposed to be money?"

"What does Tony Rolls want from you?"

"I told you. You look like federal agents, you must know Tony doesn't fly. He wants me to convince him that flying is safe. He wants to go back to the old country one time before he dies. We've turned one room of his house into a mock-up of a 747 cabin. I strap him in and sit next to him and we drink martinis out of plastic glasses for seven hours and watch James Bond movies. I tell him that's all there is to it.''

The man in the wire rims shook his head. Fritz waited for a signal to apply pain that would not invite regurgitation. The driver came in from down the hall with a handful of paper towels and started to clean the desk.

Nobody said a thing for a moment. Then Wire Rims sighed. ''We watch Tony Rolls all the time. He saw you three weeks ago in Santa Cruz. Now you're in his house with his usual gang, plus Slim Dingo. So you're playing cards. You don't play with a Visa card so where's your money?''

Drover said nothing.

''Drover, I don't want you to get into trouble. I want to avoid trouble,'' Jose said.

''Is your name really Jose Jiminez?''

''You ever think how you lose it when you get older, Drover? Ever think that you get tired of dancing? You gamble and you file tax returns. You do stocks and you file tax returns. You do . . . consulting. Consulting to known figures. You do investigations for a sports book in Las Vegas that wants to know when someone is trying to kink the action. Do you think your sports book would like to know you're consulting with known Mafia? Playing cards with them?''

''Who else is going to run casinos? You'd feel better if it was Jim and Tammy Faye Bakker?''

''I feel better when guys like you stop doing the soft shoe and tell me why Tony Rolls drives twenty-five hundred miles to see you.''

''I'm another cousin. But I'm from Reggio di Calabria, so he can't admit it as easy as if I was from Palermo.''

''You don't want to—''

Drover held up one hand. ''I don't want to fuck with

Uncle. If I fuck with Uncle, Uncle will fuck me so bad it won't hurt anymore. Is that the gist of the speech? I heard it before. It's like yelling at a kid; after a while, he don't listen. You guys yelled at me for a long time. I get audited every other year. I know the whole song, Jose, and I don't give a shit for it. You lean on me because the Tony Rollses don't get scared and you end up trying to shove someone like me around. I won't call B. Raymond Mitchell this time, but next time you'll make me mad and B. Raymond will have your little assemblage investigating transvestite activity among illegal Mexican soybean pickers in the San Joachim.''

Wire Rims made a tent of his fingertips and looked at Drover. He sighed. The guy with the paper towels threw them in the metal wastebasket on the far side of the room. The walls were unmarked by signs, photos, notices, or any other example that showed the office was used on a regular basis by anyone.

"What if we cut you a deal?"

"I don't need a deal."

"You walk out of Tony Rolls's place with his money and you don't need a deal?"

Drover shaved his chin with his left hand. "You already got a dealer. Inside Tony's house. Joe Camp? Degnan?"

"I don't know what you're talking about," Wire Rims said.

"I got a plane to catch," Drover said. He started to stuff his clothes back into the bag.

Fritz looked at the boss. The boss didn't move and didn't strike his tent. "Careful, Drover. Go careful. You might need friends."

"Nobody needs friends. It's a luxury, like owning a dog. I might get a dog someday when I get tired of friends."

"You don't want to talk about this." Wire Rims broke

the tent to move his hand around the room. Drover looked around.

"Nice view. Too bad it's raining."

"How'd you know we were watching the hotel?"

Drover said, "Three white men in sports coats sitting in a Buick. Come on, Jose. I knew it wasn't the mod squad."

"Give him a ride to the airport, Fritz," Jose said.

Fritz made a face.

"Does he know the way?"

"We know all the ways, Drover. Coming and going. Keep an eye out for us, we'll keep an eye out for you," Jose said.

"Sure," Drover said. "Come on, Gordon," he said to Fritz.

Wire Rims smiled. "Have a nice day."

Drover paused at the door and turned. "Why'd you want to tell me you had someone inside the room?"

"Did we do that?"

"The money. You knew. So why let me know?"

"I guess I let it slip."

"You'll never get your Junior G-Man badge that way," Drover said.

"S'long, Steve. Think about me."

"S'long, Jose," Drover said. "You'll be in my dreams."

CHAPTER 7

DROVER THOUGHT HE was sleepwalking when he debarked through the Jetway at San Francisco International. He hit the men's room, washed his face, inspected it in the mirror, and decided it was hopeless. He hired a limo and fell asleep in the backseat before the stretch Lincoln found the highway south.

The driver checked him out a couple of times in the rearview mirror. Brown hair, big shoulders, might have been a football player once. The guy looked like a bum in his rumpled clothes but the driver was used to that; a lot of people with all the money in the world dressed like slobs. They could do it because they weren't proving anything. Still, the driver had mentioned the price of the fare to Santa Cruz twice before Drover got in the car.

Muggy morning fog misted the coastline. It was warm but the damp shivered into your bones.

Drover woke as the stretch Lincoln stopped at the pier. He yawned and squinted at the yellow liverish fog. He decided to pay off there and walk to Black Kelly's place in the middle of the pier.

The midday leg stretch revived him as he trod over the uneven boards that floored the pier. The sea smell restored him. Being home—whatever sort of a bastard home this was—felt good.

He was tired from the all-night game as well as the

pounding from the federal gorillas. He seriously thought about an afternoon nap even though he never slept during the day. Maybe this would be the day.

He opened the door on the largest hamburger emporium to ever sit on a fishing pier and Kelly looked up at him as if he had gone outside for papers. Kelly had piles of money in front of him. He was deciding how much belonged to him and how much belonged to Uncle. He wore his rimless glasses when counting for the house and they were halfway down his pug nose. His black hair was oily in the funny morning light.

"How'd it go?"

"All right." Slumped on a stool. "Glass of juice, any juice."

"Our tomato is special today," Kelly said, and poured a big glassful over ice. "We have it flown in on ice daily from Sacramento."

"Salut' " Drover said. He gulped it down. It was helping. He put the glass down and saw Kelly again. "You're going to get a package tomorrow. Federal Express."

"What should I do with it, O Great Kreskin?"

"Make sure the driver isn't intercepted on the pier and make sure you put it away when you get it."

"They tell you not to send cash in one of those."

"What am I going to do? Use the post office?"

"Go to a bank."

"Kelly, you're obtuse. The money doesn't exist. It's gambling profits."

"Oh. I was just thinking of the safety of it."

"The G is leaning on me. In Chicago. Any other calls?"

"Your Vegas friend."

Without a word, Drover picked up the phone on the end of the bar and began to punch in numbers. First a Vegas number, then his credit card number. All of this was traceable, but then everyone figured that by now everything was being traced. The laziest act of the federal investigator is either taking both Hanukkah and Christmas off or ordering a federal wiretap.

The voice was familiar.

"It's me," Drover said.

"Where are you?"

"The place you left your message of concern."

"Then when are we going to have a sit-down?"

"There's a lot to say. News you can use. Maybe tonight."

"Eight o'clock. We're holding a séance in parlor B."

"Who's dead?"

"Washington Redskins by six and a half. See you."

The line went dead.

Drover held the phone a moment and blinked at it. Travel and long hours had confused him. He blinked again.

"What'd he say?"

"Is there a game tonight?"

"Washington-Los Angeles."

"Shit, that's right, the first proposed new *Wednesday Night Football* game. Who'd you go for?"

"Washington," Black Kelly said.

"The conventional is against them."

"The conventional is interested in the play," Kelly said in his calm, irritating way. Sometimes he played the parish priest, talking about angels who dance on pins. "If the game appears so one-sided that it can't generate any action, they make it seem more even. If it's so even that it only generates local action, they make it one-sided. You, of all people, should not quote the conventional to me."

Kelly wasn't a gambler but he fancied the life. He had a system for beating the lottery. It involved reading meaning into certain messages contained in certain comic strips in the newspapers, interpreting the letters as numbers, and playing those numbers in the lottery. He once explained to Drover the hidden messages contained in Calvin and Hobbes comic strip. The key was in looking for short words, preferably those drawn in darker lines, as when Calvin was screaming at the stuffed tiger. It was utterly mad—and millions of lottery players around the world swore by it as a method of winning what seemed a game of pure chance. The trouble with Drover's scorn of the method was that Kelly won a lot. It shouldn't work the way Kelly played it.

"Are you going to get a bet down?" Kelly said.

Drover gave a thin smile. "You know I don't bet. Besides, I've got to go to Vegas tonight."

"In connection with this Chicago business?"

"Yes," Drover said.

Kelly fiddled with the bottles behind the bar. His back was turned. "Did you do it?"

"What's that?"

"Cut off your pound of flesh."

"Yes."

"Are you in trouble then?"

"I don't think so. The G picking me up, well, that bothers me. But I can't figure out what they're playing at and I'm too tired to ponder right now."

"How did the poker player take it?"

"Like a gentleman."

"That'd be the day, the adulterous bastard."

"I've got to square with Foxy tonight and tell him some of what this is about. I suppose he's already heard one version. Then I've got to see Nancy Harrington."

Kelly turned. "And why would that be? To see if she wanted you after all?"

Drover's face darkened. He looked hard at Kelly and then let his eyes drop. "Yeah. Maybe you're right. It's an excuse to see her again, see how she's doing."

"Sorry, Drover." Kelly stared at him. "Put your heart

in a steel case, it works every time. I get too smart for myself sometimes. It comes with rank. I was a fire captain, you know. Makes you a know-it-all. You're doing the right thing.''

"That's what Eve said to Adam," Drover said.

For a moment, awkward silence filled the space between them. Then Kelly leaned both hands on the bar and hunched his shoulders like a lineman or a saloonkeeper.

"How about a cheeseburger with sautéed onions?"

Drover shook his head.

Black Kelly smiled, his eyes glittered, and his features blackened with pleasure. "All right, all right, I was gonna serve it tonight but I can give you a slice."

"I'm not hungry."

"Firehouse meat loaf," Kelly said. "Crisp new potatoes and boiled cabbage."

Drover said, "Bastard," and rose to find a table. He had a weakness for women in distress. And firehouse meat loaf with cabbage, even if it was really breakfast time.

CHAPTER 8

THERE'S NO WEATHER in Las Vegas and no time.

The casinos have no clock and no windows. Black Kelly once said it might be heaven because every day was the same and pleasant at that and the place was timeless; Drover thought it was probably just a rehearsal hall for the other place.

The plane banked in against the rays of the dying western sun and touched down on the hot tarmac just after six P.M. The plane was full of two kinds of people—those headed to a vacation and those heading for a fix. Because it was the middle of the week, the addicts outnumbered the tourists.

Bright desert sun blinded him outside the terminal and even when he was in a cab heading for the Strip, he saw spots before his eyes. He slipped off his sunglasses and opened *The Las Vegas Sun* and turned to the sports pages. The sports pages put the world on hold for him. Always had. They had the conventional skinny on the experimental *Wednesday Night* game and it didn't look good for the Redskins. The paper carried a syndicated thumb-sucker about pro football ruining itself with too many appearances; a piece like that was almost obligatory at least once a season. Drover didn't believe it and neither did the NFL.

Shamrock Casino Hotel was toward one end of the Strip,

not the most imposing casino but with enough outside lighting to illuminate Peoria, Illinois, for a winter.

Drover walked through the lobby. Everything was green and shamrocky, like Saint Patrick's day in a Polish saloon—the spirit was there but the main business was something else and in a different nationality. The slots were singing their tedious song for blue-haired ladies in walking shorts punching in the chips. The business of gambling knows no time, so no one keeps time. Clocks are banished from casinos because they are irrelevant.

Jimmy followed the corridor beyond the elevators and back, toward the kitchens. The path was familiar and odd. One thing led to another and he was in the alley behind the casino. He crossed it.

Just behind the casino was a two-story office building where Fox Vernon had his sports line service. Inside his sober offices, young men—and a few women—fed information into Zenith computers that translated finally into facts that someone could base a reasonable line on. The place looked like a mutual insurance company office but the business was pari-mutuels.

Foxy's Line was carried in a hundred papers across the country (and sixteen abroad), was the base for three private newsletter lines, and was the check against balance that the big casino sports books used to look again at their own lines. Fox Vernon was respected in a town not long on respect for anyone. He kept to himself, he ran it on the square, and he didn't want more than he could hold in two hands. Besides, he was a genius.

That's what they had said twenty years ago when he picked up his Ph.D. in mathematical theory at the University of Chicago at the ripe age of twenty. He was enough of a genius to be distracted by the vagaries of the real world.

Fox had devised an improved basketball line while an

undergraduate and, shortly after getting his doctorate, been visited by three men from the Chicago Outfit who wanted to buy his brain. As Fox later explained it. He decided no to that, but the gambling life—the sheer math beauty of it—fascinated him to the point where he decided to work in Las Vegas for one of the more famous independent oddsmakers. Now he was on his own, one of the seventy-plus legal sports books in town. He had published two books on the science of sports gambling only because he understood it and because he had met Drover.

Drover knew how to write. Fox Vernon was like the mainframe computers that use zero and one to create all the languages of the universe. Drover was on the level of a battered Royal typewriter. His words had blood in them and flesh and Fox Vernon understood that in his distant way. Their first meeting had been pure chance but not the others. They could use each other; they both knew that instinctively. Fox saw the numbers and not the names; Drover could be the other set of eyes for him and the sports book.

Drover worked for Fox off and on, when it suited him or it suited Fox to use him.

There was nothing on the walls of the large, cubicled office—except for a clock. It might have been the only clock in Vegas. Time was reality, Fox said once, and his office was not about dreams, hopes, hot streaks, or glory. Time was money, Foxy had said without realizing the was uttering a cliché.

Here and there in the white office, in the other cubicles, employees without Foxy's Spartan and unsentimental idea of furnishings put up a bumper sticker or a playful saying or a clip from a newspaper. Fox Vernon allowed these touches of humanity, even to a vase of flowers on National Secretaries Day. But the kidding around stopped at sports. No sports clippings, no pennants, no souvenir game tickets taped to the walls. The only rule was: nothing about sports. Nothing. Sports was not a game, it was a way of making a living.

Drover entered the room and stood by the door a moment. Fox Vernon himself was sitting at a keyboard while a young assistant stood behind him. The Fox was playing with a line, extrapolating from stats and bringing up news accounts on the Nexus system.

Nexus was the new way of researching newspapers. It was, like everything else in the practical computer world, absurdly simple: You typed a word or two, put them in a time frame, and hit the blat button. Moments later, every story containing the key words paraded on the screen, culled from newspapers like the *Los Angeles Times, New York Times, Washington Post, Chicago Tribune,* and a score of others. No more poring through morgue clippings, making your brainbox the sorter instead of the machine. Because of the machines, it got hard to hide the unexpected, the hidden injury, the drunk-driving arrest that made only the local papers, the divorce filing, anything that changed the expected performance of players or teams.

Drover thought the Fox was too much of a teacher to make him feel comfortable. He had known the Fox for five years and familiarity had not bred content. The Fox put him on edge; he realized he had the same effect on the other man. They were so completely different that they actually worked well together. Drover was the watcher, the human element that saw sports as sports and understood the complex human relationships that determined games. Fox was the Fox.

The assistant tapped Fox Vernon on the shoulder and he looked up and saw Drover. He didn't smile. "Just a minute." He did something else with the keys, turned to his assistant and said something, then rose and beckoned to his office.

Drover entered and Fox closed the door behind him. He was a man of small gestures, good manners, and a rather shy smile. He wore a subdued sports coat all the time because the eternal indoor temperature of Las Vegas was seventy-one dry degrees. The heaven factor again, as Black Kelly would see it. His hair was sandy going to white and his eyes were gray. Drover sat down on a straight chair with a leather seat and Fox Vernon sat across the desk from him. There were absolutely no decorations in the bare, white room. Keep it simple, stupid.

"You saw Tony Rolls in Chicago," Fox Vernon said.

"I saw him."

"What does he want?"

"He says there're a bunch of guys on the Chicago futures exchanges who are setting futures lines on pro football games and making their own book."

Fox Vernon's face was blank. His hands were in the prayer position. He said nothing.

Drover watched him. "He wants to know about it."

Fox sighed, let the hands drop to the desk. "I suppose I'd want to know about it. How can they make futures and book blend together?" He held his hands together.

"How do they book the price of soybeans and pork bellies? I don't know. I called a guy in Chicago, used to work for the *Sun-Times* business section, he gave it to me slowly, like I was an idiot. I am an idiot. The action is in the play. They put together a basket of games for the coming season. Not the playoffs, nobody can figure that until it happens, but they basket twenty games out of six hundred games or so. They put the odds on the games based on some Vegas early lines and their own gut guesses. So you got twenty games. It sounds like playing Yahtzee for what it's got to do with anything, but different strokes for different folks." He knew the game but not the key players. Tony Rolls didn't know them either.

"Okay. You got twenty games.

"You buy the whole basket. You put up a future contract. You are not risking your money to start with, you are trying to risk some other chump's money. The word is, two guys set up the pool three, four years ago. Maybe longer. They pick the games in the basket. Not just Chicago games, they go all over the chart. Some are cinches, some are close. It's the old football parley card only it is much bigger and goes over a whole season. Got two, three games a week."

"But I don't understand, how do these guys make any money?"

"They got one set of odds on games set early, at the beginning of the season. But as the season goes on, they can middle their bets with other chump bets or they can hold on to the bet—a cinch bet—and they can also lay off bets with regular bookies. The way I get it from the *Sun-Times* guy, two guys in the CBOT set up this thing and printed the schedule and everything. The other traders are using their system and then these others, these fifty guys or so, are either gambling on their own or, if they really don't like a game, they lay it off on some chump who wants to use them as bookies. Or they go to a regular book and dump the game that way, bet against whatever it is they don't like in the basket they bought."

"So it's a bunch of amateurs pretending to be bookies."

Drover shook his head. "You don't get it, Foxy. These traders *are* bookies. That's what traders are. Only it's legal to do it in grain and not legal to do it in football."

"This is a diversion for them."

"Yeah. Except Tony Rolls is interested now because he thinks enough money is changing hands in this amateur handbook that it is important enough to fix something."

"He thinks like a criminal."

"He is a criminal, Fox."

"You're consorting with known criminals."

"At least I don't watch porn movies in my basement."

Fox shook his head. "So you took it on yourself not to tell me you went to see Tony Rolls." The voice had a dreamy quality.

"I figured you'd find out. And Tony Rolls came to see me. That's the way it started."

"You stop being useful to me if you get tainted by them. With them." Everyone knew who them was.

"Tell me," Drover said. "I was a writer by trade one time. Sports. On a big paper. I lost my trade because a two-bit federal attorney in L.A. decided growing up on the West Side of Chicago and eating Italian beef sandwiches with known criminals was cause for execution. I wasn't with them then, Foxy, not in Chicago, not in L.A., and I'm not with them now but I won't wear a dress and sing 'Take Me to St. Louis' to prove it. Not to you, Foxy, not to anyone."

It was the only time he ever sounded this way, when the subject inadvertently veered around to people Drover knew or people Drover was supposed to have known in a past life. Fox knew he was right but this was different; that's what Fox said to himself.

"I want to be careful," Fox said.

"Foxy, lose me. I can make it."

"I don't want you to lose yourself."

Silence after that. Las Vegas hummed to itself through the walls, through the fluorescent, through the scan of computers.

Drover leaned forward. "The point is: Where's the action going? Not for this week but, say, for the next two months? Or, where did it go? That's futures, isn't it?"

"There's just not that much action—"

"Sure there is. If Tony Rolls takes the time and effort to run an errand to a straight geek like me for his cousins, then someone, somewhere is worried. Tony talked about 'killing the golden goose.' He isn't much given to metaphor but I catch the drift. Someone is worried that these cowboys on the Chicago exchanges may be squeezing a little profit out of the game at the expense of the game.''

Fox decided. He stopped praying with his hands. He slammed his palms down on the arms of his straight chair and leaned forward.

''I trust you, I think I know you. You suddenly didn't waltz into Tony Rolls's house to do him a favor and me too at the same time. Tony gave you something, had something on you, something that pried you off that pier in Santa Cruz.''

''It didn't involve you.''

''Everything you do involves me.''

''You bought my eyes and ears, not my soul. I thought we understood that a long time ago.''

''You playing with the Outfit—''

''Play with them? I played with them since I was six years old.''

''That isn't what I mean.''

''Listen, Foxy. You grew up in Evanston. Your daddy was a captain of industry. Your friends were Albert Einstein and Chauncey DePew.''

''Don't do that class warfare thing you do. I can't help it if I was born to the manor. But I won't apologize for eating on china either.''

''Nobody asked you to.''

''We were talking about the mob. Those guys have never done a thing without getting mud all over it.''

''I told you, Foxy, I played with them a long time ago. We lived on Erie Street. On this side of our six-flat was Terry O'Connor and now he's a captain on the Chicago department. On the ground floor was Mrs. Guidotti and her son Tony who's battalion chief in the fire department.

Her other son Marco runs the semi-legit side of the restaurant supply business for the Outfit. And don't forget
Perkins, whose old man was a book. Per went semi-
straight. He got into advertising. Now right above us, on
the third floor, were twins, brother and sister, Marie and
Dominick LaMotta. Dom LaMotta ran prostitution and
gambling for the Outfit in Schiller Park until last year when
his head was found blown off in a drainage ditch in Elm-
wood Park. Down the street was my best friend, Larry
Tischman, who is now accountant-in-crime for Cook.
Lake, DuPage, McHenry, Will, and Rock counties in Illinois and everything north to Milwaukee and Madison in
Wisconsin. See, I played with them; they were in my
neighborhood. Childhood pals. Friends of my youth. I
went straight, as I thought, the way Terry O'Connor and
Tony Guidotti and Jim Perkins thought they did, and became a newspaperman and moved around and covered the
fun and games and was having a ball when a little piece
of shit in L.A. decided all my neighborhood friends meant
I was a bad boy too.''

Fox had heard it. Not often but he had heard it. He had
checked up on Drover before he offered him a job. Drover
had turned down the job. Then he courted him and offered
him a retainer. Drover had taken that. All he did was what
he did when he had been a sportswriter in L.A.—except
now he wrote his stories just for the eyes of Fox Vernon.
And the stories measured the way people looked when
they played and what the rumors were and what all the
thousand subtleties that surround a game—and affect the
point spread—might be. So that Fox Vernon didn't get
caught. Fox didn't get caught often anymore; Drover had
good eyes and a natural instinct for what was really going
on. When he told you a story about a team, there was just
that much more if you caught the subtleties. And Fox did
have all his hearing intact.

"All right. What are you going to do?"

"Wait for you. You check the computers for the futures action. I can go down to LaSalle Street in Chicago and try to pick apart the operators but I would look like a sheep in wolf's clothing down there. It isn't my style. It might be easier to see which games are causing the biggest action and look for the losers in them," Drover said.

"They're not going to register their bets with the Chicago Board of Trade, Drover."

"Futures, Foxy. Do I have to do all of your thinking for you?"

Foxy looked startled. Drover grinned. "That's what we call humor, Foxer. Futures trade happens in the future. If the bets have been made, the pool is closed. The question is: Where's the money? This has to be a cash market because nobody is going to charge on credit on an illegal line. Not unless the traders who set this up have also hired mob muscle and since the mob is confused, I don't think that's the case."

"Then what's on your mind?"

"Where are they going to put the action? I mean, if they're running a futures line and they take in two hundred thou, where do they bury it? Or five hundred? Or what?"

"Where it'll do the most good."

"And if they're going to fix the futures line, say a one-time sellout, they're going to fix a game. And how can they fix something that far into the future? I mean, they have to be laying money down right now with the books on some future game at future odds, locking in the odds while the price is still high."

Fox nodded. "Sure. We look for the futures action on the Vegas books. Anything higher than normal."

"The chumps bet on who is going to be Super Bowl champ at the beginning of the season and get thirty to one or something. That's gambling. What the futures guys are going to be doing is not gambling."

"It's not even mathematics," Fox Vernon said.

"So get those little gray drones out there on the case and start searching the boards. You got the connections, not me."

"No. Not them. This is between us for now."

Drover said, "That suits me."

"When do you want it?"

"Tonight, I've got to get some sleep."

"Stay up all night?"

"Two nights."

"That's what I heard. You win?"

"I did all right."

"Poker isn't your game. I've seen you play."

"Guessing isn't yours," Drover said, and got up. "Don't worry, Foxer. I won't lose my way at this late stage."

"Just so you know I know," Fox Vernon said.

Drover said, "I never thought it any other way. Just so you understand something, Foxer. I play it straight as much as I can but don't lean on me. Not about friends or neighbors or acquaintances or the kind of catsup I spill on my tie. I come and go and if we're going the same way, we can ride together. Just don't give me little sit-downs and lectures. Everybody wants to be a classroom teacher. Well, I decided a long time ago to drop out of school. Okay?"

Fox thought about it. His clear gray eyes thought about it, resting on Jimmy Drover's face.

"Okay," Fox Vernon calculated.

Drover was deep in sleep in a double bed in a plush, whorish bedroom on the thirteenth floor of the Shamrock Casino Hotel when the phone rang. Actually, the room was 1402 because you don't call a spade a spade in

Vegas—or a hotel floor by its right number—unless you can make money on it. All the comp rooms were on thirteen.

He picked up the receiver on the sixth ring.

"I thought you might have gone out to party," Fox Vernon said.

"What time is it?"

"There's no time in hell, Drover, don't you know that?"

"All right."

"They've hidden the action but we found it because we were looking for it and because my boys and girls are very good at what they do. It's three in the morning."

"That answers one question."

"The other is who. New Orleans versus Denver on November fifteenth in Awlins. All the money known to man is going conventional on Denver. Denver is a better team, Denver is going into the Super Bowl this year, Denver has a running game finally, Denver is . . . how shall I compare it to a summer's day? Still, it's so early that no one is busting his butt to make a bet on this one, with Awlins at home field and all and injuries to come. . . . But that's what the futures trade was about, wasn't it? Guessing the future?"

There was a tone in Foxy's voice.

Drover said, "But what's it really about?"

"Futures money slipping through into the regular markets all over the place, just dribs and drabs, here and there, they aren't booking it themselves yet. But it's definite, Drover. Very definite. And you will have to see how many friends you have at the Denver Press Club."

"Actually, I'm a member."

"Good. Then get out there, sleeping beauty. Because all the money they're putting down is on New Orleans, a team that should not even show up for this one."

CHAPTER 9

WHEN JOHNO HARRINGTON married Nancy Payton years ago, the neighborhood was still a neighborhood of sorts. Not Bedford Falls or Wistful Vista but as much a neighborhood as Southern California ever can stand. You could have driven over to Disneyland and seen spaces. When you went to the top of the Magic Mountain, your vista would not have been office buildings stretching into the desert. Thirty years ago, this was where Christ lost His shoes; now He would have lost His car in the sea of parking lots that is the soul of Orange County.

Drover flew into Long Beach and then rented a blue Pontiac 6000. It was just after ten in the morning and the roads were in the same perpetual gridlock they were always in, rush hour or no. He touched and tapped, touched and tapped as the four-cylinder growled pretentiously forward all the way down the serpentine highway. It was easier to get to Mecca than it was to Nancy's house.

Which turned out to be a stucco bungalow with red tile roof, a dusty front lawn, a broken driveway with a broken-looking Honda in it, a California suburbanscape that would not make any real estate brochure. The house seemed a thousand miles from the ocean and a thousand miles from everything else, except for the minimarts and self-serve gas stations that crowded all around. Shopping was always five minutes away, as long as you had a car.

He parked in the driveway and walked up to the front step. There was just one. She opened the door before he got there.

Nancy said, "You made good time."

"I could have been in Japan by now."

"Good time for here." She stared at him with those frosty, sharp eyes that were neither blue nor gray but just Nancy's color. She wore a blue denim jumpsuit and could still get away with it. She wore earrings and blue slippers. The earrings in the middle of the morning were the only concession; no makeup, no lipstick.

Drover noticed. No come-hither. No go-away either.

They stared at each other a moment, standing apart, and then she was in his arms. Neither of them knew who started it.

They just held on, not kissing, not feeling, just holding on. And when the hug was over, she took a step back from him, watching his eyes.

"Come in."

He stepped inside. She closed the door behind him and looked at his back. She almost smiled.

He turned to her and it seemed the most natural thing in the world. So they kissed each other this time. Like old lovers more than old friends. They were both, of course.

She broke it and stood apart and her eyes, dull a moment before, were shining. But that might mean tears and he didn't want tears again.

She said, "I thought I'd see you after . . ."

"I didn't know you wanted me to. I honestly didn't know what to do. So I did the next best thing—"

"You came to check on your loan? I've got a job with Quigley Southland Bank. Dumb job for a college girl but I'm not a girl anymore. Anyway, I fixed the car—you see how much you need a car here—and I'm going to DeVry Institute to study computer programming."

"Are they teaching you anything?"

"It's hard to tell. I think it must be a phonier racket than doctoring."

"Except a lot of doctors actually know what they're doing."

"But they're not telling anyone else. I kind of like it. I might end up as the Queen of Sheba of Computer Programs and strong men would kneel and worship me."

"Strong men already do," Drover said.

They had moved into the kitchen. The house was on a California plan endlessly replicated to the architectural impoverishment of the country. It was so cute that it faded fast with age; cute has nothing in common with maturity.

"Coffee?"

"Sure."

She poured out two cups from a Mr. Coffee pot and sat down at the table with him. The table contained the remnants of that day's *Orange County Register,* a textbook on—Drover guessed—computer programming, and a plate with a half piece of buttered toast.

"Are you hungry? Can I make you something?"

"I ate on the plane. That'll put me off my feed for the rest of the day."

She smiled at that. She had a deep smile, full of secrets, set in wide lips and hidden behind straight, white teeth.

"I came to tell you something and to bring something along."

"I don't need anything."

"I had a chance to do it to Slim Dingo."

She caught her breath. Her face went white. For a moment, she looked stricken.

"There's no trouble for you in this," Drover said. "Apparently, a lot of people knew some parts of what happened. Not all of it, maybe, but some of it."

"About what I did—"

"No. I don't think."

"But you don't really know."

"Nobody's got secrets in the long run," Drover said. He said it while stirring his coffee. Stirring coffee seemed the most interesting thing in the world.

"I didn't want you to—"

"You never said a word to me. I know that, Nancy. The thing is, the opportunity came up. Revenge isn't always handed to you. I wondered about that for a while but I got over it; I couldn't figure out what the setup would be and why it would be worth it. So I took Slim. In poker."

"You?" Her hand shot to her mouth to hide the small *o* of shock. Drover felt annoyed.

"Everyone acts as though I can't play anything better than crazy eights. I *do* know how to play poker, Nancy. I learned in college, along with writing a new lead and the five W's."

"But you beat Slim—"

"Well, maybe I cheated."

"Drover—"

He grinned. It was a shy sort of smile but she couldn't meet it with one of her own.

"Just a little—"

"He's a bad man. A dangerous man. You shouldn't have messed with him."

"He certainly keeps bad company."

"Why did you do that?"

Drover put his hand on the table. "I wanted to give you something. It'll be in the mail tomorrow, Federal Express, less my stake money. It's everything Johno lost with a little juice added. It doesn't make up for Johno but it gives you a start. You can get out of here, go up to the city, try something else. Slim Dingo owes you at least that. I'd have cut off his finger and brought it to you but the moment didn't seem right. And fingers don't have much real value at the grocery checkout counter.''

He had said this deadpan, as he said most things. His voice was flat, hardly trying, and it put people at their ease or on guard, depending on what their intentions were. He studied Nancy in these few seconds, to see where it would put her.

What did he really expect except tears?

He went to her and held her and she sobbed, lifting and setting down each sob like a weight.

''Nancy. I'll do anything for you.''

''No. You can't do that. Not anything.''

''I already did.''

And she pushed her face up and looked at him. ''No. If I thought that, I would tell you to kill him. Go kill Slim Dingo and cut off his balls and bring them back to me in a jewelry box. That's *anything* and you won't do it, so don't tell me that.''

And he saw it, through her teary eyes, just what the frost was for. It came from inside her. Maybe it had always been there but it was there now, making her as cold as her voice. Drover saw she wasn't kidding in the least. And Nancy saw at last that Drover understood. She had changed. It wasn't just Johno killing himself or prostituting herself for Slim Dingo. It wasn't just facing forty or going back to school or the bank vice president putting the hit on her all the time. . . . It wasn't any one thing. But she had built up a layer of ice around whatever Old Nancy had been and it was what people saw as New Nancy.

She folded her arms across her chest. She rested her behind on the edge of the single kitchen counter. She tilted her head and stared at him and didn't blink.

''I knew what Johno was when we got married,'' she said. ''I knew and I loved him anyway. That happens. A guy just turns you on and you know this is going to be a disaster in the long run but there it is. I didn't love you, Jimmy. Not that way. I don't know why. We had some laughs. I wanted to try it out with you. I liked you enough to make love to you. But I didn't love you, Jimmy. You wore it on your sleeve for me but that's what happened. I went to California and married Johno because I had to. People do what they have to do, they never stand a chance."

"That's bullshit, Nancy."

"You could do all the knight errant things and I still wouldn't love you," Nancy said.

" 'Nice of you to drop by,' " Drover said.

"Nice of you to drop by."

"Well, okay, Nance." Drover got up. "Wait for the package. It will be here, absolutely positively, by ten-thirty."

"I didn't know they delivered to people without a zip code," Nancy Harrington said, still cool and still apart.

Drover smiled. "Okay, Nance. You can let it drop. I got the hint. You cried and you shouldn't have, it was the only thing wrong with it. Otherwise, two thumbs up. I won't bother you but you know my phone numbers. I can be at your service in less time than it takes to tour Knott's Berry Farm. Otherwise, *vaya con Dios*. I'm not a lovesick sophomore anymore, kid; I'm older and wiser and sadder, just like you. It happens to everyone but everyone doesn't put a cake of ice on it. Don't be bitter, Nance. Put cream in your coffee, take aspirin when you get a headache, cry at old movies."

"You sound like Dr. Ruth."

"Okay."

Silence.

"God, Jimmy, you're the last person in the world I want

to be mad at. Why did I say what I said? Sometimes I don't know who I am.''

"You're Nancy. I'm your friend, Jimmy. Let's let it go at that.''

She took a step toward him.

He smiled and held up his hand. "Friends.''

"Friends,'' she repeated.

"On the other hand, I won't let you look at my sleeves again.''

"Oh hell, Jimmy—'' She went to him and threw her arms over his shoulders and they had a good hug this time, full of good fellowship that suppressed all his love. She really was his buddy, he thought, and he still was the guy with hearts on his jacket.

CHAPTER 10

SLIM DINGO SAT at the wheel of the very presentable gray Silver Shadow Rolls-Royce convertible—a car considered ostentatious everywhere but Southern California and Texas—and tapped the beat of an unheard tune on the ivory-colored steering wheel.

The Rolls was parked in the asphalt lot of a minimart just across and down the street from the faded white stucco house with the red roof.

He and the other man watched the blue Pontiac 6000 turn around in the dusty lawn and creep back to the road. It took a couple of minutes for it to find an opening and shoot out southbound toward the freeway.

"Short visit," said the second man.

"You figure he poked her?"

"Come a long way if he didn't," the second man said.

Slim Dingo snapped his toothpick. That was his property and now he'd paid for it twice and it was too much. "He's gonna give her what he won off me."

"Ain't that the truth," the second man said, and he was grinning hard. "But he didn't bring a package."

Slim slipped a new glitter toothpick between his thin lips and fished around for the right position. He looked at the second man a cool moment. It was Poker Parlor Number Three, appraising and unafraid and a little contemptuous of the other. What he got back was strictly downtown

74

L.A., which was seedy and surly and needed a shave. The PI was named Rollins and he didn't wear a tie and his fedora needed a cleaning. Slim Dingo used him for errands and for tails and things like that.

"The guy you wanted me to check on, this guy Drover, was a newspaper guy in L.A., six, no seven years ago, wrote a column, sports column, then he had bad luck with the U.S. attorney who was then named Flaherty, a hot dog, I knew him; went after this big gambling ring, you know, the usual federal bullshit. Got fifteen Sicilians and nine other guys and put six hundred counts on them and announced it on the TV. He was running for a senior partnership in Winshop and Downs—"

"I heard of them," Slim Dingo said.

"So, to show he ain't prejudiced only against dagos, he ropes in a genuine WASP newspaper guy named Drover."

Slim smiled at that, thinking about the little prick getting nailed once, and going to get nailed again.

"See, I unnerstand that Drover ain't in the environment, he knew this guy Tony Rolls from on account he grew up in Chicago where all these guys lived."

"And that Guinea bastard Tony Rolls fucked me. Fuck him," Slim Dingo said in a calm way.

"See, I think Tony wants Drover to do something for him so he set you up. Drover is doing something, I don't know what, but I can keep on it if you want me," Rollins said. He was always figuring out days, days of expenses, days of watching, days and nights when the meter was running and then the other days, when nothing was going on and his checking account was made of rubber.

"So that's where Nancy Harrington lives," Dingo said. "That fucking cunt." The words were surprising. Slim Dingo was normally not so coarse but $130,000 was $130,000 and now that cunt had it—or would get it soon.

"Whaddaya want me to do," Rollins said.

"I don't need nothin', not now, now that I seen where she lives, know she's got the money. I can take care of that little gal myself. Package must be coming in the mail."

"I can help you if you want."

Slim Dingo smiled like a lizard. "Take care of her myself. You did good, Rollins, got a good eye." He peeled off seven hundred from a roll fastened by something gold. "You parked over here?"

"Behind the Ralph's," Rollins said, letting the cool money warm his hand for a moment, staring at it, wishing there were more hundreds.

"And this here Drover? I forgot, thinking about Nancy just now, what was it happened to him?"

Rollins stared at the money and then came out of it. He slipped the hundreds into the inside jacket pocket and pulled out a red dime-store notebook. He flipped it open. "Yeah. When he got hit with the indictment, the rag he worked for panicked and suspended him and when he beefed about it, they fired him. This was seven years ago. Then he got a lawyer and the indictment against him got dropped along the way. One of those conspiracy bullshit things because he was on a recording with Dominick D'Allesandro, you know him, but it turned out it wasn't nothing, just talking about the Dodgers. . . . So the paper was wrong but they didn't hire him back because they said a journalist has other standards or some bullshit. Fucking papers, biggest whores I ever met in my life was newspapermen. Anyway, I talked to Vinnie Vitale works for the paper, I can usually get a good line from him."

"One of your whores," Slim Dingo said.

"Well, Vinnie is all right but if he saw a tip sitting on a bar, he'd glom it for himself. Drover, this guy, got his lawyer that got him off to sue the paper and he wins the suit and wins some serious money. Then he ends up living up north in Santa Cruz and he works for this book in

Vegas, guy named Fox Vernon. But it's real casual, like not all the time. He goes out to games and looks around. I mean, is that a life or what? Fucking bastard.''

"Yeah," Slim Dingo said. He put another toothpick on his lower lip. "Nice life, all right. Too bad he went and blew it up at the end for a broad."

Rollins caught it but didn't bat an eye. Slim Dingo was changing what this was about. This was about some money and now it was about a broad—taking care of a broad himself, a mean bastard—and now it was about some guy ending his life. End meant end and Slim Dingo didn't use words he didn't mean.

Rollins knew how to keep it inside. He knew cops in the old days would put a bullet in someone for a grand, just figure it was one worthless life getting paid off by another. He knew who did it and who said they would do it and then took the money and dared the guy paying for the hit to do anything about it. So what was one more dead body? Rollins knew what Slim Dingo was saying out loud just now in this air-conditioned Rolls-Royce with leather and wood on everything.

"Go on, Rollins, call you in a few days," Slim Dingo said. "Got a gal I gotta talk to, talk some sense into her, make her see the error of hanging in with bad companions. Once she gets a package. I can wait."

"You think Drover had her in on it from the beginning?" Rollins said, opening the door.

"Don't matter. She's gotta pay because she played," Slim Dingo said.

Rollins understood all that as well.

CHAPTER 11

IT HAD SNOWED in the mountains during the night and they were white and beautiful, cupping Denver on the flat plateau like a painted backdrop.

The United 737 dropped through the crystal clear air down from the mountains and across the city to Stapleton International, which is due east of downtown and far enough away from the mountains to make landings seem routine.

Drover picked up the rental—a Dodge Omni this time, guaranteed to deliver a thousand miles a gallon—and remembered the way to the city. Interstate 70, flat since Pennsylvania, gets its second wind in Denver just before tackling the next thousand miles of real mountains. It snows a lot in Denver but the weather and people are generally warm and without expectations good or bad—unless it's the Denver Broncos. With the Broncos, they always expect good things until Super Bowl Sunday.

The Denver Press Club was not the logical first place to start. Newspapermen are gossips disguised as historians and their information is often as shaky in truth as the last issue of *Pravda*. But you had to start somewhere and somewhere was at the team that was getting all the action, the secret action from an outlaw line on the futures exchange in Chicago. Why the press club? Drover felt bad, felt bad about Nancy, felt bad about never having her again, about his lost youth, first love, and all the other silly things that really cut deep. So he wanted friends and neighbors around and Black Kelly was out with a party of deep-sea fishermen the next two days.

The Denver Press Club is an unprepossessing two-story building on Glenarm Place with a secret tunnel to help poker players escape police raids. The cops don't raid anymore but the legend lives on. It is a place for self-made legends; Damon Runyan and Gene Fowler were members in their time. It is shanked just south of the glittering downtown and across the street from the much grander athletic club. Not that it matters; the biggest athletic events in the press club are picking up the tab, putting it on the cuff, and drawing to an inside straight.

The *Rocky Mountain News* and *The Denver Post* were represented at the bar, along with admen, PR men, and a couple of ladies nobody carded.

Drover pulled up a stool and Dusty Baumann nodded at him.

Dusty had red hair, freckled hands, and a deep and lingering thirst. He drank beer until it backed up on him, usually before 1:00 P.M., and then switched to see-throughs. It was see-through time.

"Come to cheer on the Big Orange?" Dusty said. He was a sportswriter for the *News*. He could have been a columnist but he turned it down because he said he hated the idea of writing even when he had nothing to say.

"Check them out," Drover said.

"They're on track. Super Bowl express. Can't miss." Dusty Baumann spoke the way he wrote.

The bartender came over and Drover joined the club with Red Label on the rocks and soda back. He bought a drink for everyone at the bar and that made him instantly famous and friendly.

"Cheers," Dusty said without looking cheerful. He

sipped his vodka martini as though it were a new taste experience. "The Super Bowl."

"Super Bowl," answered Drover.

"Of course, when we get in the Bowl, Denver'll lose. Written in stone somewhere. Denver gets in, Denver gets left at the altar."

"I know the syndrome, Dusty."

"That's right. You're from Chicago. You've seen the Cubs. You've smelled the Sox. You've suffered, son, I'm not saying you haven't. Still sitting on that pier in Santa Cruz?"

"Good a place as any."

"Come out next month. We'll take a weekend up in Vail. Aspen. Somewhere."

"I don't ski."

"Fuck skiing. Find girls. Make love on the slopes."

"Anything bad going on with the Orange?"

"Nothing. It's eerie. Someone should be hurt by now. Someone should be rumored to have nose candy stashed in his locker. The coach should be kicking ass and taking names. But no. Not a damned thing. Serendipity. Sickening. How do you write about a team that's just plain as good as they look?"

"Come on, Dusty. 'Any given Sunday et cetera.' "

"I don't want to hear that Rozelle crap. Nobody can beat Denver in the foreseeable future. They do San Diego Sunday. A joke. The Chargers ought to send in a cancellation and turn back tickets. The Bears? Come on. The Jets right after. . . . I mean, the Jets. Then New Orleans. The only two things in life I look forward to at the moment is the Broncos beating the living shit out of the Saints in that lovely Dome they got down there and the second thing is getting crazy on Bourbon Street."

"You assigned to the game?"

"Yes. They're sending Parker to suck his thumb on it and me to do the grunt work. I like it better that way."

They ordered another round. Drover liked Dusty Baumann because Dusty represented the disordered and lovely past of American journalism. So did the Denver press. Dusty knew bullshit and he knew real things and he loved both but he kept them straight in his head. One was not the other and vice versa. He was an antique of sorts, just like the old Press Club and the saloons off Larimar Square and the Brown Palace hotel with its balconies and the lobby where cowboys and computer salesmen mingled. Denver wore its past with comfort, like broken-in cowboy boots.

So if Dusty thought the Broncos were a lock, why was Chicago money drabbing and dribbling into the market on the New Orleans Saints? Tony Rolls smelled a fix but couldn't pick a day. Fox Vernon, with his mathematical approach, saw a day but couldn't see a way.

"How's Moneypenny?" Moneypenny was a defensive back.

"Humongous as usual. Eats live chickens for breakfast. Pulverizes bricks with the sides of his hands."

"And Thompson?"

"Our gazelle. A national treasure. He's leading the Crippled Children fund again this year. Still lives with Mom in Tucson in the off-season. Goes to mass on Sunday before the game, even in godless climes like Sodom City."

Drover punched another button. "Gascon."

"Gascon. What do you want to know about Gascon?"

"How's his love life?"

"Fucked up as usual. His wife divorced him before the season, you know."

"I read it somewhere."

"Probably a newspaper."

"Probably."

"You read the *News* out there?"

"Doesn't get circulated."

"Your loss. You should live in the Queen City."

"Gascon."

"Got a girlfriend or five. He can handle it. He is simply getting better, Drover. Did you see last week's?"

"I was watching on the big screens at Shamrock. I was interested in the Bears, paid more attention to it—"

"Bears. What a chauvinist Chicago people are."

"That's ungrammatical."

"I ain't paid to talk, only write."

"Let me get you another leg to stand on."

"Are you trying to get me drunk?"

"Gascon," Drover said.

Another martini, another Red Label rocks. Someone else wanted to buy. Dusty never got drunk, which was physically impossible but there it was. He said it was his Prussian liver that did it all.

"All right, Drover. Gascon. Step into my office."

Drover got up and bent an elbow next to Dusty Baumann. Baumann did not look at him but at the rest of the bar. He judged it was self-occupied. His voice, never loud, dropped a notch.

"I know this and now you know this. I know a guy knows a guy says Gascon and the GM had a sitdown a couple days ago. Not about broads but about the GM wanting to discuss the subject of blow."

"Gascon doing drugs?"

'Put out that word and everything changes. But no, I honestly don't think so. Partridge, the general manager, is as loopy as Nancy Reagan on the subject. He fixes you with this idiot grin and breaks into sermons on the subject. He does not smoke, drink, snort, fuck, suck, or use enough breath mints, the latter my opinion only. I want to help you out, kid, but you don't seem to know where you're going, do you?"

"No."

"So what's really going down? Does Vegas suspect a fix? Or are they hoping?"

"The outlaw line will probably open with Denver up by nine. The next day, it might go higher."

"Prudent men. Denver is gonna kick ass in Awlins, you heard it here first."

"What about Gascon?"

"You could buy me a rainbow trout at the Brown Palace and I couldn't tell you different, Drover. Gascon is a fun guy. He's into girls. Lots of girls, every color girl on earth. I can't say he's never done a line but that's not his style. He doesn't go to Snow City for recreation."

"Snow City?"

"The Big Nose Candy Capital. Aspen."

"Oh."

"He likes Wild Turkey neat and girls undressed. He bangs stews and cheerleaders alike. An equal opportunity stick man. I spent time with the guy. I seen him naked in locker rooms. It's a big one, Drover, really big."

"Watch it, Dusty. You're turning."

"Never happen. But I'm observant. Gascon is a normal, healthy, egotistical, twenty-six-year-old professional football quarterback who can throw like Joe Montana could on his best day and has the line and receivers to make this old heart of mine sing. Denver is not gonna blow the Bowl this time, I don't care if they put in two National Conference teams against us."

"The good reporter is a cool, neutral observer."

"That kind of crap talk kills newspapers. We are there to cheer our young men on. You worked for one of those cool papers, didn't you?"

"Once or twice."

"We can't lose with Gascon and Company."

"Can you win without Gascon?"

Dusty looked at him.

"What do you know, Drover?"

"I don't know anything yet. I know I want to know something. Something is funny."

"Well, life is full of laughs."

"Where does Gascon live?"

"Right here. Downtown. Out Seventeenth toward Union Station. He's a party cat and he likes big-city living. Hates mountains. He walks them home sometimes."

Drover smiled. "Can someone talk to him?"

"You? No way. You're banned from football, what could he do, being seen consorting with known gamblers?"

"I don't gamble. I watch games."

Dusty Baumann squinted at his glass and then at Drover. Drover signaled with one finger and more drinks came up. When the barman walked away to the far end, Dusty Baumann said, "What game are you watching now?"

"The game of Dead Cert."

"How's it played?"

"Dead Cert. The Lock. Denver plays the Saints in four weeks in the Crescent City.'

"Ah, you still have that colorful way of talking that we sportswriters cultivate."

"Dead Cert." Drover was staring at the back mirror of the bar. He was seeing himself but he looked right through that image. There was something else he wanted to see. "Gascon can get clotheslined by the Bears secondary and see double for a few weeks. Moneypenny can pull a hamstring."

"He don't have hamstrings, man. He's the Michelin Tire Man. We proved it. We scientifically dropped him from Moffat Pass and he bounced when he landed."

"Gascon gets called in by the GM about drugs."

"It was bullshit. I sniffed and sniffed and I smelled it good. I can still smell."

"But why now? I don't know, Dusty."

"How come I'm feeding you and you're not feeding me?"

"I'm an old friend. I bought you a drink. I don't know, Dusty, I really don't."

He paused, stared at his own brown drink. "But I hate the idea of a Dead Cert game that people are betting the wrong way."

It was all he could tell him now.

CHAPTER 12

THE FEDERAL EXPRESS van pulled up to the white stucco house at 10:10 the next morning and the man in the blue uniform climbed out. He had the Courier-Pak in hand and walked up to the front door.

Slim Dingo had guessed right again. He had been watching. He was a good guesser. Came from playing poker. Besides, he had logic on his side. Drover had left Chicago without the money on him. Therefore, he had dropped it or stashed it. Since Drover didn't go back to Chicago, it was logical that the drop had been mail. Mail or one of the private couriers. Either to himself in that rathole he lived in on the Santa Cruz pier or direct to Miss Nancy. Miss Nancy indeed.

He thought about that blonde fluff naked. She was in her thirties or forties but she carried herself. Tits were nice and she had pinkish nipples. He had liked all her parts and told her so. Now he was going to see her again and it was going to be double pleasure, taking back his money and giving her some instructions. Some lessons. Yes sir, that was nearly as good as the money but the money counted too. He'd see the widow and have a little sitdown with her when it was over, he would explain the new and revised rules of human behavior to her. After all, she had it coming, not as if she were a real lady. She was a whore, proved that when she went down on Slim to save that worthless slimeball husband of hers. Proved it now again, stealing his money with that prick, Drover.

Slim Dingo didn't even have to check out of the motel. Everything was arranged.

He popped a gold-colored toothpick in his mouth as he slid behind the wheel of the Rolls. Heat rose in waves already and it was still morning. The flat commercialscape stretched out between the thin ranks of orange trees.

Above him, the desert sky was turning from early blue to, eventually, afternoon brown. The air conditioner didn't make a sound, which is what you pay so much for.

He thought about what he was going to do the same way he thought about cards around a table and who had what and what the play would be. There was the money and the girl and that punk who took him and maybe Tony Rolls too, maybe see just what kind of clout the old man had in Vegas with the wise guys.

Slim Dingo thought he was a superb hater.

CHAPTER 13

GASCON SAID, "COMIN', honey lamb," and opened the door on a surprise.

It was just about going-out time and he had on a terrific purple shirt, sweater, gold chain, small earring in the left ear, purple silk socks, black loafers, all very laid-back and waiting to get laid.

Drover figured Gascon figured he was a disappointment. Something about the frown forming on his lips.

"Hey, man, who are you? I was expecting someone—"

"My name is Drover."

"Do I know you?"

"You're going to."

"What's that mean?" Not laughing but not quite snarling. The accent was lost in the swamps south of Baton Rouge. His curly hair was frizzed as well and as black as Louisiana oil.

"I want to know about Partridge and you and what you talked about this past week."

"Hey, fuck you, man, who the fuck are you?"

"NFL Security," Drover said. He held up a card.

"I got rights, I don' gotta talk to ya—"

"You don' gotta do nuttin', including playing next week," Drover said. He pushed it on the accent. Nobody likes a smart ass. And Gascon looked big enough to put him through a brick wall. Which is why you have to establish the relationship right away. You shit, me boss.

Gascon took a step back. Drover took a step forward. They were in an apartment on the nineteenth floor of a steel-and-glass building. Union Station was down there and Mile High Stadium was over there and downtown D was there. The lights beckoned. The playing was to commence.

"I want to ask you a few questions," Drover said in a softer voice. No need to push it. Gascon was a millionaire and, according to Dusty Baumann, the cocksman of the Western World. But he was still a kid and Drover was a man and the NFL Security was something nobody messed with, least of all a player.

Drover shut the door and they stood in the foyer for a moment and then Gascon led him into the living room. A wet bar divided the front room from the tiny kitchen and that's where they headed.

"Who put you on me to hassle me? Old Lady Partridge call you in?"

"One of the first things we learn at Dick Tracy University is never to reveal our sources," Drover said. He sat down at the bar. "Siddown, Gascon, this won't hurt."

"I don't do drugs."

"You just say no."

"Fuck you. Gimme a test. I never flunked yet. Y'all go after some of those boys you know is walkin' around on cloud nine, shit, you can see it in their eyes when they're in the pit. Y'all can get as many cokeheads as y'all want if y'all was honest about it."

"Who put the bee in Partridge's bonnet?"

"Old Lady Partridge is crazy, man. He cain't stand success. Best fuckin' quarterback in the league, best team, best ever'thing and ever'body signed to contracts and the asshole can't let well enough alone. How do I know what got into him Wednesday? Asshole. Maybe his old lady wanted a fuck and she already had her quota for the year used up.''

''You got nose whores around you?''

''Shit.'' Gascon almost spat but then realized he'd have to clean it up himself. ''Do I look like I gotta buy broads with blow?'' He couldn't spit but he sneered. ''I'd show you my cock but I'd be afraid you'd want to suck it off.''

Drover smiled at that. ''Gascon, I want to tell you a story.''

''I ain't in the mood.''

''Guy was a quarterback on this golden team and one day someone puts out the word on him. Why'd they do it? Maybe somebody was working the angles. You know, Vegas, stuff like that. Maybe somebody wanted to set up the golden quarterback so that a long-shot bet turns into a sure thing. You wanna fix a game, fix the coach or the quarterback.''

''So talk to Schultz.''

Schultz was the coach. Drover shook his head. ''You don't get it, Gascon, that's because you're so in love with yourself you're driving down the freeway looking in the rearview mirror instead of through the windshield. Somebody put the bee in Partridge's bonnet and it was specific. It was about drugs. And someone else saw to it that the same bee got buzzed in the sports department at at least one paper. But this is all by way of the windup. You get me? If you take the test right now, are you gonna pass?''

''Fuck yes. I ain't even had a drink in two days, how's that grab you? More I can say for you.''

''I forgot to use Listerine before I came over. Sorry.''

''I don't care if you was shootin' up in a Chinese whorehouse, just don't put your problem on me. What newspaper you say got wind of me using drugs? I'll go over and cut some sportswriter a new asshole. Shit, what do I need with blow? Broads come just looking at me, let alone before I do anything. I got money and bought me a farm in Florida for fun and when I get done throwin', ole CBS or ABC or someone is gonna say, 'Gascon, honey, with your big blue eyes and honeysuckle voice, come on over and give Brent Musberger a hand with the mike and we gonna make you rich doing it.' I ain't got shit for brains, I ain't no fuckin' lineman, I'm a fuckin' quarterback. Shit. *The* quarterback of this generation.''

''Well, there was that Italian fellow in San Francisco.''

''Hey, you know what I'm saying, I'm just saying it differently. I don't need it. Don' do drugs, don' do muscle builders, nothin'. Don't need to.'' He smiled and Drover had to smile despite himself. ''I was born perfect.''

''Humpty Dumpty,'' Drover said.

Gascon stared at him. The bell rang. It was probably Honey Lamb.

Gascon said, ''You gonna keep interrupting the perfect evening I have planned?''

''Not at all, lover boy,'' Drover said. ''Remember what I said. Look over your shoulder the next couple of weeks. Especially before New Orleans.''

''What about Awlins? Saints ain't piss ants. We could beat 'em drunk.''

''I ain't kidding, kid. There's bad out there and it's pointed at you.''

The bell rang again. Gascon stared at him and walked around the bar to the door. Honey Lamb was only a nine because of a slight overbite that, in reality, made her look even more attractive. She had the Lee Remick look from *Days of Wine and Roses* and you really wanted to get drunk and dirty with her. All this registered with Drover in less than a second.

Honey Lamb gave Gascon a big one and she seemed to quiver on her teetery heels while doing it. Drover felt envy

but let it slide. After all, he had a better mind than Gascon
and years of experience.

"Who's he?" she asked when she finally noticed
Drover.

"A man from the league, Honey Lamb. This is Lori
Gibbons. I forget your name but that's all right. Must not
be important."

"Drover," Drover said. "I was just leaving, Lori,
though after seeing you, I leave with regret."

That charmed Lori into a smile and that lovely overbite
came on display again, dazzling a hundred feet of track in
front of her. Gascon slipped his arm around Lori and just
glared at Drover.

"Remember what I said, Lenny," Drover said to Gascon. He took a card out of his sports coat. "I got a number
if you need me. Day or night, twenty-four hours."

"Is that right? Why the fuck would I need you?"

"Don't use that word, honey."

"Aw, Honey lamb, I forgot." He patted her bottom in
a different way than most football players patted each other
on Sundays on national television. "Man is askin' me if I
use candy. You ask Lori here, is my main squeeze, ask
her."

"I wouldn't spend a second with Len if he was using
anything like that," Lori said. She said it so you believed
it. Especially if that overbite caught you. Or the wide blue
eyes. Or anything else on her list of weapons.

"What do you do, Lori?"

"I work for United. Flight attendant."

"You based here?"

"Yes I am," she said, forthright. Gascon was frowning
very hard now, wishing Drover straight to hell.

Drover said, "Okay, Len. Lori. I told you, Len. Watch
out. Someone is out there in the dark."

"I look like I'm afraid of someone? You get hit some-

time by Dan Hampton, ole Dan'l get you on the blind side
and one minute you're passing and the next minute this
guy is trying to drive you to China straight through the
earth, and you get up off the ground and spit out a tooth
or two and then throw a touchdown pass next play, you
think someone like that is afraid of some booga-booga shit
like you're puttin' down?''

''What's he say you should be afraid of?''

''Asshole Partridge ask me this week if I'm using drugs.
Some asshole tells some other asshole and now this asshole from the league is coming to put the spook on me. I
say test me or shove it up your ass, I ain't afraid.''

Lori looked at Drover. ''Why'd you want to roil Len?
He hasn't done anything, believe me, I'd know. We go to
dinner, dance, have a drink. I mean, Len is as good as
gold.''

''I don't doubt it, Lori.''

''You got anything else to say or you just wanna keep
staring at my girl's tits?''

Lori blushed. ''Len, watch what you say.''

''Yeah, Lenny, watch what you say.'' Drover was tired
of it. He didn't know what to make of it. But he knew that
Gascon was so heavily in love with himself that Lori was
probably a beard for masturbation. ''See you around, kid,
and keep your nose clean. Nose. Clean. Get it?''

''I'd pop you one if it wasn't for the good of the team
to restrain myself.''

''A patriot,'' Drover said. ''S'long. S'long, Lori. I'm
transferring all my business to United from now on.''

Another dazzling smile. Drover opened the door and let
Gascon slam it behind him. Out in the darkness once
again. Groping for the bad thing.

CHAPTER 14

BART BRIXTON, WEARING eleven hundred dollars on his back, walked into La Tour at 7:00 A.M. Thursday. He let the faggy maître d' lead him to the occupied table by the window. People who showed well got window tables so the peasants on North Michigan Avenue could gaze at power and wealth on display. It was a good day to be seen. Rain glazed the sidewalks and made the hurrying masses that much more miserable. Inside La Tour all was warm. Even the orange juice exuded sunshine. Breakfast was ordinary and ran a double sawbuck per but La Tour was the place where power "did" breakfast and cut deals that spread from the city of Chicago around the world.

"Bart."

"Tommy."

"Coffee, sir?" said the hovering waiter. Bart deigned to touch his cup as a signal. Coffee was poured, the waiter retreated like an altar boy, and Tommy Sain stared at the other man. If you didn't look close, they were two of a kind, both in their thirties, both immensely sure of themselves and sharp about it. They had begun their fortunes on the Chicago Board of Trade. Now they were going to add to it on other exchanges of chance.

It had been Bart's idea from the first.

"How much did you manage to put away yesterday?" Bart said.

"Another sixty thousand. In five pieces in Vegas and I layed off ten dimes with a book in Denver."

"Nothing local."

"I got your instructions, you don't have to repeat. I can even recite the times-twelve table," Tommy Sain said. He was annoyed. He didn't forget, he didn't need to be reminded.

But that was part of the game. Tom was the weaker, Bart was the leader. Tom deferred, Bart commanded. It was almost sexual as all relationships usually are but neither Tom nor Bart was homosexual. It was just that one guy goes first and keeps reminding the other guy he trails.

"That means we've got two hundred thousand to go," Bart said. "I figure another two or three days."

"Shit. That really is pushing it," Tommy Sain said. "I dunno—"

"Look, Tommy. I've got the other end. Our party is going to make the setup after this weekend's game. San Diego is wired and ready to blow up. As soon as our boy gets back to Denver, the little birdie gets in the commissioner's ear."

"That's the part I don't understand."

"You wanna understand everything?" Bart smiled. He was a big man with red hair and the eyes of a con man. It was part of his charm, this sense of his being a con man. He'd smile at the ladies and they knew they shouldn't trust him and he was smiling in a way that encouraged their mistrust. That was the charm. He had the manners of a con man. He listened to the ladies, he deferred to men, he seemed attentive but there was laughter in everything he did. He didn't really mean it and he was sharing the joke with anyone smart enough to get it. This was a form of flattery that really worked—Bart was always telling you that you were smart enough to understand that this was a con game.

"I want to understand the parts I got to understand," Tommy said.

"Nobody ever understands everything," Bart said. "You go along for the ride. You don't take a course in aerodynamics before you get on a plane."

Tommy smiled. Bart forced a smile out of everyone. Charm, that's what it was, laid on thick like mayonnaise and, hell, you knew mayo wasn't good for you. But you had to have it anyway. Bart wasn't good for you but a room lit up when he was in it. Like now.

The waiter returned. Rain was splashing against the big picture windows and against the peasants hurrying to their 8:00 A.M. jobs. Chicago was an 8:00 A.M. town. The bosses arrived by car at 10:00. The workers arrived by bus and on foot at 8:00. Only in the very different environment of the world's biggest commodities and futures exchanges did big shot and gofer arrive for work at the same early hour. Which is why Tom Sain and Bart Brixton were early risers and eaters.

When he got his orders, the waiter moved off. Bart said to Tommy, "I've got an in. If I explain the in to you, that makes two of us know it. I don't see why I have to. Just know that I can do it. When the commissioner gets his ear filled, he's going to act. He has to act. It's his job to. Beside, what's it to him? If they run a test and Gascon is clean on drugs, so much the better. If they're looking for cocaine, they aren't going to find it. But they're going to find the other thing. Yes. They are definitely going to find the other thing."

"How can—"

"Trust me, Tommy. This is the score. We hit the way we're supposed to, we can just about pocket the chump change and fold our little betting parlor and quietly walk."

"With two million dollars each," Tommy Sain said. It was the part that dazzled him from the beginning when

Bart Brixton first proposed it. Two million. The betting pool inside the board of trade exchange was four years old and it was just good fun, everyone agreed on that. Some guys made money and some guys lost money but it was nothing serious. A few thousand each way each week. Not like the money lost to cocaine dealers or by betting wrong on sow bellies.

Tommy Sain ran the pool as a hobby and part-time job. He was a trader as well but the pool represented a substantial bit of income every fall from the juice he charged—the 10 percent "vigorish" for booking the bets. Ten percent on every bet. He bet himself on the games but not in his own pool. He liked sports, he knew bookies, he liked to gamble. He really liked to gamble. If there was a flaw in his makeup—and he didn't look flawed at all, not in his custom-made suit, not with his dark good looks—it was the gambling thing. He would be calm and careful for months at a time, doing some small betting with one of his bookies, dropping a few dollars here and there, when, suddenly, it would come on him, this need that was almost physical. And even when he knew it was coming on him— could almost feel it like a fit coming on—he knew he would succumb to it and do what the demon inside told him to do.

He would lose himself for a long weekend in Vegas, pushing the limits, gambling until his money was gone and his credit was no good. And then, purged of the de- mon again, he would wake up from his nightmare in a strange, flocked-wallpaper hotel room, sometimes with a naked woman beside him, and he would feel drained and dirty. He would crawl back to Chicago and resume his role as a trader of future things, making money for himself and those he bet for, holding himself in check until the next time he went insane. It was a dangerous way to live

and the longer he lived this kind of life, the more dangerous it got.

Bart Brixton had pulled him out of a hole once or twice.
Tided him over. Now Bart Brixton had put the scheme to
him and Tommy, despite his weakness, saw that it would
work. Just one time. Maybe with that kind of walkaway
money, Tom could check himself into a program, get this
monkey demon off his case. He could look at his problem
rationally when he wasn't being possessed. Like now. He
was calm, he made small bets now and then, he read the
sports pages without going insane. Close down the pool
after this season, stash the two million in Zurich, go to a
shrink and talk himself out of this obsession.

"Tommy, timing is what this is about. I already put a
bird in Emil Partridge's ear."

"The GM at Denver? Are you crazy? What are you
messing with him for?"

Bart smiled but there was nothing pleasant in it. The
con man eyes didn't care and that made them most dangerous. "Listen, asshole, I know what I'm doing. You do
your job half as good as I do mine and this thing is a lock.
Partridge called in Gascon for a chat about his drug problems. And I circulated a rumor out to the Denver newspapers as well. They aren't going to print anything, so
relax. You don't understand how to set these things up.
The world feeds on rumors. What do you think runs the
market? We ran long last year on orange juice. January
orange juice. Man, it was beautiful."

"You did January orange juice? I didn't know that. How
come you didn't let me in on it?"

"I let you in on a lot of things. I saved your ass a couple
of times, Tommy, when you went over the edge in Vegas.
Remember? I know you remember."

"I remember. I told you thanks a million times."

"So I didn't make you suck my knob, did I? So don't

give me shit about not telling you about January orange juice.''

''Shit, Bart, I was just talking.''

''You were just talking and I was explaining to you that I know how this thing works. The world is a rumor waiting to be believed. Partridge was part, the newspapers in Denver were part, now we got to get to the upper level.''

''So how are you going to get him to take his medicine? Gascon.''

''Gascon's already been taking it,'' Bart Brixton said. He liked that one, the dumb look on Tommy Sain's dumb face when he pulled a gotcha. Tommy Sain was an addict and Bart Brixton had nothing but contempt for addicts. The guy was a gambler. When he was gambling, he couldn't lose enough. It was like Frances. Frances was one of his girls, a nice-looking model with those model bones and that porcelain skin. Skinny but nice tits, tits were back in the world of modeling. She was also his coke whore. She'd go down on dogs if he told her to. All that beauty and she wasn't worth a shit. Four, five years, she'd be sucking shines in the alley for blow. Addicts. Worthless usually unless you had a use for them.

''Gascon got it in his Wheaties. Guy ate Wheaties for breakfast, I'm not kidding you. Cut up a banana on top, milk—used two percent milk—and sugar. Like he was ten years old still. Did it for a girl. Well, he's really got the breakfast of champions now. Got that muscle builder to make him big and strong and leap tall buildings in a single bound. He just doesn't know it yet.''

''How did you do it?''

''See, you're doing it again, Tommy. I show you a way to make money and you want to take it apart and examine the wheels. Let it go and just know that I did it and when I tell you something, it's done.''

Breakfast came. Eggs and bacon and new potatoes.

Toast. Bart Brixton looked at the plate, looked at Tom Sain. Tommy was getting on his nerves all of a sudden. The waiter went away.

"You're not getting crazy, are you, Tommy? That money itching you all of a sudden?"

"I'm not getting crazy."

"You blow this, Tommy, I swear to God—"

"It's under control, I'm not getting crazy."

"Listen, Tommy, I want that money laid off by Saturday or it comes out of your side of the split. Don't fuck around with me and don't ask me a million questions. There's gonna be heat when this hits. And after, there's gonna be heat if they figure out this was a setup, that this was a fix. But they won't. But the Outfit, now those guys don't like to get taken, they don't like their lines fixed unless they are doing the fixing. I don't need any partners except for you. Everyone else is a salary to me. But, partner, you do as you're told. You understand me, am I going slow enough for you?"

"Shit, Bart, don't talk like that."

"You finish your breakfast, asshole, and spend the rest of the day thinking how you're gonna lay that money off and you do it and you come back to me and say you did what I told you to do. You understand me, Tommy?"

Tommy let his eyes go down and focus on his uneaten eggs. "I understand, Bart."

"Fuck," Bart Brixton said, getting up, getting ready to walk out on the scene. The con man eyes glittered but the light was cold, colder than the day. "You fucking better."

CHAPTER 15

NANCY HARRINGTON HURT all over. Her ribs hurt most and she knew she had been broken.

Her face was bad. Both eyes were bruised and that made her eyes look haunted. Hell, she was haunted. She had met the devil.

The first thing Slim Dingo had done was hit her, even before he told her he wanted the money. She had picked up a knife on the kitchen table and come at him, remembering Johno, remembering the humiliation of that weekend with Slim Dingo. She was going to kill him.

He had got a very small cut before he made her drop the knife. Even after she dropped the knife, he twisted and she had to scream. He pulled her hair. He beat the hell out of her and he enjoyed it, every minute of it. Just beat her and beat her, slamming her around the house from the kitchen and into the bathroom and then into the living room. She even pleaded after a while and it made him beat her more. Then he wanted the money. She went to the cupboard and took down the envelope and gave it to him and he hit her again. Then he counted the money in front of her with her standing there, sobbing because it hurt. He raped her more than once and in more than one way. Then he talked to her, lying there naked on the bed, her ribs hurting and bleeding all over.

"What I did to you goes for what I am going to do to

your partner. Whoever the fuck this Drover is. You, Nancy honey, are now permanently on my list. When you look better, I want you to come see me at the ranch like you came to see me when you wanted me to let up on Johno. You come on by and if you do good, I'll let you sleep in my bed. If you don't come see me, I'll come see you. You understand, honey?'' The voice was just as even as it always was, a poker voice, but the Texas charm accent was too clipped. Slim Dingo was now the devil out of hell. "You do good and I won't put you in a cathouse where you will spend your days and nights balling every asshole with a double sawbuck in his pocket. You do good and I'll sort of let you live. You do bad and you'll get beat up again and then maybe beat up all the time. I got plenty of time to beat you up. I got friends would enjoy beating you up. You talk to a cop, you are dead meat, you know that, you know the way it goes. They put you in some half-ass witness program, we get you. Besides, what are you gonna say? Say that I beat you up and raped you? Shit. I got pictures of you when you came out to the ranch for me. Remember that weekend? That was a lot of fun, Nancy, we could have fun again. Did you like getting beat up?''

She shook her head because he wanted her to answer. She moaned because she had to.

For a long time, maybe a day, after Slim was gone, she thought about what she should do. She was humiliated and afraid. She thought about everything. And she thought about Slim Dingo and how she was going to kill him. She thought about cutting him open all the way from his balls to his neck, just letting him die that way with his guts hanging out.

She thought about the cops. She was Johno Harrington's widow. Johno was a gambler, a bum, a no-good. What was she but his lay? And then she accuses another gambler

. . . uh, oh, I don't think we wanna get in this, do we, officer? Besides, Nancy knew what it was like on this side of the law. People on this side of the law had no right at all and certainly no right to go over to the other side.

Besides, if she went to the cops and then found a way to kill Slim Dingo, they might arrest her. She was nothing, just some broad who'd been around too many tracks.

Then she decided.

She called in sick to work because she was sick. And then she found the card he had left her.

She called one of the numbers.

CHAPTER 16

Fox Vernon met him in the lounge of the Shamrock Casino. Fox drank ginger ale.

Drover took a stool and ordered Red Label. He stared at Fox and waited until the drink came.

"It's Denver."

"You're positive."

"I got a feeling."

"You do good vibes," Fox Vernon said. "I'm going to put it off the boards."

"You do that and I can't move. You do that and Tony Rolls and his crowd start whacking people. I need a little time. If they do the fix, we can find out how and why and who."

"We're not policemen."

"I don't want a fix. I happen to like football."

"I like it as a mathematical calculation. Fixes tend to screw up arithmetic. Guys who like to think two and two can make five give me problems."

"The G. There's something about the G in this. That's what I can't figure out. Somehow, this is connected. The G picked me up in Chicago and they knew, they were sitting there and it was like they had been inside Tony Roll's house. So they know something. And why put me in the middle of it?"

"I told you to be careful. Your problem becomes my problem."

"Foxy, this may be more than one game and one guy. This may be the beginning of the end for a lot of us. If football starts stinking, a lot of betting goes away. Tony knows that and so do his cousins. He wants someone outside the environment to find out something his wise guys can't find out. Except they know it's coming from the Chicago commodity exchange, from some brokers. How many guys? Fifty? Hundred? Maybe that's the G angle. Maybe not. I just don't know and I don't like swimming at midnight in dark rivers."

"There's a lot of money in play on this."

"Gascon. They're going to get Gascon. And it's going to be drugs. I can feel it like my own skin."

"I don't like this at all."

"Gascon is going to like it less."

"Is Gascon doing blow?"

"He comes out and says no. His girlfriend backs him up. He said he wanted a test. But there are rumors around Denver. He's an arrogant prick but he's being set up. There's too much rumor not to be fact. I want to talk to NFL Security."

"Did you talk to Gascon directly or is this stuff from your . . . sources?"

"I told him I was NFL Security."

"Wonderful. Now you want to turn yourself in."

"I want to save that jerk's ass. I'm one guy, what am I going to do about however many guys are setting this up? Me and you think it's the Denver–New Orleans game but maybe it's some other games in the basket. Denver is down on the basket for three games, one already in the tank. Denver against Los Angeles and Denver against New Orleans. Denver–Los Angeles can be iffy but there's no if with Denver and New Orleans. New Orleans isn't there.

But this gets back to seeing things too small. Maybe it's Denver but what if it's six or seven games, maybe other teams? What if those traders were fixing six, seven games? And how many guys would that take? I mean, we could be talking a conspiracy of forty, fifty guys.''

"Take it easy, Drover. You're into exponentials. Go back to basics,'' Fox said.

Drover looked at his drink.

"Why is it Denver? And Gascon?''

"A hunch,'' Drover said. "And the action on your computers.''

"All right. I like hunches as long as you don't do them too often. If Denver, why more than one game?''

"You mean they make enough on Denver in one game to make it worthwhile?''

"You told me futures is about using other people's money to buy commodities, make bids on what will be. So, extend the logic: One or two guys are using other people's money to put money on a sure thing. Fix a game.''

"One game,'' Drover said in a slow voice. "The guys who set up the book in the first place. They got fifty or so customers and the fifty or so spread out their risk with a thousand or so others. But the inside guys are two guys who absolutely know that a game is going one way and they won't have to pay off for it so they can use all the money in the book to go the other way. The guys running it are going to bet New Orleans. New Orleans can't beat Denver, even the pope knows that.''

"Stranger things have happened,'' Fox said.

"Maybe they make two, three, four, five, six million. Whatever it is, it isn't big change as these things go but it's big change for one or two guys. It's worth fixing a game for five or six million. Guys get killed for a hundredth of that kind of money.''

"Millions," Fox said, seeing millions in mind as clearly as ordinary people remember sunsets. The lounge was dark and there was music that might have had a melody. The girls with big breasts and high heels walked around in shiny dresses, being available. Luck was a lady every night.

"You got names on the guys running the book?"

"Not yet. Tony Rolls doesn't have a lot of clout with traders. It is an illegal book after all and if he stirs around too much, suddenly he's in the sunlight. Tony wanted me in the first place because he wanted someone coming in from left field. He doesn't want a goombah going around leaning on people, drawing attention to himself, to Tony."

"You're the left fielder."

"It makes sense. I should to go Chicago. Tonight."

"The stock market is closed for the week," Fox said.

"Good time to go. Friday night is loose lips night. North Side party time. The traders are coming down off the high, doing their recreational lines of coke and hitting on girls and talking too much about too many things."

"You know these guys."

"I was on the paper in Chicago. The thing about Chicago is that everyone knows everyone else after a while. Media, traders, lawyers, all the swinging dicks."

"You keep revealing parts of your life so that I have to figure you're seventy years old by now."

"You could feel that way after some Friday nights," Drover said. "The traders come on like outlaws, you know, Jesse James. They make their own rules, they're living on adrenaline all week, they got to show guts every hour of the trading day, they tend to all this macho stuff after school is out. That's where Tony should of looked for his conspiracy, except guys like Tony don't go to places like the traders go to."

"When do I hear from you?"

"I like your idea about two guys or three guys doing one game and splitting the pot. That makes sense, it would keep the conspiracy numbers down. A neat in and out. I'll do twenty-four hours hard in Chicago, try to get a name or two names. Then I'll fly to San Diego for the game Sunday. I want to watch Denver getting set up. Maybe I'm wrong but Denver and New Orleans has got to be the game. Also, I want to check on a chick named Lori Gibbons."

"Who's she?"

Drover told him.

"Maybe she was the way to get to Gascon," Drover said.

"You don't trust a lot, Drover. I like that."

"Foxer, the way she looks, she could get Gandhi in trouble if Gandhi was still around. I know a guy in Chicago with United Airlines, I can talk to him."

"You got any place you don't have a guy?"

Drover smiled. "Calgary. No connections at all. Covered a rodeo there. Hate rodeos, hate cow wrestling. I think it was a rodeo, come to think of it, maybe it was just what cowboys do on Friday nights in Calgary. The cows begin to look pretty after a while."

"You must have been desperate for a column."

"Had a managing editor came from Wyoming, thought cowboys were normal. So I humored him. Also don't have any wires in Montreal. Did hockey there and baseball, but I never understood French," Drover said.

"French is easy," Fox said, meaning it. He stared at a girl at the end of the bar who stared back, waiting. Fox said, "A lot of guys will be unhappy about this. A thousand guys in a book and a game is fixed to fleece the customers and that will make some people very unhappy."

"Look, Foxer, just keep your mouth shut and set your little lines. Let the wise people handle this."

"And are you talking to us when you talk about the wise men?"

Drover stared at his brown drink for a moment. He thought about popping Fox just once. "You know who I'm talking about, Fox. You want to do ten rounds again on that?"

"I don't fight."

"I don't pick them."

"Good point."

"Just so you know."

"I got a call for you. Two hours ago. Call Black Kelly. Anytime, day or night. That was the message."

"Why didn't you tell me when I first came in?"

"I wanted my information first," Fox said, as if that was a perfectly reasonable explanation.

"Listen, Fox. Just one time. If Black Kelly ever calls me here, you tell me, even if I'm in Timbucktu. Especially when he says 'day or night' "

"Drover, take it easy—"

"No. You tell me. Never, ever don't tell me." And Fox Vernon saw that Drover's face had turned white and the eyes gone wide with shock.

Drover slid off the stool and started out of the lounge. Fox had never seen him move with such purposefulness. What was the message? Anytime, day or night. That was it.

Fox reached out and signed his name on the bill and calculated an exact 18 percent tip in the process.

He sat and finished his ginger ale. In the splendid green-and-gold lobby, Drover tapped in his credit card number in a pay phone and waited. He heard Kelly's rumbling voice about the time Fox finished his soft drink and left the lounge.

CHAPTER 17

THE MAN WHO called himself Jose Jiminez was waiting for him.

Slim Dingo took off his Western hat and set it on a saddle that was used for just that purpose inside the front door. Everything was Tex-Mex. Tile floors, whitewashed walls, turquoise things, heavy oak tables, leather couch, the works.

Jose Jiminez said, "You got the money."

"Got the money."

"Anything else?"

"Knocked off her pussy, if that's what you want to know."

"You give her a hard time?"

"Not particularly."

"I told you. You don't make waves."

"He stole my fucking money. He stole it from me. He cheated. And he gave it to that two-bit whore. Fuck this all to hell and gone. I do a job for you, don't say I don't do a job for you."

"You know why you do a job for me."

"All right. We can cut out calling ourselves names."

"Just so you remember who you're working for."

"Hell and gone. If I forget, you'll come around to tell me. Anything I tell you working out?"

"It's just intelligence, Slim. Intelligence is its own reward."

"They find out ever, they'll put me on a meat hook. They'll peel my skin off."

"We got programs for that. Don't worry. Someday you can be Swedish if you want."

"I don't wanna be Swedish. I wanna be let be."

"That's in the past, Slim. You were very naughty and you got caught out. Now you work for Uncle and Uncle lets you keep your money. Now, don't fuck around with this guy, Drover, and that woman, Nancy Harrington. I don't want this complicated."

"I'd like to whack Drover. Have him whacked. Get a guy from Phoenix or somewhere, just go up to Santa Cruz and turn him into shark food."

"Look, Slim, I want you to do what Uncle tells you to do and not start on your own. I want you to be in Vegas next week playing cards with Sam DiFrenzo and his associates and I want you to wear the necklace like you always do."

"Every time you wire me, I get the jumps."

"Listen, these wise guys haven't paid attention to technology. We got wires thinner than linguine. That's all you need. They do a body search on you, what do they find? Lint in your navel. Relax. Law enforcement wouldn't be the same without those clever Japanese. Don't ever worry."

"I worry all the time about you guys. Y'all would make a nun worry."

"Watch your mouth, I don't wanna hear no shit about Catholics."

"Yeah, I know. All you guys got to be Catliks."

"Just like all you assholes gotta eat that shit chicken fried steak every night or you'll turn black or something."

"Hey, take it easy. Let's not call each other names, pardner."

"Okay, partner, just so you know which side of this partnership is on top. Just so you don't forget. Just so you don't start running your own little vendetta when you should be sticking to business. Okay, partner? Am I coming through okay?"

CHAPTER 18

BLACK KELLY HAD fought a fire in Chicago when he was 41 years old and already a lieutenant. He had gone into a six-flat on West Roscoe Street and gone through the smoke, looking for people. He had found them, huddled in the back, in a second-floor apartment, in the kitchen, and the stupid bastards had bolted shut the back door against burglars. The smoke was black and they were going to choke to death because they could not open the back door. He had picked them up and brought them back through the hall of smoke and saved their lives, one by one. There was a baby and there was a terrified girl of two and there was a boy, five, who was already overcome by smoke, and there was a woman of twenty-five who was the mother of all these children. She was unconscious as well. She had fled the flames in the front and gathered her children about her and stupidly she had simply prayed to be saved. Black Kelly and the paramedics worked on her for twenty-five minutes before she opened her eyes. She said, in Spanish (because she was Mexican), "Where are my babies?" And they were all alive. And who did she thank? The Mother of God. Kelly, his blue eyes turned meat-red by smoke, had felt both good and bad in that moment, exactly the way he felt now. The nearness of the tragedy shook him so that he could not savor the sense of helping save another person.

He had taped Nancy the best he could and made her drink some homemade soup. He had put her on his couch because it would have embarrassed her to be in his bedroom.

He had covered her with sheets against the cool night air rolling a healing breeze through his open windows. The ocean smell was a balm and she eventually fell asleep, even in her pain. She looked like hell and he had fretted until Doc Sage came and examined her and she had two broken ribs but Kelly had taped them right and that the other stuff would just heal in time but that she should really get checked out in a hospital and she said no, she couldn't do that.

She had wanted Drover and Drover was out of pocket, so Kelly had flown into Long Beach, rented a car, and been at her door in less than three hours. Kelly had convinced her to go with him. She hadn't even locked the house; the house wasn't her house anymore, not after that man had invaded it and invaded her life. It was as though her will had been beaten out of her.

Drover got in at 3:00 A.M. He turned the key in the front door of the bar and opened it. He closed the door and locked it. The building had three entrances and his own apartment was separate from the bar but he and Kelly had agreed to meet here. Kelly had pulled the shades and the bar was silent, the music had stopped and the laughing people were gone, and there was a single, bald night-light illuminating the remains of the nightly party. The bar was littered with used glasses and a couple of bottles. Leroy the swamper would clean all this in the morning.

Kelly opened the door that led to the back and the stairs.

"How is she—"

"Sleeping. Doc Sage gave her pharmaceuticals."

"Is she all right?"

"No, she's not all right. A sadist beat the shit out of her."

"I got to go to Chicago but I got to see her."

"What are you going to do?"

"You take care of her, Black."

"Who are you talking to? I ever send you a bill? She's my daughter from ten o'clock this morning."

"I can find Slim Dingo. That'll take a day."

"And what's that going to do for her?"

"She said I wouldn't do anything for her. I couldn't then. I can do anything now." He said it flat, not for Kelly but for himself. And Nancy.

"Slim Dingo in Chicago? Is that it?"

"He's on hold. I got twenty-four hours for Chicago and then I go to San Diego."

"What's going on?"

"Fix," Drover said.

"Shit. Who they want to fix?"

Drover told him. He had just enough time for a shower and a nap. And to see Nancy and tell her it was going to be all right or whatever other lie came to mind.

"I don't see how they can fix this guy Gascon. They going to inject him against his will?"

"I don't know what anybody is going to do. Maybe I've got the wrong guy."

"But you don't think so."

"Money buys a lot of things. Lot of people. There's a stew for United I want to check out named Lori Gibbons. She's playing house with Gascon. Unfortunately, all this is on deadline."

"Did it ever occur to you that this might be something coming out of New Orleans?"

No. It never had. Drover stared at Black Kelly. He reached for the bar phone and punched in a Las Vegas number.

Fox was up.

"Anything funny out of New Orleans?"

Black Kelly was watching him as he spoke on the phone.

"Lemme see," Fox Vernon said in a sleepy voice. Drover heard the buzz of the computers.

"Nothing. We're putting it off the boards. Sim's was the first. Everyone is getting a smell of the game."

"Action from New Orleans?"

"Just the hometown bets."

"Maybe somebody is holding."

"Maybe."

"Good night, Foxer."

"Good night."

Drover looked at Kelly.

"Go on up. I put her in the living room." He was talking about Nancy.

The apartment was softly lit so that its unfamiliarity wouldn't frighten Nancy if she woke suddenly. The sleeping pills from Doc Sage had worked well enough but Nancy wasn't sleeping deep. There was too much hurt for that.

When he saw her, Drover did not speak for a moment. He sat on the coffee table next to the couch and he touched her hair. Her face, in sleep, had regained some composure but the swelling around her eye was as ugly as broad daylight.

She looked at him. Then she looked away from him. He touched her hair again in a soft, clumsy gesture of sympathy.

Nancy turned to him again. "He was watching the house. He told me that. He said he knew I was going to get the money. He knew about the money. Did you tell him?"

"I never thought he'd come after you. I never told him about you."

"He said horrible things after he beat me. He raped me. I guess you could call it that. After a while, I was going to do whatever he wanted me to do."

"No, Nancy, don't—"

"How did he know about the money?"

Drover stared at her. "I don't know."

"I can't go back to that house again. I'd see him in it, the way he was. . . . One day you're here and the next day you're so far away that you can't ever go back to where you were. I thought about killing him. I'm going to have to do that or I won't be able to . . ."

"Nancy, take it easy."

He handed her a glass of water and held her head as she drank a little. She fell back on the pillow. "When you weren't here . . . that friend of yours came all the way down, just like that. I was afraid of him too at first. And then he took me here. I don't even know where here is."

"Santa Cruz. On the ocean."

"I can smell the ocean. You can't smell the ocean down there."

"You don't have to go back, Nancy. I just want to tell you. Stay with Black and I'll be back Sunday night, I got a job to do."

"And what about Slim, Drover?"

He stared at her for a long moment before he answered.

"Anything. I'll do anything for you."

And she understood.

CHAPTER 19

THE COMMISSIONER WAS talking to Hugh Maddenly. Maddenly wanted one of the new franchises. The NFL was on the verge of expanding again, striking a balance between lowering the quality of the game because of the expanded player pool and giving the suckers what they wanted. What America wanted in the last decade of the century was saturation sports on TV, starting with football.

Hugh Maddenly had made a small fortune by buying companies, stripping them of profits and assets, and then spinning them into component parts. He was a patriot and a civic booster and a man the commissioner thought might be good for the game.

"Thing is about drugs," Hugh was saying. He took a quick, ice-cold sip of his bourbon and ginger ale before continuing. "I got nothing against the Bushes but that crap about saying no to drugs was just a load of crap. Thing is, we got to get to the people using drugs, selling drugs to our kids, and we got to turn over some place big into a prison."

"Like what?" the commissioner said. He was being polite. He never liked to talk about drugs. The party chatter around them was about other things. These were people with money, the kind the commissioner liked to be part of, and the event was something noble and worthwhile having to do with dyslexia or something and there was a mound of beluga caviar shaped like a football and here he was, the commissioner of professional football, listening to yet another boring lecture of What to Do About the Drug Problem. But Hugh did want a football franchise and he could afford it and you did things like this for The Good of the Game.

"Mississippi, I'm serious. At first you'd think I'd be kidding but when you look at the thing, you can see how it makes common sense. Mississippi is so far down the economic ladder you'd have to goose the place to get it to the first rung. But what if Mississippi went in the prison business in a big way? Think about it. I'm talking the whole state, one end to the other, and just full of federal prisons for drug offenders. I am talking serious construction projects and lots of jobs. And just think about it, Commissioner, the thought of going to jail for five or ten years for carrying heroin around and not just going to prison, but going to a Mississippi prison! There'd be some serious second and third thoughts on that. You gonna scare them by sending them to a candy-ass liberal prison? Hell no. I'm talking Southern sheriffs and guard dogs and cattle prods and the whole nine yards."

"That's very interesting, Mr. Maddenly. A state full of prisons." He was looking around for escape.

"Not just any state. It has to be Mississippi. Those poor people would be getting jobs for themselves and we'd be solving our drug problem. Say we got to lock up five, ten percent of the population . . . well, you gotta bite the bullet once in a while."

"Some good players come out of Miss—"

"Lord, don't I know that? Let 'em keep comin', I'm not talking about shutting down the schools. We need those schools to keep giving us those ball players. But their mommas and daddys gotta have jobs and this is one way to end the economic problems of a region of the country that has been down so long it looks like up. I was in Washington just last week, I was talking about it to a couple of senators, they seemed very interested.''

''I'll bet they did,'' the commissioner said. There. The woman in the white satin gown. ''Excuse me, Mr. Maddenly, I just have to have a word with her—Oh, Frances? Frances?''

Hugh Maddenly grinned. ''I'd like to have a word with her myself.''

Frances Downes turned. The face was the face you saw when you looked at Bloomingdale's or Marshall Field's ads. She was Saks, too, when it was required. Like all models, she was too thin but there were curves here and there that made the size four more than acceptable. Take this little number, a satin thing she had just thrown on and would sell in a couple of months to a store that resold it to lesser mortals. Frances Downes gave the commissioner of football a full, fine smile that cost six thousand dollars once upon a time.

''Hello, Commissioner, I knew you'd make it,'' Frances said. They gave each other a kiss that wasn't. He introduced Maddenly who just gaped at her and they moved off after a moment as though they had a secret to share.

The room glittered but didn't glare. They were in the Parker Meridien Hotel in New York and the very best people in the world were present. It was French, affected, and quite striking and some of the money raised by those present would actually trickle down to do good.

''When are you going to let me rescue you, Frances?''

''And make an honest woman of me?'' She laughed the way a chandelier tinkles. There was music to her and her blue eyes were bright. ''I'd rather live in sin with you. It'd be more fun.''

The commissioner smiled at that. ''Where have you been, I haven't seen you since summer—''

"A lot of work in Europe this summer and now, in the fall, the catalogue bits. I've been in Chicago all during September. Work, work, work, and the weather has been so lousy, rain every day."

"And I suppose that means . . ."

She looked troubled for a moment. "Yes. Bart. I've seen him. In fact, that's what I want to talk to you about."

"Lucky Bart Brixton."

"Lucky Bart," she repeated in a suddenly dull voice. Her eyes were suddenly far away. She looked at the smile on the commissioner's face and realized she had almost betrayed herself. She cranked up a *Glamour* magazine grin and took his arm. She led him across the room. The other man in a standard tuxedo had red hair and eyes that might be laughing behind your back.

"You remember Bart," she said to the commissioner, and there was an awkward moment. The commissioner had once dated Frances before he was named to the top job he now held. Frances had represented a sense of class and fun to him that he hated to lose but now they were in worlds that rarely converged. This party—and events like it—were the only times those worlds collided and he didn't want to share his few moments with her with a man he vaguely saw as his rival.

"Yes, Bart, how's it on the commodities game?" That note of bonhomie was meant to be as false as it sounded. The two men shook hands in a feel-my-grip way.

"Doing every one I can and those I like twice," Bart Brixton said. He smiled when he said it as though he didn't mean it.

"Bart came all the way to New York today just to be here, just to see you," Frances Downes said. She said it brightly, in a quirky and insincere way. Unfortunately, her presence always dazzled the commissioner into believing anything she said. "He called me last Wednesday and said he had to be here."

"Is that right, Bart?"

"Yes, sir," Bart said. He turned to Frances. "Frances. Will you excuse us a moment?"

She looked at the commissioner and then at Bart Brixton. She smiled again and turned to go dazzle some other part of the room.

An orchestra was playing underneath the polite buzz of the mob. It was the charity mob and they knew each other and went to each other's parties and kept the dress designers in chicken noodle soup. Bart broke through the buzz. "Something to say," he said.

His voice wasn't very loud but it was loud enough to make the commissioner drop his grin.

"So," the commissioner said. "Are you going to tip me off to some stock? I don't know a thing about the market except that people like me can never make money in it."

"Oh, you'd be surprised," Bart Brixton said. He let the silence settle. "But it wasn't about the market, not at all."

"Was it about Frances?"

"You can't seem to make up your mind about her, can you?"

"You see her a lot?"

"I see her. She's in one world, I'm in another," Bart said.

"I'll bet it keeps you busy." The conversation was about to dissolve like wet tissue paper.

"Some people who work on the board are betting hard against Denver over the next couple of weeks and it doesn't make sense. I don't bet—unless you call what I do gambling—ha ha—but, seriously, I wanted to tell you. I know you've got your regular sources, the books in Vegas, whatever, but I just want to tell you. I don't know a who and I don't know a why but you know I played football, almost made it with the Vikings, I like the game just the way it is.''

"So do I," the commissioner said. He tried a little smile. "Appreciate the tip, Bart. Always look into things like that."

"It just doesn't make sense, betting against the best team in the NFL."

"Well, you know, on any given Sunday, any team can win. You know we try for that, for parity—"

"Gascon is the best quarterback in the game."

The commissioner caught it. He let a pause fill the space between them for a moment.

"Is that a name?"

"It's a name," Bart Brixton said. "That's all I've heard. Check it around. See if money is going down on the teams that play Denver. Say between here and the New Orleans game. I'm in the rumor business, you know that. We hear that there's a freeze due in Florida, we scramble. May only be rumors, I don't have any gambling sources."

"I wish nobody gambled," the commissioner said.

Bart Brixton grinned and the con man eyes clouded over. "Now, you know that's as full of shit as anything. If nobody gambled on football, who'd watch it?"

"The integrity of the game. That's what we've got to sell. That's what they pay me for, to make sure the game doesn't sell out. We never want a Black Sox scandal," the commissioner said. He believed it in a dogged way, the way a religionist holds on in a world full of atheists. On any given day, there might be more doubts than beliefs, but you stuck with it.

"Nobody wants a scandal. Nobody wants anything to hurt football."

"No. And that's why Vegas doesn't make my job easier.

Over a billion dollars in the sports books. More than seventy legal books. That doesn't make anything easier.''

"And what's the illegal? Twenty-five billion I saw in the paper the other day. Twenty-five billion dollars and not one cent of it taxed." Bart grinned. "You think I might be in the wrong racket? Get into sports gambling and all I'd have to worry about is the IRS.''

"I don't know much about it. I know it makes the police part of my job just that much harder.''

"That's why I came to the Apple. To see you. And seeing Frances in her pretty party dress made the trip worth it too.''

"I appreciate what you're passing on," the commissioner said. "Now I've got to mingle.''

"I understand. Thanks for hearing me," Bart said. He was still smiling and he held it long after the commissioner moved on to another crowd in the charity mob. The little bird had whistled its little tune and now the dance was just beginning.

CHAPTER 20

"TELL ME," DROVER said.

The guy was into his third sheet. His eyes had that dead look that comes after too many stingers. If he wasn't a remarkably clear talker at this stage, Drover would have moved on. Drover was tired, the bar scene tired him out, listening to too many people wore him down. They were in the Green Door Tavern in the gentrifying loft district of River North in Chicago. This place was intense and loud and full of advertising signs of another era. It was trendy and trendy was where Drover was conducting his daylong search for a name. This guy with the fifty-dollar haircut and holes in the knees of his jeans might be the guy. He was a trader on the commodities exchange named Alex Thompson and he had remembered Drover as a writer from his Chicago newspaper days. Alex Thompson wanted to know why Drover had left Chicago and why he never saw his name in the papers anymore and Drover had explained he was writing books about gambling and he wanted to know about gambling on the exchanges, in confidence of course, and one thing led to another.

"One guy is Tommy Sain. Tommy Insane," Alex Thompson said. "Nice guy and a fair trader but every now and then, he disappears."

"Drunk?"

"Not particularly. He gambles. He gets a fit every six,

eight months and goes out to Vegas to lose all his money at the crap table. When he's finally broke, it's like he lightens up and comes back to work the pits. He's been doing it for years.''

"Married?"

"His wife is," the drunk said.

"Why'd you pull Tommy Sain's name out of the hat?"

"You were talking about gambling. Everyone on the exchange is a gambler. But if you're talking about gambling gambling, then the list narrows. I mean, everyone puts down a bet but Tommy Insane, he runs a book.''

"Really?"

"Really. Been running it a couple of years in the football season. Doesn't do the other stuff unless you count the Final Four which is a funny kind of book in itself. Just football, just the pros. Oh yeah, he'll take action on Notre Dame, all the guys went to Notre Dame insist on it. He charges the standard ten percent juice and I think he makes a fair amount of money on it.''

"So I should talk to him if I want to know about gambling in the exchange.''

"He'd be a good starter. He parties around but most of the time, he keeps his nose clean. Not a bad guy, Tommy, I don't know why I was just bad-mouthing him. But he's got a gambling problem and he's gonna shoot himself in the foot some day.''

"Where's he party?"

"I dunno. I've seen him at the usual places on Division Street, you know. Catch him on the Street, he's listed. He might talk to you, might not, I mean, it is illegal after all. But don't mention my name.''

"I don't tell," Drover said.

"I wish you were still in the paper.''

"There's always someone else to feed the goat. John Carmichael, Dave Condon, Warren Brown, someone else was always coming along behind them. Like to see guys like Jerry Holtzman and Ray Sons hanging in there, gives it continuity,'' Drover said. He had named names in his pantheon of sportswriters, a shrine of the heart he carried around with him to remind him where he once had been. Somehow, it always softened the pain because he had once been part of them, no matter how short his stay.

''What do you think of the Bears Sunday?''

''What are they, eight underdogs? The over-under is thirty-four. Stick with that,'' Drover said. ''Over, way over.''

Alex looked like a child who had lost a friend. ''That bad, huh?''

''That bad.''

''I took them anyway. I liked the spread.''

''Mayonnaise is a better spread at this point,'' Drover said. ''I appreciate the name, Alex. Buy you another drink?''

''Naw. My limit is sixty and I think I've been over-served. A wise drunk knows his way home. When's this book on gambling coming out anyway?''

Drover always gave a figure exactly fourteen months away. It sounded more definitive that way. And people usually forgot fourteen months had gone by in case he ever ran into them again. The great gambling book. Frankly, the idea of it bored him. He knew gambling, he knew what it was about, he had made bets, but the sport was the thing to him. He could watch a pickup basketball game outside Cabrini-Green projects and be enchanted. Those black men driving under netless baskets, their bodies glistening with sweat, were the pure beauty of the game sometimes lost in the welter of the commercial world. Sport was what they did and what Drover would rather watch and what Drover, in his brief time, would rather write about.

''I want to read it. Read anything you write. You were

good, buddy, really good," Alex Thompson said, and shook Drover's hand the way a drunk will, forgetting he had done the same thing a moment before. "Hope you go back into the business."

"Thanks," Drover said, dropping a tip on the bar.

"Really mean it," the drunk stumbled on. He wanted to keep shaking hands but now it was time to make the next move and Drover was threading through the crowd, beneath the din, out on to Orleans Street.

"Orleans," he said to himself, reminding himself. It was late and he was tired and the flight to San Diego was scheduled to depart at 7:00 A.M. sharp. He hadn't found his friend with United Air Lines and he hadn't done a million things. He had called Kelly four times to inquire about Nancy. She was getting Firehouse Kelly, including Firehouse pot roast, Firehouse vegetable soup, Firehouse coleslaw, and Firehouse mashed potatoes. She was keeping it down and she looked better and she cried in the afternoon over nothing. Kelly said it was going to take a lot of time.

Fox Vernon said the action was still trickling in from Chicago. He said there wasn't an unusual thing from New Orleans. Drover said there should have been by now.

He saw a cab and waved it down and headed for the Drake. He could count on a solid five hours of sleep before his flight and, if he was lucky, three on the plane. The week of travel was having its cumulative effect.

The streets were wet. It had rained yet again and made Saturday that much more of a hang-around day. He had found a lot of traders and even bumped into a couple of newspaper friends from the old days but he didn't have time for friendship. The meter said $4.40 by the time they reached the canopy of the seventy-year-old hotel. He didn't have any spring left in his step.

He opened the door of his room on five and didn't remember leaving the light on.

He hadn't.

"Hello, kid," Tony Rolls said. "You're a hard man to track down."

"I didn't know I was being tracked."

"You were in Vegas yesterday."

"That's true." He stepped into the bedroom which was crowded by the wheelchair, by Tony Rolls, and by Vinny, who was sitting in one of the stuffed easy chairs.

"What'd you find out?"

Drover looked at Vinny. Drover shrugged. "Nothing. You gave me a week, what am I supposed to find out in a week?"

"You wrote for a daily paper or what? You never have deadlines?"

"Not the kind that kill."

"When are you gonna tell me somethin'?"

"When I got something."

"Why are you in town?"

"To make it easier for you to ask me questions."

"Don't get smart," Vinny said.

"Take the under on the Bears game."

"I need betting tips from you?"

"That's from Fox Vernon. I couldn't handicap a soap box derby."

"They still got those?" Tony Rolls said.

"I don't know. I'm tired, I got to get sleep."

"Mr. Rolls asked you a question," Vinny said, doing his muscle.

Drover decided. Vin was on his nerves. "All right, Tony, I got something for you. Tell Arnold Schwarzenegger to take a walk."

"Take a walk, Vin."

Vin made a face. He got up and walked. The door closed.

"What's up?"

"What's up with you, Tony," Drover said. There was no question in the tone of his voice. Everything was done flat.

"What are you asking me?"

"Who's got a wire on you?"

Tony made one of those "whaaaaaa" looks.

"I leave the game with my money, I barely had time to count it before the G picked me up. They were interested in the money and in the game. They knew everything about the game. What I haven't been able to figure all week is why they knew about me being the winner. And knowing it like this, from Jump Street."

"They get your money?"

"No. But that isn't the point. I leave your house and less than an hour later, a car full of G got me, take me in, punch me around, keep asking about the money. There was Slim, you, me, Joe Camp, the Irish guy, Vin. And then there was the room itself. Are you sweeping for wires?"

"Of course."

"Well, I just gave you something to think about, Tony. Now let me go to sleep."

"Why are you in Chicago?"

"Fox. He wants me to eyeball the Bulls, get ready for the season."

"Is that right?"

"Jordan is the franchise again. I could watch him play basketball twenty-four hours a day. God made racehorses, sunsets, and Michael Jordan to remind us of grace."

"That's poetry like you used to write in the paper."

"Yeah. Before I got associated with your association."

"That wasn't me. That was shit went down in L.A. Little turd. You got cleared."

"I got cleared but I'm not cleared. So don't crowd me, Tony. You and I both know what this was about. Something bad going down, Foxy wants to know as much as you do. I want to know. I come out here to see if I can get any names on the exchange."

"You got a name?"

"Not one."

"So what are you gonna do?"

"Put on my pj's and go to sleep."

Tony gave him a wise look. "I don't crowd you, Jimmy."

"I appreciate that."

"Everyone is anxious."

"Yes."

"All right," Tony Rolls said. "Call Vin out of the hallway."

The muscle got to the wheelchair and pushed the large man into the hall of the quiet midnight hotel. Tony looked up at Drover at the door.

"About the other thing, I appreciate it," Tony Rolls said.

"Don't mention it. And I mean, don't mention it," Drover said.

"I got you," the old man said. And Vin pushed the wheels down to the elevator banks. They got on just as Drover was closing his eyes for five fast hours of sleep.

CHAPTER 21

DENVER WAS KICKING ass and taking names.

The Broncos put silence into the crowd on the second play from scrimmage.

Gascon just faded into the pocket and the grunts at the pit pushed back. The pocket started to collapse around Gascon but he didn't seem to care. Say, he might have five or six hours back there to set up his pass. Nobody was going to touch Lenny Gascon today, he was invisible and his arm was made of twenty-four-karat gold, it was as simple as that. The pocket collapsed in slow motion around him and still he waited, looking for inspiration.

The crowd eventually roared again, after the shock wore off, and it was asking the San Diego Chargers to get that boy with the earring in his ear and tear him a new asshole. The crowd was also asking the Lord to strike down dead the son of a bitch linebacker Moneypenny. In short, sixty thousand laid-back Southern Californians were acting like a bunch of beer-soaked cheeseheads in Lambeau Field in Green Bay, Wisconsin. Football on Sunday makes all men brothers and a few women too.

Serious miracles were being asked for both inside the stadium and up and down the West Coast where the rest of the world was watching and out in the big sports books in Vegas where entire walls were sacrificed to forty-five-inch TV screens bringing in every football game known to man for the pleasure or pain of the assembled sports bettors.

But all the people who knew that San Diego did not stand the chance of a Popsicle in hell of winning knew it was over when Gascon, having combed his hair and checked himself out in a three-way mirror, decided to throw that darned football about sixty yards up the field.

It wasn't a matter of just throwing it. But it was the way it was thrown. The football suddenly turned to Stickum and there were matching brass handles to boot. The football spiraled the way it did on the Jack Armstrong show, it was a deadly heat-seeking missile and when it sensed the heat of the receiver Chambers at the other end, just inside the goal line, it went plop into his large, greedy hands and stuck there. 6–0.

It got worse.

Drover saw people he knew in the stands and people he didn't. He moved around, watching and waiting without knowing what he was watching and waiting for. Gascon and Company were doing Rout City. They were stacking up San Diego's defense like poker chips on green felt.

He bumped into Dusty Baumann just before halftime and sat down next to him. Dusty was filling out sheets with weird notes to himself.

"Howdy," Dusty said when the gun went off. He wrote something else down. "Thirty-five to zip. Color it orange. Almost boring in his perfection, isn't he?"

"Gascon gives good quarterback."

"Gascon. The boy worries me. League apparently is gonna take him up on his Budweiser challenge, test his urination process tomorrow."

"When did you get that?"

"Half hour ago from a pal in NFL Security. Seems the commish got on the blower from New York and ordered it up. Sort of a semi-surprise, you might say, but the boy is cocky. Maybe that. Maybe the commish isn't a Broncos fan. Hard to believe but there are still three or four people in New York City who still think the Giants got a better team.''

''Why?''

''Why what?''

''Why would the commissioner order it out of the blue?'' Drover asked.

''Beats me. Lord works in mysterious ways.''

''This is getting funnier.''

''Well, you were sniffing around that boy before, what do you think?''

''I think he doesn't, as we say, do.''

''He impressed you?''

''Either that or he's the dumbest airhead ever to put pads on.''

''Gascon ain't dumb. He invests, he's got stock, he even learned a thing or two in college.''

''Like cheerleaders wear underpants.''

''Only some of them and only some of the time,'' Dusty said.

''How would you know, you only write about it?''

''I got a vivid imagination. Have to have to be a sports-writer and make what the dummies say read into English. I'm surprised you came out to this game.''

''Nice day, sunny Southland. His girlfriend is named Lori Gibbons.''

''Nice to know. Which one is she?''

''A stew. She's got a face like Lee Remick when Lee Remick was a tad younger.''

''I don't know her. But she's one of many. Len Gascon believes in sharing himself. Mrs. Gascon finally decided to object and that's why Len is batching it.''

''Who was Mrs. Gascon?''

"Your usual knockout. Cheerleader. Became a model. She got tired of him getting tired of her. Girls who wouldn't look at a sportswriter, they jump in the sack like that with anybody who can get into spandex pants on Sunday. Hard to believe they don't admire brains."

"It's a shocker all right. Who was she?"

"Name was Deanna. Something. Lives in Denver still. Does some modeling still but she's really too big. You know. Bazooms. Modeling you got to be boy-shaped to get ahead."

"I never saw them too big."

"Well, you're just a tit man. So it's a big secret about the testing but you aren't gonna tell, are you?"

"Does the *Post* know?"

"Maybe. I'm not gonna give it away."

"I'll leave you to your hieroglyphics."

"See you at the club."

He moved on down the press rows and kept searching the crowd for faces. He recognized a couple of gamblers, the sort called outlaws, with Vegas pale faces and suspicious looks. He wondered sometimes if these guys went to Suspect School to learn how to look like one.

The game resumed, to the dismay of the Chargers. The brilliant sun that always seems to hang over San Diego faded a bit but maybe that's just the way it looks when you cheer on a team and you know their heart isn't in it.

Gascon was finally relieved in the fourth quarter as an act of mercy on the part of the Denver coaching staff. His substitute was a fifth rounder from three years before who looked great in college and immediately forgot the techniques of football when he hit the pros. He could throw like a quarterback, carried girlfriends like one, even talked like one on the rare occasions when someone in the Denver press corps decided to fill in the blanks on a slow news day and talk to the Great Forgotten. That was his unfortunate nickname, given to him by a *Denver Post* writer trying to make his quota of words on a no-injury-report Tuesday. But he just couldn't seem to have any luck. If the offensive line gave him a hole to walk through, he would get to the line just when it was having second thoughts about the opening. The Great Forgotten was a nice kid and thank God Denver did not have to count on him for anything.

The game ended around 49–7 which neatly helped all who had bet the over and the ones who were not tempted to switch to San Diego when Denver was made a two-touchdown favorite. Kicking ass and taking names; it was just terrible what happened out there. The only satisfaction the San Diego people had was that it was snowing in Denver at the moment and they would be enjoying their usual spectacular sunset while Denver dug itself out.

Drover found his way down to the Denver locker room. His neck tag said he was Hamilton Burger of *The Denver Post*, one of the many credentials he kept for such purposes. The only thing he had to do was to stay away from the real *Post* guys.

Locker rooms are all the same. They are all weary with sweat after games, the only smell that's left when the adrenaline is all leaked out. They are damp and men with too-large bodies are walking around naked, trying to get to the showers. Locker rooms contain the true smell of athletic battle: The smell was weariness mixed with the afterglow of having been cheered to a supreme effort by your fellow, lesser mortals, the ones who only stand and watch. Naturally, the locker rooms of winners smell a little better but winning is always roses and the fertilizer comes from the other side of the wall.

Locker rooms are also much smaller places when tele-

vision reporters shove their equipment in and get naked
men to do a sitdown, shooting them from the neck up.
Athletes resent this technique because it is not becoming
for anyone to be interviewed on live television naked. Especially when the guy asking the questions wears a sports
coat with the number of his station on the lapel, in case
he forgets.

That was going on now. The athletes put up with this
invasion because they were paid to do so. Because they
want to be in television when it's all over, be a John Mad-
den or something. Because one hand scratches the other
and getting on live TV after the game can translate into
doing Chevy commercials for the local dealer if you can
actually navigate through sentence structure without losing
what the point of it was.

Gascon did it because he loved it.

"I felt like Patton out there," Gascon was saying. "I
was gonna tear up France and then kick butt in Germany.
You ever see that movie?"

"Like Patton," chuckled the television reporter, ad-
miring Gascon's vivid sense of history.

"San Diego came to play but we came to win," Gascon
said.

"And win you did," TV said.

"Shit, kicking ass is more fun than being the only boy
on a hayride," Gascon said, and live TV had to blink and
take it. That Gascon. What a card.

Even in victory, there were all the hurts. The players
unwrapped their bodies and some did it cautiously,
afraid of what they'd find. Some players found bruises
on bones and some found blood when they urinated.
That'd heal, that's what the game was about. Some of
them celebrated victory by putting in their store-bought
teeth they had kept on their locker shelves and grinning
at each other. Some just sat on the bench in front of

their clothes and stared at the floor, waiting for that second breath that had always been there before to come back so they could negotiate a shower. Football players know the best they're going to feel in a season is the morning they drive up to training camp in their Corvette convertible. It goes down from there and the punishment is a half year in the making. When the season finally stumbles off to the Super Bowl and the losers are home, the healing begins. If it heals enough, you get a chance to go back on a bright summer day to training camp and start beating up your body all over again. When the healing never quite catches up with the calendar, it's time to find a job in what the squares call the real world.

Drover had seen it all; he had written about it with affection and tenderness and a quiet humor that came from somewhere he thought was probably God. He could write in his day, no mistake. He was nominated for a Pulitzer once for just describing games. Now he could just witness, take a look around at things, just watch for one man in Vegas and see things as they really were and keep the words inside his head. Sometimes he wrote sentences but never on paper, just in thoughts.

What he saw now, on the other side of Gascon hogging the cameras, was what he had wanted to see, to check on Dusty's tip.

The guys were NFL Security and they didn't travel with the team. They even looked a little sour about something. NFL Security guys are a cross between FBI semi-suave and major league umpire blackjack-law-enforcement. Probably the sourness came from being called on their day off to tap the kidney of a stranger. Gascon had called it heads; now let's see what it was.

Dusty was right.

Somehow, in that moment, Drover had a very bad feeling. Somebody had it in for Denver and that's why the New Orleans chump money was accumulating in all those Vegas handbooks. Gascon was sure the coin had heads on both sides.

But it was going to turn out tails when it hit the grass.

CHAPTER 22

MAGGIE SAIN SAID, "You wanna call this off?"

She said it out of the blue, just like that, sitting across the kitchen countertop from him, a half cup of Monday morning coffee in front of her. Maggie Sain was pretty and smart, about thirty-three by the calendar and eighty-seven by experience. She had her warrior makeup on and she was ready for her workday down at the magazine.

"You always start up about this."

"I see you, what? Two, three hours a week? If I'm lucky? Lucky Maggie. You're watching football, okay, I can handle that for a Sunday. But what happened to Saturday night? In fact, they don't play football every night of the week. I checked. And I'm not even talking about Friday night when you never got home. I hope she gave you herpes at least."

"Are you unhappy with the Miata I bought you?"

"I could buy a Miata if I wanted to. You want the Miata so you can fuck it?"

"So you got all the money in the world and so do I. Is that supposed to make us unhappy?"

"No. You losing yourself every day is making me unhappy. I feel like I'm living in *The Honeymooners*."

"Look, I don't wanna call it off."

"So where are you going tonight?"

"I'm gonna watch *Monday Night Football.* I got some money down. You wanna come watch?"

"And when's the next time you're going to flip out and go to Vegas?"

"I got a problem. I admit it. I'm going to get help on it. Believe me I am."

"You got all kinds of problems, Tom, and I'm one of them. I'm going to leave you, Tom. I am this time."

"You left before."

"I left and came back. This time is called the triumph of reality. At last. I see where this is. This is no place, Tom. I really mean it."

"You said that before."

"Oh, you're going to try to charm me into staying. 'Duh, you said that before.' "

"Maggie, I'm under pressure right now—"

"So am I. So is the world. But some people actually stay married. People under intense pressure actually manage to get it off with each other from time to time. You can still get it up, can't you?"

"You've got a thing about moving out."

"I've got a thing about it this time. This time it's the last time. Okay, Tom, you can turn off the charm. I just had to tell you. I really just had to tell you."

"Maggie."

Tommy Sain looked at her. He didn't want to lose her. He even loved her. He just didn't have time for her right now. There were too many pressures and they were all coming from Bart Brixton. He didn't know why he'd gotten into this. And the fucking Bears got beat and he had the under when he should have had the over. A dime. An entire dime on that game.

He wanted to tell her.

But Maggie was slipping on her go-to-work raincoat now

(distinct from her go-to-party one) and she was staring at him with hard blue eyes. Daring him to say something.

What could he say? What could he ever explain to her about Bart and the New Orleans connection he had had to use to lay down the last two hundred dimes. That's where I was, Maggie, I was in New Orleans Friday night after work, putting two hundred dimes into the network through a guy I knew, the last-chance guy to keep Bart off my case and that hadn't worked so well, the only way to keep this thing working. But what could he tell her?

Maggie solved the problem temporarily.

She slammed out the front door.

CHAPTER 23

NANCY WORE SUNGLASSES that Sunday. That helped and meant she was really going to get better because she cared now how she looked. She washed her hair. She hurt but not as much. The Firehouse meat loaf—made with tomato sauce, mushrooms, and green peppers and onions—was amazing. It was all amazing. She had never eaten Midwest family-style firehouse food. Black Kelly, she thought, was the sweetest man in the world. He had babied her and that was what she had really needed those first two days.

A mild roar was rising from the bar beneath the apartment. They were watching football on five television sets. San Diego was over; Nancy could hardly wait to see Drover.

The Bears were stumbling in the mud at Soldier Field in Chicago. The Giants were pounding on the Steelers in New Jersey. The great weekly festival of NFL football—a glorious circusy mess of games upon games—was on. The gladiators, lions, and Christians were duking it out on hundred-yard fields made either of carpet or grass. Dallas was at Houston today, an occasion in Texas of equal importance with the siege of the Alamo. The country was rendered temporarily insane by reason of football from Green Bay to Georgia.

Actually, Nancy usually liked football.

She had gotten into the game for the sake of sharing

something with Johno. But after a year or two, she realized
something shocking: She knew more about the game than
Johno did. She kept the fact of her superiority a secret
from her husband and even pretended not to read *Pro
Football Weekly.* She suddenly smiled, remembering with
a little heartbreak how she would sneak her reading of the
Weekly in the bathroom, hiding the paper behind the toilet
paper shelf. Johno was so vain about so many things it
would hurt his pride to think that his Nancy could handicap football better than him.

Kelly was in the bar all afternoon—football Sunday is a
big bar day everywhere they have them—but he came up
now and then to check on her, to see if she wanted anything. She felt as though she were five years old and sick
in bed with a cold. She had brought out the mother in
Black Kelly.

It was a perfect day, as usual. Sea gulls hung around on
jets of wind, waiting for garbage, and the hard bodies still
littered the October beaches. The weather did change from
time to time in this part of California but perfect days were
never enthused over the way people in Chicago or New
York or Boston do.

Drover got there by seven. The games were long over
and now the analysis was creeping in. Coaches were explaining victories and finding good things in defeat. The
players were on their way home, sometimes home being
two thousand miles away. The TV sportscasters were
showing the same three or four seconds of key footage
over and over, slowing it down, running it backward, asking their guest player or coach What It All Meant.

She hugged him in front of the forty-inch Magnavox and
didn't say a thing.

There was nothing to say for a while. Neither of them
wanted to go back to the bad things that had been done to
Nancy in the white stucco house near Disneyland in Ana-

heim. The perfect day became a perfect evening and the sunset, for which God made the Pacific Ocean, started its show.

He took her for a walk down the pier to the very end where you can see the sunset the best. The night gets very purple very fast and she shivered. He gave her his jacket. Knights in shining armor are always doing things like that.

"I thought about it," she said. "I was mad, humiliated. I was sick with myself. For that weekend I stayed with him. For what happened now. It's not the money, I just wanted to strike out. That's when I told you I wanted to kill him. I'm still mad, still mad as hell, but I don't want to go on with it. It's not about the money. I just don't want to do anything with him, he's an evil man."

"How did he know about the money?" It was a question for himself. "Even if he could guess, how could he guess so fast? I mean, he was there waiting for you."

"I know. That's what scares me. I don't want to be scared the rest of my life."

"You won't be. It'll never happen like that again."

"Can you promise that?"

She still wore sunglasses and there was something lost in that question. He wanted to find the little girl who asked it and tell her he could promise her the world and it would be true.

"Nancy. Stay here. With me."

She stared at him.

"I need you," she said to him.

"You got me."

"My friend."

"Just like the James Taylor song."

"I called and you came."

"Kelly came. But I'm here."

"I'm not afraid here."

"And we've got sunsets for you."

She kissed him. Gentle but a real kiss and he really held her, gentle, but a real hug and not brother-sister stuff. It was a perfect sunset at the end of a perfect day.

CHAPTER 24

BLACK KELLY WON the lottery on Sunday night. It was $450.

On Monday, about the time Maggie Sain was walking out on her husband, Kelly explained to Drover how he had carefully unscrambled the numbers contained in the message inside a Willie and Ethel cartoon panel.

He did this for about ten minutes, writing numbers to correspond with letters until he got Drover's goat. Drover stormed out of the saloon on the pier and Kelly laughed across the bar to Nancy. They were friends and they were sharing a laugh and a knowing wink, which is what friends are supposed to do.

Drover walked into town. The walking around in Santa Cruz was good and maybe that's why Drover had settled there. Towns where you have to drive every place made him jumpy and feel trapped. The earthquake had been a bad thing and had torn a hole in the downtown but Santa Cruz wasn't made for whining. The national press coverage of the quake seemed to indicate it had all happened in San Francisco and in Oakland and had something to do with the World Series. Hardly anyone got down to Santa Cruz to see where the worst of the quake had happened. Santa Cruz shrugged it off the way it shrugs everything off. The Pacific Avenue mall was still not rebuilt and there was a sense of almost pioneer days uncertainty to it—but the people were the same and that suited Drover.

The walking was a way he used to put the jumble of thoughts into a list that someone might believe. He felt too damned close to whatever was going down on Tony Rolls. The G had wired his room, the G might have put a wire on someone in the room. That was the likeliest thing.

Who would it be?

The guy who wanted his money back.

But Degnan, the construction Mick, had lost. So had Joe Camp. The biggest loser was Slim Dingo and Slim Dingo had shown up three days later in California to get the money back that he knew was coming.

And meanwhile, there was the other side of the problem. How were the Chicago fixers going to fix the Denver–New Orleans game? It had to come from Chicago and it had better get in Denver pretty fast. That was all Drover knew. And Fox and the other books were getting anxious over all the bets they had agreed to at crazy odds. Somebody would crack in Vegas. The game was off the boards. The damage was done. Some hilarious odds had been set in the early action on the Denver–New Orleans game.

Not a hundred guys. One or two. Maybe this guy Tommy Sain. Maybe someone like him.

He had given the name to Fox Vernon. Fox had computers; that meant Fox had knowledge.

"I don't need a computer. He comes to town once or twice a year and does a party animal. Usually craps. When he wears out his welcome, he sleeps it off and goes home and pays his bills. A gambler junkie."

"He uses drugs?"

"I mean, he's got gambling fever. He should get treatment but I know he won't find it out here."

"He books. He works at the exchange in Chicago."

Fox did a "hmmm" and said nothing. They broke the

telephone connection. There were a lot of phone calls that day. Dusty in Denver, some others. And he called Belle Fontaine in New Orleans.

"Hiya, Belle."

"Where you at, sugarman?"

"Cruz. I thought I'd come down."

"Hell, don't need no special invite, sugar. You still a single boy lookin' for love in all the wrong places?"

"You know it."

"How's the fireman? I should get out and pay you boys a visit. It's just so damned hard to leave Awlins, once you been havin' the best, go out there and eat that California food. Y'all still eat grass for lunch?"

"You got better food, Belle, but not the best football team."

"They just broke my heart again yesterday. I was wearin' my special fleur-de-lis dress and I lit a candle for them in St. Louis Cathedral and it came to no avail. But they are handsome young men and we should forgive them their trespasses."

"Kelly sends his love."

"Tell that boy I expect more than sentiment, I want full-frontal nudity and I want it yesterday."

"Belle, I need a room tonight."

"Windsor Court hotel, best hotel in the world, I can fix you up."

"I was hoping you'd say that."

"You want comp'ny?"

"Only if it's you."

"When should I put my bells on? Or don't you want bells this time?"

"I'm still ringing from the last time."

She chuckled. Her voice was as lazy as Decatur Street on Sunday mornings.

"We'll have dinner. Say eight tonight?"

"Sounds fine, Belle. Love you."

"You say that to all the girls and I bet they all know you're lying but it don't make no difference, not to me."

"Belle, I need a little information."

"Here I was thinkin' you called me up just because you was hungry for a loving mama and all you want is to admire my brain. It makes a girl wonder why she bothers with eye shadow."

"You know of an action player named Tommy Sain?" The old shot-in-the-dark trick.

"Can't say I have had the pleasure."

"Chicago boy."

"Love Chicago boys, they good tippers. New Yawk boys too. They like to flash, if you understand."

"Who might know someone like Tommy Sain?"

"What kind of action?"

"Sports gambling. Football. A heavy hitter."

"Hmmph. I can ask my friends who have friends."

"And what do you know about Len Gascon?"

"What I know is that the National Football League is grossly unfair and against Awlins because they take one of our boys, good coonass Cajun boy that loves his mama and jambalaya and takes that sorry redneck outta here and put him in a place like Denver, Colorado. There is no justice on this earth that can convince me my po' boy is happy in a place full of cowboys that probabl' don't know a catfish from a shrimp. It's a known fact that the reason the Saints ain't never been in the Super Bowl is that they always wanna use our Superdome for the Super Bowl and it wouldn't pay off big if New Orleans had a homefield advantage. That's a fact."

"I'm sure it is, Belle. I'll advance it in Vegas next week. What I wanna know is, is Lenny a good boy or does he party?"

"Party? Ain't nobody from Loo'siana don't party."

"I mean, nose candy party."

Pause.

"Honey, Lenny parties that way, he don't do it on Bourbon Street, I mean, ain't nobody in Awlins wouldn't know that. He a good boy; y'all hear how he beat the hell out of San Diego yes'day?"

"I was there."

Pause.

"Sugar, is this serious?"

"It's downright hilarious."

"Then I'll see things with your eyes for a while."

"Thanks, babe. See you tonight."

The fourth call was to New York City.

"National Football League," said the voice at the other end of the line.

He gave a name.

"Hello," said the new voice, belonging to a man.

"When are you going to know about Gascon?"

"Whoa. We don't give that out until everyone gets it, Drover."

"All right. When does everyone get it?"

"Soon."

"Christmas is coming."

"You still with the Foxman?"

"Still."

"He's been square with us."

"He's square now. Money is going the wrong way," Drover said.

Pause.

"How's that?"

"Going to the Saints and not to Denver."

"Shit."

"Exactly."

"The commish picked up a birdie the other night at a cocktail party."

"From who?"

"We didn't ask. We don't usually ask the commish who sings to him."

"Some bad stuff is going down."

"Mob."

"No. Independents out of Chicago."

"Chicago Family connection?"

"No. Even Tony Rolls acts puzzled."

"Where from?"

Drover thought about it. "I don't know yet. When I get a line, I'll call you. But look, see if you can get a make on the bird."

"Why? So you can burn him?"

"Nobody's burned yet. We want to keep it that way."

"I dunno. That's a lot of favor."

"Think about it."

They broke the connection. He had given half a loaf. Maybe it was enough.

Now he would have to find out what he could in New Orleans, in case this whole thing was coming from two ends.

But first, there was Nancy.

Drover's apartment, in the back and connected to the tavern building, was an outgrowth of it. There was a long, big window that looked out on the sea. There were three rooms, a tiny kitchen and smallish study and the other room. He could sleep here in the other room and stare at the sky and sea. He lived in this room and it was simple and it was just enough for him. Now it was their room.

Nancy was helping Kelly out in the kitchen of the saloon in the afternoon. She now was disturbing the order of his apartment the way women do these things, but he didn't mind. Drover told her his travel plans and she listened as though she was being asked something. Maybe he just wanted to tell someone and share parts of a secret life.

"Be careful," she said.

"No, that's my line. In case Slim Dingo decides to come looking for me here."

"I've got Kelly."

"Stay close to him."

"This is real, isn't it? I mean, this scary stuff?"

"Yeah. I'm beginning to understand it a little more and it gets scarier. I don't want either of us to drown."

"Be careful."

"See you by Wednesday night, maybe Thursday."

He had his gym bag packed. He wore a sports coat in deference to New Orleans dress codes. He smiled at her, trying to make the smile last until Thursday. She had a better idea. The kiss she gave him said Wednesday night at the latest.

CHAPTER 25

BELLE FONTAINE WEIGHED two hundred pounds and dressed like Mata Hari. She screamed when she saw Drover enter her bar on Decatur Street in the Quarter and flung out her arms to him. Drover kissed her and she devoured him, pressing full-frontal dressed-upness into his chest and making sure her breasts made an impression.

Drover staggered back but held on. Belle Fontaine was a lot of things besides a lot of woman but right now she was a woman. She had an appetite for men that bordered on irrational but Drover was her pet, kind of a kid brother who might turn out to be an altar boy. She thought she had to explain everything twice to him.

When the kissing was done, to the applause of her bartender and sandwich manager, she led him by a firm hand to her table in the back. The saloon was dingy because she liked it that way. When someone complained once that the toilet was stopped up, she gave him a plunger and told him to fix it.

"Sugarman, you look good enough to put in a po' boy and eat up," Belle said. Her hair was bottle red and her eyes were green flashers. She had pretty features that had softened out with the fat. Beneath her green silk dress were rather dainty legs and feet and one of her great sexual pleasures was to have her date of the moment suck her toes.

"Got you all set up at the Windsor Court and we got a reservation for eight there," Belle said.

"I could eat," Drover said. "I've been living on airplane food for a week."

"Well, sugar, I done what you wanted, at least I think I did. I talked to Charlie and he talked to Sergeant Carey at the Vieux Carre station house and one thing led to another. I had Sergeant Carey over here this afternoon and we talked and talked. He's a good old boy and he was rattling on 'bout most anything I brought up. Like so many of our finest officers, he knows all about the criminal elements."

"Which means?"

"Well, naturally, there are people who think the Saints are going to the Super Bowl and they ain't all locked up in Algers either." Belle Fontaine made a signal to Charlie, the barman, who came over and took his order. He felt like a Dixie and said so. Belle had her usual, Chartreuse and vodka.

"There's money down on the Saints is what I'm saying, lamb chop. I guess the gamblers call it chump money. The bookies is laying it off around the country the usual way, just evening out the losers and winners so they don't end up gambling themselves, they just in it for the juice."

"I know how handbooks work, Belle."

She let her eyes laugh at him. She patted his hand. "Bless your sweet virgin ass, I believe you do know. It's just that I can't ever help thinkin' you're just a little boy yet. Y'all bring out the mother in me. In here. Between these." She gestured and Drover laughed. Belle was a party that celebrated every day of her life.

"Well, there's been some more money than usual in the last few days," Belle said.

"On what game?"

"Denver game in less than three weeks."

"Denver game. On New Orleans."

"Thats's right."

"One book handling it?"

"As it turned out. He tried to lay it off but he took the initial action. And now you bookies out in Las Vegas have put it off the boards and nobody can lay anything off. That's what they say."

"Got a name?"

"Edwin LeClerc, usually find him at the Pontchartrain. He's a good boy but he ain't no coonass, even with that name on him, he drifted down here ten years ago."

"Where's he from?"

"Up north. Still talks like that."

"Like what?"

"Like the way you talk, sugar."

"He's from Chicago?"

"Thats's what the cop had to say."

"Why'd he come down here?"

"Seems he was a stock trader? Up there? Now, I don' understand none of this, I thought all the stock traders was people in New York but I guess they got something up there? In Chicago?" She was being coy, putting question marks at the ends of perfectly declarative sentences. She fluttered her eyelids and took a medicinal portion of her green drink.

"Was."

"Seems he went to prison for a couple of years for doing something thoroughly nasty with those poor old stocks or whatever they was, the sergeant wasn't all that clear and the records on it just up and disappeared one day the way those things can happen in the Awlins police department, don't you know?"

"Stocks."

"Honey lamb, there something wrong with you? You gonna speak in one-word sentences all night? Y'all know how much I enjoy your palaver, maybe you ain't feelin' right because you been eatin' those plastic airplane sandwiches too much—"

"I'm thinking, Belle, you know how you distract me from that," Drover said. He squeezed her thigh under the table and she giggled at him as she brushed his hand away.

"Edwin LeClerc is a Garden District bookie, very high-class and only the best people place their bets with him. Now, all the books and the gamblers know each other and the cops know them too because we're all just family in Awlins after all. So Sergeant Carey, he says it was funny I was askin' 'bout football bettin' because they were just goin' on the Saints all of a sudden and the other bookies don' like it because all the action is comin' from Edwin LeClerc and they don' like to handle a rush like that. Ain't gonna handle tha' rush."

"Like what?"

"Lots of thousands of dollars over the last five, six days."

"Is that right?"

"Course it's right."

"And did anyone ever hear of Tommy Sain?"

She shook her head.

"And Gascon."

"Gascon's a good boy."

"Gascon is getting set up," Drover said.

She stared at him with true shock on her innocent features. "Who would do a thing like that to a po' boy from Loosiana?"

"I think I begin to see who and now I want to see how."

"Y'all mean someone is gonna fix the Denver game?"

"Yes, Belle."

"Damn! I put two hundred dollars on ever' Saints game at the beginning of the season. I don' mind losing my money because those fine boys just ain't as good as the other boys in those wiggly little pants they wear, but I'm damned if I wanna win because it's fixed."

"Except you got to keep it to yourself for now," Drover said. "I told you because I trust you, Belle."

She shrieked a laugh at that and kissed him good across the face. "Trust me! I ain't been trusted since I was eleven years old and found out boys had moving parts. I know you mean a compliment, sugar, and I take it that way, but if word got out that a man trusted me, my reputation wouldn't be worth warm spit in a vat of Dixie beer."

"All right, let's say we got a secret."

"I like that much better, much better, secrets are nasty things and I do love nasty things. Are you goin' over to the hotel, honey, or you gonna see that man?"

"What would he look like?"

"Gray mustache and distinguished, says Sergeant Carey, most distinguished-lookin' man in any room. I told him he must be lying because Sergeant Carey would be the most distinguished-looking man in any room and he blushed his cute little blush and laughed and I said, 'You'd look especially distinguished in my water bed with me sitting on your face,' and that made him turn redder than a coonass's bandanna."

Drover managed to get away from her a few minutes later, promising to meet her for dinner in the bar of the second-floor restaurant in the Windsor Court. He wasn't much for hotel food but there were probably five hotels in the country that put regular high-class restaurants to shame and this was one of those places.

He went down Decatur toward Canal Street. It was the

middle of the afternoon and the narrow streets of the
Quarter were filled with browsers and antique buyers. A
gaggle of black boys were tap dancing on a piece of linoleum on Ann Street to the music of a boom box. Their
taps were attached to their gym shoes. They were very
acrobatic and Drover dropped a dollar in their upturned
derby hat. That was the Quarter every time you visited
it: music and street performances, jazz bands and drunks
carrying their go-cups from bar to bar and strip joints
where ladies took it all off and wiggled it at you, and
games—gambling was in the New Orleans bloodstream
along with partying and all that jazz. Drover guessed
New Orleans was the best party town in the country and
nobody ever said no to a sports assignment down in the
Big Easy. He never had. Hell, he'd cover hockey here if
they had it.

The man named Edwin LeClerc was not at the Pontchartrain. Drover shrugged off the disappointment and
walked to his hotel off Poydras Street. He checked in at
one of the writing tables they used instead of desks and
took his bag to his room. He did an electric shave and
slapped lotion on the scraped meat and went down to the
second-floor bar to catch up on the day's *National*.

He was into a second bottle of Dixie when the man
tapped him on the shoulder.

Drover turned.

Distinguished. And gray.

"Mr. Drover."

Nice tone to the voice but there was Chicago in it, the
Chicago that starts in Streeterville and stops short of Lincoln Park, a cultured University of Chicago tone that can't
quite catch up with Boston but softens New Yorkese.
Drover's came more by way of the West Side and he had
to watch it not to drop into "dese" and "dose."

"That's me."

"Edwin LeClerc."

Hand. Drover shook it and put down his paper.

"Sergeant Carey said you were checking in this afternoon and I took the opportunity to make your acquaintance."

Soft and suave. That's what they all wanted to hear, from the Gold Coast to the Garden District. Men who showed nice were shown inside.

"I don't know a Sergeant Carey."

"New Orleans Police Department. Very nice man. He's been quite a friend to me over the years."

"How nice to have a friend."

"Do you have many friends?"

"No. I collect dogs instead."

"Friends in the environment?"

"What environment would that be?"

"Say, Las Vegas."

"What line of work are you in, Mr. LeClerc?"

"I book bets. Sports gambling."

Damn. New Orleans was always surprising you. The Big Easy all right.

"And you know Mr. Vernon, Mr. Fox Vernon in Las Vegas?" Edwin went on. "I would surely appreciate it if you could give me a moment or two of your time, sir."

"Sure. Sit down and have a drink."

"It's a little early for me, sir, I think I'll just have a Perrier, barman," LeClerc said. The drink came and LeClerc let the prop sit there.

"Now, my friend, Sergeant Carey, had a nice chat this afternoon with a woman named Belle Fontaine, runs a place over in the east end of the Quarter on Decatur Street?" That was a New Orleans question mark. "Well, Miss Fontaine was making discreet inquiries all day on behalf of a certain James Drover, a friend of hers?" Another one. "Your name came up and Sergeant Carey—"

"How did my name come up?"

"Oh come now. This is a small town, Mr. Drover. We're all family. I like to think they've even adopted me. In any case, her barman, I think his name is Charlie, he dropped the name to get a name. You gotta give to get in this world."

"And my name came up."

"To go on, it was mentioned to me. And I knew who you were right away. You were the sportswriter who got into trouble in Los Angeles that time. I can sympathize. I was into trouble once in my life too. And we're both from Chicago. I read you when you were in the paper there. I had a lot of time to read the papers. You see, I was in prison at Sandstone in Minnesota for two years, six months, and fourteen days. I'll never forget how long a time that was. Read a lot of papers."

"Some things impress themselves."

Gray Mustache did not seem amused. He went on in the same careful and polite voice. "I was a commodities trader and I slipped. Not that it's all that uncommon. The uncommon thing was, I was caught at it and they made an example of me the way they liked to do. So they put me in prison and they took away my ticket to trade. So I had to learn something else and I learned in prison. You see, I had quite a lot of money to get started in the business."

"And it's similar. The trade, I mean."

"Very similar. The principles are the same. We live on expectations and rumors. Will Russia run out of grain? Will the winter wheat crop die and drive up summer wheat? Will summer wheat fade? Will, will, will. If you pay attention, you can make quite a lot of money. I pay attention."

"Good. So do I. This is all leading to something isn't it or are we just passing the time of day?"

"You are somewhat annoying."

"You haven't seen half of it."

"You want to know about action. A lot of action going down on a certain game."

"I guess that it comes from Chicago."

"Yes," LeClerc said. Another surprise. A bookie's client list was a secret right up there with not telling outside the confessional.

"He burned you," Drover said. It was the logical guess. And it was a hell of a piece of luck.

"Maybe."

"Sure. You didn't lay off all that action because it was a chump bet from a man who is addicted to gambling and to losing his money. You knew him when. You kept it and now you're going to be burned because you'll have to cover yourself. Your friend, the sergeant, he mentioned one name to you that sent you quivering. You should have laid it off but it's too late. The game is off the boards in Vegas and nobody in New Orleans will touch it."

"And what part did you have in taking the game off the boards?"

"No part. It was another book in Vegas that took it off. Fox wanted to know why. He sent me down here to find out."

"You know more than that."

"Everyone knows more than he tells."

"I took a big gamble when I kept that money."

"And you may have lost."

"Why?"

"Because there's something funny going on about that game."

"Do you know what it is?"

"I'm waiting like everyone else."

"For what?"

"The *Rocky Mountain News* said this morning that Len

Gascon of the Broncs is being given mandatory drug tests. If Gascon gets busted, Denver is sunk, they don't have another arm.''

''I took the game off the boards after I talked with Sergeant Carey. I don't like this at all.'' The Gold Coast was gone out of the voice. This was a voice learned in a federal prison. It had edges, like a spoon turned into a knife.

''So what are you going to do about it?''

''The point is, what are you going to do about it?''

Drover said, ''If there's a fix, I got to find it. I appreciate all the help I can get.''

''There's no evidence of any fix.''

''They aren't testing Gascon because they like to see him urinate into bottles.''

''Gascon is a clean liver.''

''So everyone agrees. So he's got nothing to worry about.''

''Everyone has something to worry about.''

''Talking to you, Ed, is like riding a merry-go-round at warp speed.''

''Thing is, we should stay in touch.''

''I already work for a book. The legal kind.''

''But your work is unique. You watch the games and tell your friend in Vegas what you see.''

''It's like sportswriting only you don't have to go down to the paper.''

''What do you see?''

''Just what you think.''

''Damn.''

''You want to tell me who loaded you?''

''I can't do that.''

''It's not as though either of you is likely to get arrested. I'm not a cop.''

''But you might know cops.''

''Hey, I can't help it. I know all kinds of people.''

"Like in Chicago."

"The Outfit has a connection down here too," Drover said.

"I'm more interested in Chicago at the moment."

"Don't tell me that was Outfit money."

"I begin to wonder."

"Shit, Ed, you know where that money came from."

"Yes, I do. At least, I thought I did. It just doesn't figure."

"It doesn't figure that Tommy Sain would know enough or be smart enough or be tough enough to fix a pro football game but now it looks like that's what he did. Either that or he had insider knowledge, as you fellas on the stock market like to call it. And that means that he found out that the Outfit was going to fix the game and decided to use his old trading buddy in New Orleans to make a bet, a Dead Cert. You, having ripped off this chump before when he went into his gambling fever, decided to keep the chump bet yourself. And now you got a big loser coming up and you think the Outfit did it and Tommy Sain fixed you."

"Where'd you get that name?"

"I got nothing to say to you, Ed, because you got nothing to say to me. Read 'em and weep in three weeks."

Edwin LeClerc worried his mustache with his right hand a moment as though he was considering something. He got up from the stool instead.

"You want a number?" Drover said.

"Yes."

Drover gave him a card with three phone numbers on it. There was no name.

He put the card in his pocket and turned without a word. Drover thought that was rude.

Drover said, "Ed."

"What?"

"I don't buy Perrier water. If you were going to have a drink, I'd have picked it up. Leave what you owe."

"I don't like you."

"It shows. But that's okay. You got a good friend like Sergeant Carey already. You don't have to like me."

CHAPTER 26

SLIM DINGO DROVE down from San Francisco International in a rental Lincoln. She had defied him. She had run away just like that and she was probably shacking up now with her boyfriend in Santa Cruz. Well, fuck her. He had five days until he had his next game and he would just use the time to take care of Miss Nancy and her asshole boyfriend and put them both in the ocean. Teach Miss Nancy that he meant what he said that one good beating deserved another.

He got to Santa Cruz by four. The pier was crowded with people going out to dinner or coming in from a day of fishing. He found the place and looked inside and saw her behind the bar, washing glasses. She was alone at the moment and he could have gotten to her but it was important to be careful, there was a man involved in this too and he'd have to take them both out. Slim Dingo had a very good idea of how he could handle it but first he had to get a piece. He'd have to get a room and call down to Los Angeles and get the eye named Rollins to drive him up a piece. The eye did a lot of good work for him.

Okay, Miss Nancy, I'll be seeing you, he said to himself. She wasn't wearing sunglasses and her eyes were still puffy but she didn't look bad, not bad at all, maybe next time he'd make her look worse. If he let her stay alive at all and that would be up to her. She could come out to the ranch, she might be fun to have around, and she could think about her boyfriend feeding fish.

That thought gave him his usual rush of pleasant feelings.

CHAPTER 27

BART BRIXTON WATCHED her.

Frances Downes was on her knees in the bathroom. She had the toilet seat down and she was kneeling over it, a straw in her left nostril and a line of cocaine on the seat. She was absolutely naked and looked ridiculous, Bart thought. She was a metaphor of her life. She was in the toilet. She had gone down for him the way he wanted it and he had given her the nose candy that was her reward and now she was going down on the candy. Her life was in the toilet already.

She felt the rush of pleasure and the intense sensation of absolute clarity, a sense of well-being that comes with the first glass of whiskey or a line of coke or any vice that stimulates and soothes at the same time. Only later, after the tenth glass of whiskey or the umpteenth line does it feel so much worse than normal.

She saw that he was watching her through the open door and she saw she was on her knees over the toilet and she didn't have any clothes on. She giggled and got up and banged her head against the sink and didn't feel a thing.

She giggled some more.

She did her model runway walk up to him and he let her kiss him and rub her chest against his shirt. He had his clothes on. Sometimes he liked it that way, giving him a sense of power.

They had tested Gascon in the morning and he had joked about it to the nurse and to the doctor so that the nurse had blushed and nurses never blush.

Bart got this from the sports network. He also discovered from Tommy Sain that the Denver–New Orleans game was going off the boards in the legal books in Las Vegas. They smelled something all of a sudden but it was too late. Tommy Sain had flown out to New Orleans on Friday afternoon to see their old friend Edwin LeClerc. Ole Ed.

He frowned at the thought and pushed Frances away. "Get some clothes on, I want to go out, we'll go over to Bub City."

"What should I wear?"

"Just something to cover your pussy, honey."

"You can be so fucking crude."

"Only if I'm in the mood." He was not frowning at her but at that asshole Tommy Sain.

"You laid off two hundred dimes with Ed LeClerc? Are you crazy? Didn't he ask you why?" That's the way the conversation had gone in the beginning of the day after Tommy Sain said his wife walked out on him and he was looking for a pat on the head.

"I put down ten dimes on the Bears and Denver and the rest on New Orleans and Denver. That way, he thinks I got one of those hunches. Shit. I bet with him for five, six years, he took me pretty good once when I was in Vegas, off the wagon. I owe him one."

"You did it to Ed? And Ed is going to know? What do you think Ed is gonna do? And when he comes back to you, where does that put me?"

"Relax. He's going to lay it off. It'll look like New Orleans local booster money when it finds its way to the other books that Ed lays off bets with. Ed isn't gonna lose, he keeps the juice and he evens out the bets."

"What if he holds the bet himself because he thinks you don't know shit about sports betting?"

Tommy had said, "I know a helluva lot more than you do."

Bart had wanted to paste him right there in Binyan's in the south Loop. The old, paneled restaurant was full of traders, legal crapshooters, and they were all hunched over tablecloths talking deal. "You're making signals, for Christ's sake. Ed's got your name and a hundred and ninety dimes on a single, meaningless game."

"You said I had to lay it all off by the weekend."

"Because that was the timetable."

The timetable. The little birdie in Denver twitting to the *Post* and the *News*. The little birdie getting to Partridge of the Broncs. The little birdie in New York, right into the commissioner's ear, thanks to Frances. And Frances, dear Frances, dear doped-up Frances who had to keep her weight down by inhaling Colombia's great export, she had been the key to it all without realizing all of it.

What if it came back to her and she got scared?

He watched her shrug into the dress. She didn't wear underwear on dates. She said it just got in the way. She had endearing qualities and she was sexy, there was no doubt about that. So it wasn't really that much trouble to lay Lenny Gascon. She felt a little bad about betraying her fellow model, Deanna, but then, Deanna was not Mrs. Lenny Gascon anymore. More than once when she was married and Frances had gone to see her in Denver, Lenny put the hit on her. Laying Lenny was easier than laying linoleum.

That's where Bart had picked up the idea in the first place.

He had looked at Frances and her life-style and looked at her friends and then he had looked at Tommy Sain. Here were two people on the verge of self-destructing and it didn't put a dime in anyone's pocket. With their connections, it should.

Bart Brixton, the young con, used people and knew the uses of power better than anyone he had ever met in his life. If Frances was going to nose candy hell, then get it for her and get laid on a regular basis by a fashion model whose tongue wouldn't quit once it got going. And if Tommy Sain was on the edge of falling out of the commodities game for the Vegas game, then use him. He had the informal book. And Frances had once dated the commissioner. And Frances, who could have laid just about any man she wanted, could certainly get to the legendary stick man of the Denver Broncos.

So it had formed in his mind from the spring until now. Just one game, one game far removed from Chicago, a game that was so one-sided it shouldn't be played and Bart Brixton saw that he might be talking about five million dollars. Five million dollars was small enough change not to sting too many books across the whole country so there was no chance of comebacks to him.

If Tommy Sain hadn't fucked up.

"You're an asshole," Bart had said to him.

"I'm ready, honey," Frances said now.

"You worry too much," Tommy had said.

"Is something wrong?" Frances said now.

Shit.

He kissed her instead. Her eyes were cocaine bright. She was wired and he needed to put it out of his head for a couple of hours.

"Let's watch the *Monday Night* game," he said to her.

"Whatever you want to do," she said.

He knew that was absolutely true.

CHAPTER 28

DINNER WITH BELLE Fontaine was a feast of eight courses of which Drover took part in three. Belle modulated her laughter in the elegant dining room but did not limit the frequency of it. She was full of gossip about New Orleans, low- and high-life, anecdotes of events that can only be allowed in a city that prefers to live on the streets day and night.

"Whacha gonna do now, sugar thighs?" she said at the dessert.

"Take you upstairs and jump on your stomach."

She laughed a little too loud but it was late and nobody cared. A jazz trio was playing in the lounge and over-dressed men and underdressed ladies, the latter wearing variations of the little black dress, were sitting around on overstuffed chairs, getting dreamy and ready for bed. The lounge was an open room without the cheap dark lights and dark woods. It might have been someone's expensive living room and spilled out to the dining area.

"Honey, I begin to believe you ain't been laid lately."

"A couple of weeks."

"Time is a most precious commodity and should be used wisely and well and a man of your looks, finesse, capacity, and not to mention dong size, should be engaging in the lively art of fucking on a regular basis. I just might take you up on it."

"I'm serious."

"You haven't been serious since the Vietnam War."

Drover gave it up. Even after a bottle or two of Medoc, you couldn't fool Belle. "I talked to LeClerc and it all begins to fit. Chicago, my hometown."

"Y'all going to Chicago, just got here?"

"Have to. Plane is out of here at eleven, got to change at Atlanta."

"I gone through the trouble of reserving your room and I thought we could do the game where I'm the wheelbarrow and you're the gardener and now you're going to Chicago?"

"I'll be back, Belle. It's just coming down faster than I can pick it up."

"Did you do yourself any good here?"

"Got to see you again, had a lovely meal, spend the evening, have a nice nap, lovely room, and now maybe I'm close to the end of whatever it is that's going to happen."

"The fix."

"Our secret."

"Our secret."

"I can leave you the room key in case you want to get lucky with someone in the room."

She smiled. She really was pretty. "Luck has nothing to do with it. I am a beautiful woman who knows sex back and front, you might say, and that's all any man wants or even deserves."

"A feminist."

"Hate them with a passion because they keep giving away the secrets. Hell, I was born liberated, no sense drawing attention to it."

They left it at that.

The Delta flight bumped a bit over Alabama. The Chicago connection took off late. Not even homeless people want to spend more time in the Atlanta airport than they have to. But Drover thought there is no sadder place on earth than O'Hare Airport after all the bars and restaurants have shut down and the cops were hustling the homeless out of the terminals. He called the Drake but it was full. He finally got lucky with the Raphael and recited his credit card number.

The cab driver wanted to talk about how he had lambs slaughtered for him in Indiana and how lamb was the centerpiece of his native cuisine. He was from Jordan. Drover listened because he would listen to anybody, especially at nearly three in the morning. Conversation gets more precious in the single-digit hours. The driver smelled like lamb and so did the cab.

Drover called Fox from his room. Like many people in Las Vegas, Fox kept late hours. It was past midnight there, a time when action is just beginning.

"Any word on Gascon?"

"Yes. The news isn't going to be good."

"Positive on drugs?"

"Anabolic steroids."

Steroids.

Drover held the phone a little too tight and it started to shake. "He didn't do drugs."

"The trouble with steroids is that you can be given them. Players get shot up all the time. Someone could have slipped him a conditioner. Didn't even have to do with our little problem, it might have been innocent. Except I don't think so."

"Too many little birdies. A guy in N.O. named Edwin LeClerc."

"Book," said Fox Vernon. He knew everyone.

"Was a trader on the Chicago Board of Trade before he went to jail for some insider stuff."

"What about him?"

"He's holding the bag. Action on the Denver game. It had to come from Chicago. I guessed a name and I thought he was going to pee. He's stuck for it because he didn't lay it off."

"Tommy Sain," Fox said. He was as good as Drover when he put his mind to it.

"Bingo. So I'm in Chicago instead of jumping on Belle Fontaine's stomach."

"She must be some woman to pull off carrying two hundred pounds on her ankles and still getting men to do bad things to her," Fox said.

"She is. She put me on LeClerc and LeClerc is hot, he sees the books have taken the game off the boards and he can't lay off his bet which looked like a sure sucker bet a few days ago. I am going to see Tommy Sain."

"What are you going to do?"

"Talk to him."

"About what?"

"About the Outfit. About Tony Rolls."

A long pause. "We are not involved in the crime syndicate."

"Neither is Tommy Sain. This might be possible, this could be, this might be, it is . . . a home run! Sorry. Quoting Harry Caray runs in the Chicago bloodstream. But Tommy Sain has to get scared first. I hate to scare people because I never believe it myself but then, what the hell."

"This is going down tomorrow, the announcement on Gascon. The commissioner wants cameras at eleven. That means a one-month suspension. Gascon misses the Saints game. The Saints, I hesitate to say it too loud, have suddenly got a chance."

"Shit. I saw the Forgotten Quarterback mop up the fourth quarter yesterday. He throws like a girl."

"There is a running offense."

"There's no quarterback, Foxer. It's like when Payton was running for the Bears before McMahon came along. Payton was the greatest runner in the game but he was all they had. Give it to Payton one, give it to Payton two, try a pass that was sure to fail and then kick. That's not offense. Denver is dead and I don't believe for one minute that Pretty Boy Gascon used steroids. Said it himself, he was born perfect. I got to get a line on this and the line is in Chicago today. When this is over, I am taking a week off and not traveling anywhere."

"Use good judgment, Drover," Fox Vernon said.

"I'll use a case of it. Excuse me, I've got to go sleepy."

"Night night," Fox said.

CHAPTER 29

MISS NANCY LIVED in that apartment on the second floor behind the tavern, overlooking the ocean. She worked in the afternoon for the fat Irishman in that tavern or restaurant or whatever it was. She stuck close to the Irishman. That's what was taking time, she was sticking close to this guy and the other guy, the bleeder, Drover, he wasn't around. Maybe the Irishman was poking her on the side. Maybe anything, Nancy was a tramp and back at the ranch, he could put that to good use. He finally had decided he was going to sell her to one of the houses in Nevada where prostitution was legal. Had to get her to the point of sale first and that meant conditioning and training. It was like you did with a horse. You had to break it first before you could build it up.

Slim Dingo checked in by phone on Tuesday morning, about the time that the NFL commissioner announced that Len Gascon was to be suspended for four games for the illegal use of anabolic steroids.

"Goran."

"I'm checking in like you told me."

"Where are you?"

"In L.A."

"You getting ready for the game this weekend?"

"I got my necklace and ever'thing." He hated this FBI guy worse than niggers.

"We'll keep an eye out. Check in same time, station, tomorrow."

"I know the routine."

"How's the weather?" People in places like Chicago always asked questions like that when they pierced the rain clouds and reached out to California.

"Smoggy."

"Yeah. It's a real smoggy place."

Asshole, Slim thought, hanging up the phone. He had a couple of days of freedom and Nancy was going to get careless, it was bound to happen, and she'd take a walk on the beach or go over to that boardwalk they had and then she would disappear. Just disappear, without a trace. Rollins, the eye, had brought him a piece and his own Rolls-Royce and the eye had taken the rental Lincoln back to the airport. It was perfect. He'd put her in the trunk. He'd drive her back to the ranch. That would be the beginning of her training, being in the trunk of his car all that way.

And then he'd hit Drover.

CHAPTER 30

"FEDERAL BUREAU OF Investigation?" Tommy Sain said, turning the card over three times. "What do you want with me, Mr. Cleaver?"

Edwin Cleaver. Eldridge might have been pushing it.

Drover took the card back and put it in his wallet the way G men do, very carefully and neatly. He wore a white shirt and sober blue tie for the occasion and his shoes were polished.

"We want to ask you about interstate gambling," Drover said.

The statement left a large hole in Tommy Slain's forehead, right above his brown eyes.

"Specifically, about a very large bet you placed recently with Mr. Edwin LeClerc, a known bookmaker, in the city of New Orleans."

"I dunno what you—"

"Mr. Sain, for some time we have been monitoring gambling operations in Chicago that we have code-named MOBSCAM. I tell you this in the strictest confidence because we want your cooperation as we would want the cooperation of any citizen. Now, the crime syndicate persons we are watching, and they include Mr. Tony Meathook Rolls, Mr. Vince Titcutter Alberlini, Mr. Giuseppe Joe Blood Tomano, and others, they have indicated among themselves in private conversations we are monitoring through a court-approved wiretap that they believe you are running a rival gambling operation in the area of sports gambling on the exchange. In our monitor, we have determined that there is a decision to be made to have you eliminated as a competitor.''

There. Drover paused and let the parade of federalese march through Tommy Sain's brain.

They were off the trading floor and the halls were filled with men in cloth coats running back and forth. Everything was marble walls and marble floors. This was the great commodities game and the traders and runners were in full cry. The place could have been a bank except for all these crazy people in funny-colored jackets running around. The madness overwhelmed silence. Yet Tommy Sain suddenly seemed lost in a world of utter silence.

''Mr. Sain?''

''The mob? The mob wants to kill me? For what? What did I do?''

''I don't know Mr. Sain. But they perceive you as a threat to their monopoly over illegal gambling. If you are running a book on this exchange, you are in violation of federal laws governing both interstate commerce and illegal gambling. Do you have a gaming tax license?''

''I don't know what to say.''

Drover gave him Federal Agent Number Three. It is both bland and menacing for its blandness. The eyes look sad.

''Mr. Sain, can we find some place more quiet.''

The office Tommy Sain opened was wired for computers and not much comfort. They found two chairs and used them.

''Agent . . . Cleaver?''

''Yes.''

''Agent Cleaver, this comes at me like a bomb.''

''And a bomb might be one of the ways they would use

although they're partial to the old-fashioned one-way ride, it's simplest and works extremely well.''

Drover wasn't letting any warmth enter the room. Tommy Sain rubbed his arms as though he could feel the chill.

''Tell me something, Mr. Sain. Why did you go all the way to New Orleans to place a bet on the New Orleans and Denver game? And with a person who had crime syndicate ties?''

''Jesus Christ.'' He was going to get the shakes, exactly the way he sometimes did when he had to go to Las Vegas, when he knew he had to do it. Jesus.

Drover waited. Silence in interrogation is used by cops and the G but Drover had learned to use it as a sportswriter with eager-to-please general managers and athletes who wanted to fill up the silence with words. Sometimes you got something good out of silence.

The line of sweat on Tommy's forehead was good, just above where the bullet hole was.

''I bet. I bet sometimes. I know Ed, knew him on the exchange. You gonna arrest everyone in this country who makes a bet?''

''Only the ones we catch.''

''Did Ed tell you?''

''We do not reveal our sources.''

''Am I in trouble?''

''Do you run a book here?''

''No, absolutely not.''

''Then you don't need a gambling tax license.''

Silence.

''But am I in trouble? I mean, you said you heard the crime syndicate wants to kill me.''

''They don't use the word kill. They say 'whack.' They want to whack you for something you say you don't do. That's very unusual. The crime syndicate usually does not interfere with people or persons who do not interfere with them."

"Am I going to be protected?"

"Would you like our protection?"

"Do I need it?"

"Have you perceived any change around you? Men following you? A strange car parked on your street at home?"

He thought. God yes, there were strangers all around and he had seen them and never given them a second thought.

He wiped his brow.

Drover slipped into Federal Agent Number Four which is a variation on We're All in This Together. "Look, Tom, if you can see your way clear to cooperate with us, I think we can assure you absolutely of our protection. Believe me, a situation like this is what we're faced with all the time. But we need a cooperative attitude."

"Cooperate about what?"

Back to Agent Number Three.

"Look, I want to cooperate. I gotta think. I gotta talk to someone. My lawyer."

"You have the right to the advice of counsel." He had picked that up on an old *Perry Mason*. Drover got up. "Think about it, Mr. Sain. There are men out there who would stop at nothing to get their ends." That was Phillips Lord from *Gangbusters*.

"But you heard them. You taped them. You heard them say they were going to kill me. Whack me. Can't you arrest them?"

"And endanger MOBSCAM? MOBSCAM is part of an ongoing program of intelligence which is more important than any one person or one incident. Besides, murder is not a federal crime."

"Tell the police—"

"We have reason to believe certain police officials are themselves targets of our investigation."

Tommy Sain stared at Drover.

"Shit," he said.

"Here's a card. Call anytime, day or night. It's an eight hundred number and will not cost you. I'll be back to you when you call. Think it over, Mr. Sain. And have a nice day."

CHAPTER 31

LENNY GASCON WAS looking for a hole to crawl into.

He called Lori Gibbons but she wasn't in and a recording said she would call him back as soon as she could.

He called Partridge finally and the old lady wasn't in to him. The fucking general manager wasn't in to Lenny Gascon, the million-dollar spear chucker who, until eleven this morning, was leading the glorious Denver Broncos to the Super Bowl. He called his agent in Los Angeles. His agent sounded pissed.

Agent Pressman said, "I'm into a couple of deals, Len. But you're number one."

"I know that."

"Thing is, kid, we stay away from the press. Stay away. Don't think you got friends on the papers because newspapermen are assholes, they smell blood and they rip into the carcass first. Keep your head down. Why'd you get tested? You never told me this. Do I have a phone number? What am I, chopped liver?"

"I didn't figure I gotta check with you ever' time I pee."

"You should of called me. I would of told you."

"It wasn't nothing. I didn't do nothing."

"So that means they just, out of the blue, decided to test you?"

"Out of the blue."

"Incredible. You got one year on your contract."

"What do you think? This is about the contract?"

"Everything is about a contract," the agent said.

"Shit. I can't do nothin'? You gonna come see me?"

Pause.

"I'm your pal, of course I'm gonna come see you. But I got to clean something up. Say tonight, we can do dinner and talk. Cheer up. What's a suspension? I gotta call around on this."

He finally went down to Deanna's house. He wasn't going to risk calling her. His phone was off the hook to *The Denver Post, Rocky Mountain News, Associated Press, New York Times,* and every TV station between here and Osaka but he knew that Deanna had personally fixed it so her phone was always off the hook to her ex-husband.

Lenny wore his orange Izod, black leather trousers, orange silk socks, white tennis shoes, and Chanel for Men.

Deanna Lu Glascott, formerly Deanna Gascon, wore white rayon trousers, white blouse, white scarf, knee-high black nylons, and three-inch heels. She was heading for lunch at the Denver Athletic Club, a high-class place that overshadows the rowdy Press Club just across the street. She looked good, better than he remembered her looking when she was his wife, but that was the thing about wives. They always looked better on someone else's arm.

"I'm late, baby," she said, and tried to brush by him. Her house was south of downtown in a tony section that had mountain views out of every window. When he saw he couldn't even kiss her, he appealed to her motherliness.

"I got suspended."

"I heard on CNN. You're the top story at eleven. There must not be any news in the world."

"Honey, I'm down. I'm so down a hole looks up,"

Gascon said. "My fucking agent is calling around, whatever that means."

Deanna was a natural blonde rendered ashen by hair coloring. Maybe she was a little large for modeling but in the real world a size six is a size six, even if it photographs as an eight in the world of fashion. Deanna had done a nice score on the divorce and achieved a certain cachet in the small world of Denver society by being the ex-wife of the star quarterback of the Broncos. If she got laid now, it was on her own terms and in her own time and place. At least two men in the banking community had proposed marriage to her without even going to bed and trying her out because to be the second husband of Deanna Gascon was closer to immortality than they'd ever get making bad mortgage loans. Arthur Miller must have thought that way after Marilyn divorced Joe DiMaggio.

Deanna tapped her front tooth with a painted fingernail and looked at him. Gascon looked more miserable than he had the time Ole Miss had stomped his ass into the swamp in his junior year. That was the time she had fallen in love with him. He had needed a lot of cheering up after that game and after all, she was a cheerleader.

"Why'd you take those things they said? Take steriods?"

"Steroids. I never took none. I never took nothin' but an aspirin in my life. I didn't need that shit, I was born naturally strong."

"I'm glad to hear you say it, babe. It wouldn't have been natural to have two minutes of conversation with you without you telling me what a great hunk you are."

"Shit, Deanna, honey, I got no place to turn . . ."

"Oh come on, this is your ex-wife talking, you go pull that line of bull on some bimbo off an airplane or something."

"Honest, honey, I never took no steroids, I been framed by the commissioner."

"Get a lawyer. I did. They work wonders."

"Shit, I ain't talkin' 'bout the divorce, I took care of you—"

"I like to think I took care of myself."

Damn. She realized she was doing it again. They were talking and she could outtalk Lenny any day of the week but there was this fatal weakness she had. Bankers were all right and diamonds were forever but look at him. She hadn't felt a hard belly in a year.

"Aw, honey, anythin' you say is okay but don't leave me 'lone. Not now. I got a hurt, I gotta figure out what to do."

"What to do? Get a lawyer, that ain't bad advice. You didn't take steriods—"

"Steroids."

"Don't correct me, Lennart W. Gascon, I ain't your wife no more and I can call it anything I want. If you didn't take those things, then you need a lawyer."

"I called Albert Broccoli—"

"Albert Broccoli handled the divorce for me, not for you."

"Thas's what I thought. He did all right for you so I thought he could do all right for me."

"What did he say?"

"He's in Italy on vacation."

"There's more than one lawyer in the world."

They were standing in the foyer next to the table that held the vase full of silk flowers Deanna had bought in a shop off Larimar Square. It was a silly place for an argument because it brought them too close together.

"Deanna Lu, I'm lower than pigshit. I just wanna play football and this shit has me stumped, I got no one to turn to."

"So you turn to the woman you cheated on."

"I never cheated but that once."

"Honey, wasn't a day went by that you weren't sniffing for mushrooms," Deanna said.

"Honey babe—"

"Yeah, it's honey babe time, huh."

He made a clumsy move and held her.

Deanna thought: hard as an oak tree in winter. Damn.

He thought: She's putting on ass and it suits her, she feels like a couple of honeydews under silk.

"Oh, babe—"

She pushed him away. Oak tree or no.

She looked hard at him. "We are a thing of the past, Len. I'm sorry for your trouble but I don't want you messing up my bed covers. I'm not that sorry. You gotta have someone who can help you. You want me to try to get you a lawyer?"

It slapped him in the face. He wiped it off and looked at her. "You got a heart of stone."

"You carved on it enough to know what the material was made of."

"Well, I guess your well is dried up, so I might as well move on."

"You drank too much from it," Deanna said.

"Bitch," Gascon said.

Yes, Deanna thought with a sudden burst of happiness. She was turning into a stone-cold bitch with Lenny Gascon. About time.

CHAPTER 32

THE WOMAN RAN on the rocky shoreline of Lake Michigan. She had started at Belmont harbor and now she was closing in on the Oak Street Beach which is just across the street from the Drake Hotel and two blocks from the Raphael. The man sitting on the green graffiti-slathered bench watched her run. She wore a pink sweat suit and pink jogging shoes. Her hair was pulled back in a pink yarn braid.

When Drover stood up, she slowed down and then stopped. Her fine features were glistening with sweat and her overbite managed a smile.

"You were the man from the National Football League—" Lori Gibbons said. She acted as though she was reminding him, as though any man would ever forget her.

"Lori, I got to talk to you. I went to the apartment where you're staying over with Monica—"

"How did you know where I was?"

"The airline. You're here for an interview on the Tokyo route. Everyone thinks a lot of you, Lori. I mean, at the airline."

Dazzle. Then a frown.

"Why are you here? Is it about Len?"

"You don't listen to the radio?"

"I hate radio and television. I listen to music. Why should I? Was Len in an accident? Is this about Len?"

Drover said, "Sit down."

They shared the public bench. The lake was cold, huge, and heaving like an ocean in an arctic clime at the end of the summer. The rest of the day was beautiful, the kind of weather made for runners.

"Two hours ago they suspended Len. For using steroids," Drover said.

She just looked at him. What was a pleasant little smile puckered into a little frown.

"Then that's why you went to see him that day. You were trying to get something on him. You talked to him about cocaine. Why would you want to do this to him?"

Drover thought about it. Her eyes were hostile with loyalty.

"My name is Drover. I'm not with NFL Security. I told Len that to get him to talk to me. I liked the way he talked. He's an arrogant guy but I think he's on the square. I don't think he took any steroids either, Lori; I think he was set up."

"What do you mean you're not with the NFL?"

"My name is Drover. I do work for a man in Las Vegas. All legal. We think a game is being fixed and it involves getting Len Gascon suspended for a few weeks. That's what happened two hours ago in New York. They announced it."

"Len doesn't do drugs."

"I don't think he does either."

"I don't understand—"

"Steroids. He was given steroids by someone and he didn't know it."

"He loves his body, he wouldn't do anything to harm it."

Drover almost smiled. He thought better of it.

"Who knows Len? I mean, close. Besides you, Lori? Who could get him to take steroids? Someone in the coaching staff. He mentioned taking medication for some hurt or other?"

She tilted her nose exactly the way Lee Remick did it in *The Days of Wine and Roses* when Jack Lemmon got on the elevator. Drover tried not to let it distract him.

"Len doesn't hurt. Len takes a shower after a game. He got taped up once. Len is careful about getting shots. He hates a needle. He said he had a tooth pulled once without Novocain because he couldn't stand a needle."

"Then what about someone else? Close to him?"

The frown made it harder.

"Len has girlfriends, if that's what you mean. I'm not his wife and I don't intend to be. He's sweet and funny and . . . well, he's what I would call beautiful, but I'm not interested in becoming the wife of someone like Len Gascon. He won't settle down until they put him under a headstone in one of those funny graves they have down in Louisiana."

It startled him. He shook his head. He had one picture of Lori Gibbons and Lori Gibbons had just smashed it beyond recognition. Women were constantly amazing him and he thought it must be because he had grown up in the protected environment of the chauvinistic West Side where girlfriends were what you took out on Fridays and wives were for Saturday.

"You think one of them did this to him?" Lori asked.

"I don't know what I think. I think Len got a bum deal. I think this is a setup and it involves sports bets that were put down by someone in Chicago."

"I hate gambling."

"I want to help Len," Drover said.

"Why?"

Her eyes blinked. The question was pure innocence and it came out of a steel trap of a mind.

"I work for a sports book in Las Vegas. We got word that some people in Chicago wanted to fix a game. The Denver and New Orleans game. A game that would have been a sucker bet until Len got his ass in a sling two hours ago."

"Because the Great Forgotten throws like a girl," Lori said.

"I couldn't have put it better."

The overbite now concentrated on worrying the lower lip. She squinted in the sunlight and the fine sheen of sweat on her face put sweat in fashion.

"He dates a girl from Continental, I know that. Her name is Melanie. She's out of Los Angeles."

"Too far. I need a Chicago connection."

Lori stared at him a moment. "There's me."

"That's why I wanted to talk to you."

"I don't do drugs, give drugs, sell drugs, sleep with drugs, dance with drugs."

"The guy told me that."

"What guy?"

"The guy I know at the airline. He said no one can understand why you're a stew and not a brain surgeon."

"Is that supposed to be funny?"

"No. It's a statement of simple adoration."

She smiled then. "I want to live six or seven lives, like a cat. This is one. I travel and meet people I wouldn't meet otherwise. In my next life, I'll cure cancer. Actually, I'd like to play fullback but that's probably beyond the realm of possibility."

"How can you stand Gascon?" It was just curiosity and she frowned before she answered.

"He's pretty. I thought I said that."

"I could do situps," Drover said. "Stop eating meat-loaf."

"No." She touched his cheek. "You're too much of a smart ass. My life only needs one smart ass. That's me."

"That's as nice a turndown as I've ever gotten."

"Oh, you haven't got so many," Lori said.

"Give me some more names, Lori," Drover said.

"If Len got suspended, I have to call him," Lori said, suddenly hiding her overbite with her left hand. "There's going to be no one to help him."

"Lenny isn't going anyplace," Drover said.

But she got up. "No, I've got to run back, I've got to call him—"

"I can give you a ride—"

She smiled. "No thanks, this way is better. For both of us." Another little smile. "I don't think you mean him any harm. I appreciate what you told me." And then she was off, jogging north on the rocks and it was all Drover could do, even in sports coat and white shirt and tie, not to follow her.

Fox said, "Gascon called twenty minutes ago. I said you'd call him back."

"He wants a friend," Drover said. He was standing in his underwear in the room at the Raphael. It was 3:00 P.M. and the perfect Chicago weather was holding. The sun had been shining for six hours in all and many thought it might set a record for most consecutive hours of sunlight in October.

"You got his number?"

"First thing I wrote down in his apartment. How's he doing?"

"Jennifer took the message. This is all going down the way we thought."

"Still puts us out a little cash."

"It's hard to lose one but that's life. There's enough chump money normally bet on Denver to equalize it even with What's His Name in at quarterback. Hope springs, as the philosophers say."

"But a fix is a fix and it smells bad and it hurts the game."

"I don't like it because it hurts business. People lose their confidence in football and then what do we do in autumn, bet hockey?"

"A fate worse than being Canadian."

"What do we do?"

"I put the fear on Tommy Sain. He's going to crack. I'll call Lenny but I can't hold his hand right now. I think I'm too close."

"What about his squeeze?"

"You mean Albert Einstein? She's fine. If she's in this thing and I guessed wrong, I'm going to go straight."

"You liked her, huh?"

"I did offer to adore her the rest of her life, if that's what you mean."

"It must be fun to run up an expense account on me."

"What's the spread on Sunday?"

"Denver is still up by seven."

"Put me down for five dollars. Against."

"I thought you don't gamble."

"This isn't gambling."

"You think Denver is that bad?"

"I think Len Gascon is that good."

"All right. I'll take care of it."

"Call you later."

CHAPTER 33

Pork bellies were up the limit by noon.

Not Tommy Sain.

He was pumped. He called Maggie at the magazine and told her.

"What did you get into?" she said.

"Nothing. A bet. That's all."

"So that's what you did Friday night."

"You accused me of sleeping around and I was in New Orleans."

"Making a bet. A stupid bet. You don't have any bookie around here?"

"A guy used to work on the exchange. I bet with him before."

"You went down to New Orleans to make a bet?"

"It's only an hour-fifty flight."

"Are you insane, Tom?"

"I made a bet."

Pause.

"What kind of trouble are you in, Tom?"

Another pause.

"A guy from the FBI came by."

"Oh God, Tom, what did you do?"

"I didn't do anything. I made a bet."

"The FBI? That's not anything? Are you crazy, Tom?"

"Maggie. I need you."

"You need a psychiatrist."

"Maggie, I didn't do anything."

"A guy from the FBI came to see you and you didn't do anything."

"Maggie, Maggie."

Another pause. Marriages are filled with them. The unspoken places are shared with either pain or joy, nothing in between.

"Baby," Maggie said. "What's this about?"

He told her. Husbands are like that at times. He only told her about the FBI guy and making a bet with Edwin LeClerc. Not about the other stuff. It was enough.

When it was over, she said, "Shit."

"Exactly."

"I don't believe I'm married to a man who is going to get killed by the crime syndicate."

"I don't want to get killed."

"Nobody does, baby."

Pause.

"What can I do?"

"You can call him. He gave you a number."

"I can't do that."

"Why can't you?"

"I got a job. An FBI guy can pull my ticket."

"What are you going to do?"

"I just don't want to do the wrong thing."

Another pause.

She understood. Women who wash dirty underwear, make stew out of leftovers, diet after the second child, kill mice, and smile on rainy days understand.

Maggie said, "What's his number."

CHAPTER 34

DROVER KEPT THE room at the Raphael but took the five o'clock flight to Denver. He took two hours but gained an hour. Airline bookkeeping.

It had snowed for about an hour in Denver. There was slushy white stuff on the streets but it was warm. Someone said the sun shone 324 days a year in Denver and people skied in short sleeves but every football picture shows Mile High Stadium covered in snow. However, those are TV pictures and they can't tell you about warmth or depth. Television was always full of lies, even about games.

Lenny Gascon was a basket case. Agent Pressman had not shown up when Drover knocked on the door of the apartment on the nineteenth floor. Len Gascon showed him in with a boozy step that came from Wild Turkey. It was hard for a hot dog to hide from the media all day on the worst day of his life. Especially when even his sweet-ass wife, which he had had, turned him down.

"Lori said she talked to you in Chicago." He said it as though he was amazed conversations took place out of his presence. "She said she thought you were all right."

"I'm better than you, sport, at the moment."

"There's something about you wants me to deck you."

"I grow on you."

"Fungus grows on things."

"Stuff you learn living in swamps in Louisiana."

"Asshole."

"Perfect."

Drover helped himself at the wet bar this time. Len Gascon looked as though he had already overhelped himself. The phone was still off the hook.

"Make yourself at home."

"Len, I asked you before. Did you do steroids?"

"My coach in college wanted me to beef up. I told him and I will tell you. God gave us these bodies to live in and not to fuck up."

"I believe you. Lori believes you. That's two of us. Unfortunately, there's the NFL."

"Fucking assholes. They fixed the test."

"They do not go out of their way to screw themselves. It does the league no good to draw attention to the recreational habits of its denizens."

"I didn't do nothing. How can I test positive?"

"Someone set you up."

Gascon liked that. He sized up Drover the way a lineman sizes up the next guy he's going to hit. "Like your people? Vegas people?"

Drover saw it.

"You called me, kid, not the other way around."

"This a fix some of you guys are setting up?"

"It's been set up, not by me. Someone set you up. Gave you some steroids. I don't want it any more than you do."

"Is that right? If my agent was here, which he is not, fuck his ass, I would like for him to talk to you."

"I already have an agent. Wrote two books. And I'm too old to play football."

"You are a wise ass."

"That's what Lori said. Or words to that effect."

"You trying to hit on her?"

Drover threw the glass at him.

It missed but that wasn't the point.

Gascon stared at the crazy man.

Drover came over to him and shoved him with both hands into a hand-tooled leather couch that had the Broncos emblem engraved on the skin of an animal. Center cushion.

Drover said, "I got a neck out to here on this and I'm listening to drivel from an asshole? I fly out to Denver for this? I could be in California. It never snows there."

He let it go down. Then: "Okay, asshole, heavy money has gone down in the past couple of weeks, days, on New Orleans over Denver. You are now, officially, out of the game. The Saints are still pros. They show up, put on spandex, flex and groan and punch out your center. You got a limp pussy at quarterback as of eleven o'clock this morning and that's because of your big mouth. You wanted a test and you got it. And someone is going to make money and it isn't me."

"You lied to me, said you was with Security."

"What's the matter, baby, nobody ever tol' you a lie? They tell you that winning for the Gipper was the God's Honest Truth? I told you to watch your ass, didn't I?"

Drover stared through him.

Len looked at his shoes. The ploy had worked in high school when Coach Talbert had chewed him out. Eventually, Coach got tired of looking at the top of his head.

Drover didn't stop staring. Len Gascon looked up. His eyes, widened by Wild Turkey, looked lost.

"I dunno what to do."

"That's because you're twenty-six years old. The only thing you're fit for is to be a grunt in Vietnam except we called off that war."

Softer.

"Gascon, someone gave you that shit."

"I know it."

"Who did it?"

"It wasn't Lori."

"Someone in the training room?"

"I don't take no needles. I got a regular doc, not that quack they got to tape your ribs and tell you it's natural to bleed when you piss."

"Then who did it?"

"I dunno."

"Then you're just fucked."

"Lori wouldn't do this to me."

"I believe you. Her. Who else you sleeping with?"

"I don't cheat on her."

Drover laughed out loud. "You were born cheating. Your life is like the centerfold of the *National Enquirer*."

"I dated around. When Lori was out of town."

"Who you date?"

Len shook his head. "A gentleman doesn't tell."

"I told you, you're not a gentleman, you're an asshole."

That did it.

Gascon came off the couch.

Drover clipped him. It was a right to the jaw as the ringside announcer would say. Drover had help from a half bottle of Wild Turkey being turned into carbohydrates and empty calories in Gascon's liver but it was a nice punch.

Gascon sat back down on the couch, aided by the thrust of the punch. His mouth had a little blood on the lips, about what you would expect after a football game. Gascon didn't take notice of that, only the punch.

"You hit me."

"Is that what you say to Dan Hampton?"

Gascon grinned. "Exactly. When ole Dan'l hit me, I was shocked. I told him so."

"I bet he apologized and lit candles for you."

"He said he would."

"So will I. Now tell me about it."

"I got nothin' to tell. I don't do drugs. Ask Lori. I'm set up by people or things I don' even understand."

"You wouldn't understand Tinkertoys. You know about steroids?"

"Yes, I know about steroids and I know nobody gave me no needles."

"It's not just needles. You can ingest them."

"You mean eat?"

"I mean eat."

"I dunno."

"I got a plane to catch."

"I did know this girl, one or two nights, Melanie."

"Who else?"

"It wouldn't be right to say."

"Gascon, you perfect asshole, nothing right now is right."

"I'm thinking. Been thinking all day."

"I bet it's the first time since second grade."

"I got a degree."

"Monkeys get a degree when they can throw footballs."

"Linemen too."

Pause.

"Girlfriend of my wife's. Ex-wife."

"Who?"

"Frances. Frances Downes."

"Who is she?"

"Model. Back east."

"What is back east to you?"

"Chicago. Also New York." He said it proudly, like wearing a graduation cap.

Drover stared into his skull.

"Couple or three times. Maybe a couple of other times."

"Frances Downes."

"Models are real skinny. My wife is skinny but don't show skinny. Thas's what she said. She's developed. She looks good."

"Frances."

"My wife. Shows good."

"Frances live with you?"

"Naw. Couple of nights. She's a health nut."

"She jog on your bed?"

"You are a first-class—"

"Why'd you call her a health nut?"

"I eat eggs for breakfast, always have, she had to have her Wheaties. Brought over a box. From the airport. Brought them all the way from Chicago, like we don't have Wheaties here."

"You are driving me crazy."

"Good."

"Where's the cereal?"

That puzzled Gascon for a moment and then he got up from the couch, went behind the wet bar full of whiskey, and produced the box.

"I always thought I might be on the box. Like Walter Payton. I tried them. They taste good."

Drover sifted the crisp cereal.

"You call these Wheaties?"

"Breakfast of Champions."

"What's this?"

"Thas's Wheaties."

"That ain't Wheaties, champ. Those little brown things aren't Wheaties."

"They aren't?"

"You never had Wheaties?"

"Po' ole coonasses, we never had nothin'."

"Shit," said Drover to himself. Frances Downes from Chicago.

CHAPTER 35

THE COMMISSIONER LOOKED at the pug-nosed security man for a long time in silence after the security man finished.

October rain was in mourning over the biggest city in America and it washed down all the narrow streets between the immense buildings until they were ready to be shined by a late afternoon sun.

"So this Drover, who works for Fox Vernon's book in Las Vegas, this Drover wanted to know who told me to test Lenny Gascon? Is that it?"

"That's it."

"I won't even ask you how he has a line to you."

"You can ask, boss. You know and I know that we like to stay in touch with Vegas, to see what the action is, to see if maybe we're getting sucker-punched or someone on our side is selling out. You know and I know what the realities are. What I'm saying is, before the announcement, I got a call from Drover who thought something bad was going down. This was more than a suspension. He wanted to know who put the bird in your ear."

"We don't do that."

"I know, sir."

Thunder applauded the magnificent storm and clouds lost the tops of several skyscrapers. The planes were still descending on LaGuardia by that usual route that took them down the Hudson and across the Bronx, avoiding the noise-sensitive heart of Manhattan where only taxicabs and buses were allowed to make noise.

"Who is Drover?"

"He was a sportswriter in Los Angeles. Originally out of Chicago. He got busted out of the racket for consorting."

"Is he in the mob?"

"No. Not that I know of. But he consorts."

"Why would he be so interested in Gascon that he called you even before we made the results known?"

"I get uneasy." The security man's name was O'Malley. He had been a cop in New York before this. "There were rumors about Gascon before you called for the tests. I checked with Partridge at the Broncs. He confirmed he had heard the rumors as well and had talked to Gascon last week. Wednesday. I called around. I talked to a sportswriter in Denver named Baumann and we sort of traded, back and forth, and Baumann said he had heard rumors. Baumann said he hadn't believed them at the time and didn't believe the results of our tests."

"Were the tests flawed?"

"No, sir. A man's reputation was at stake. Absolutely positive in steroids."

"Could someone have given him an injection without his knowing it?"

"Denver got the word, same as other teams got the word a long time ago. They want to do the crime, they got to do the time. Steroids are a no-no. The team trainer is hip to what the word is. No. Denver is a clean machine and it doesn't seem likely, any of it, does it?"

"Not when you tell me what you just told me. You should have told me a while ago."

"I should have maybe. But what would have made the difference?"

"I might have held off for a day or two."

"He still tested for steroids."

"But was he set up?"

"I checked three books in Vegas. Not Fox Vernon's. There's money down on New Orleans but there has been, just as there's money down on the Bears against Denver. But it just doesn't seem like enough money to want to fix a game by taking out the best spear chucker in the country."

"Money. With twenty-five, twenty-six billion changing hands even a fraction of the action on one game is enough to make me nervous. Illegally? I don't like anything about this, not one thing."

"Sir."

The commissioner looked at O'Malley and saw the unstated question.

"A man I met at a party. I even forgot his name, he was introduced to me. He works in the stock market or something in Chicago. That's all I can tell you."

"Sir."

"Go ahead."

"Can you describe him?"

"What are we doing, O'Malley. Investigating ourselves? Or me?"

"No, sir. The point is, we should never be afraid to look the thing in the eye. Maybe you were being set up."

"Me? I'm the commissioner."

"Like you said, billions out there. Even if it's a small time set up, the guys behind it could easily take five or six or seven million out of fixing one game, that's enough money to fix anything."

"One game would hurt us."

"There're rumors all the time. The zebras are fixing it, the quarterback dropped that ball because the spread was important, all kinds of things. Hundreds of players, all of them babies, baby millionaires with bad habits and bad girls around them. In a few cases, bad boys. This is a very volatile situation. I can be discreet.''

"I'm not saying anything against you.''

"I know, sir. But it unsettles me for this Drover to ask me about Gascon before it comes out. Why is an investigator for a book wondering? I asked around. He was out there, this Drover, in Denver last week, wanting to snoop around. I get this from Baumann, it was a trade-out, this Drover was asking about weak links on the Denver team. Baumann told him about the talk that Gascon had with his GM and it was about the same thing. Drugs. Only everyone was asking about cocaine and it turned out steroids. I doubled back on Gascon. He looks like a clean boy. He never had trouble in college unless it was women, he knocked up an English teacher.''

"He did? He was in college?''

O'Malley grinned. "I guess it works both ways, the profs want the girls in the front row and maybe a lady prof wants the guy in the back row.''

"I've heard about Gascon and the ladies. Funny thing is, I know someone he knows. Girl is a model named Frances Downes. I should tell you, I know her boyfriend, the guy who gave me the word on Gascon. His name is Bart Brixton, trader in Chicago. I wasn't going to tell you. Met him through Frances at a charity thing Saturday. You said Drover was from Chicago?''

"Chicago. And Frances Downes? She introduced you to a guy who gives you a word that turns out to be a good tip? And this girl knows Gascon in Denver? How did she know Gascon?''

"She knew Gascon's wife. Ex-wife. They're both models. Not that big a business, I guess, everyone knows everyone.''

O'Malley was studying the commissioner the way he

used to study burglars in the interview room. Sometimes you let the silence speak for themselves.

The commissioner saw it as he unfolded it and he saw how it looked to O'Malley. The trouble with cops is that they have this attitude and even if you didn't do anything wrong, you're probably still guilty of something. That's the way they look at you.

"I see what you're thinking," the commissioner said finally to break the silence.

"I'm not thinking, just letting it fall into place. The trouble is that we have suspended Gascon. So if we go into this further, we find out that Gascon was possibly, only remotely possible, possibly set up by someone, the fact is, Gascon still took steroids whether he wanted to or not. We start going back on our test results and the player's union is going to jump through that hole with both feet; they don't want testing in the first place. And there're all kinds of liabilities we could be getting into."

O'Malley stopped his thinking out loud long enough to light a cigarette. The commissioner didn't smoke, no one in New York smoked anymore, but O'Malley was still a cop in the Bronx, thinking out loud in the interview room with a burglar sitting across the desk from him. He had forgotten himself and the commissioner let him.

"The trouble is with this Drover. If Drover is close enough to be going to Denver to sniff around and calling me for a favor, then he's too close. If Drover finds the fix and we don't, we might be in worse shape than before."

"So what are we going to do?"

"I gotta get close to Drover. I think that's the thing to do. Pally-wally with him. I got to know what his next jump is," O'Malley said. "Maybe we can work something out but I've got to have your okay on this."

"Work what out?"

O'Malley blew smoke. "Figure out something. Some way to keep the test and stop the fix."

"But if there is a fix, it involves Gascon. The Broncs would have murdered the Saints with Gascon."

"Yeah. Now they got a quarterback who throws like a girl."

"So the Saints are going to dump on them."

O'Malley smiled. "On any given Sunday, any NFL team can beat any other."

There was nothing to say. That kind of shit was on a plaque on the wall.

CHAPTER 36

BART BRIXTON KNEW what he had to do. Not that he shrank from it but it was a significant thing, this killing of another person. Someone you know. Someone you can figure to a tee.

He carried the pistol in his briefcase.

The perfect Chicago Tuesday had lingered and people in the Loop were congratulating each other on the weather. Nice day, isn't it? Stuff like that.

The girls in sneakers and business suits were walking north toward home. White buses were fouling the air with diesel fumes and the Loop bars were filling with out-of-work workers. It was five and that was the time most Chicago people quit work, both the peasants who had started at eight and the bosses who had started at ten.

Bart Brixton took a cab north. The address was on Cleveland Street, in a section of the Lincoln Park neighborhood where six-flats were routinely turned into twin eight-hundred-thousand-dollar town houses and women shopped for Pampers in Mercedes 300s.

It was a lot easier since Maggie had walked out on Tommy Sain. The town house would be empty and it could all be handled as quickly as possible and with as little muss as possible.

Bart Brixton was sure he could kill someone. Not that he ever had but he was an expert marksman, he had scored very well in the shooting gallery on Mannheim in Stone Park. He knew it was a matter of just squeezing the trigger and letting the machine do the work. There was no point in threatening Tommy. Tommy was half-crazy about this FBI guy. He had babbled to him all afternoon and he was seeing shadows where none existed. FBI guy. Maybe there was an FBI guy, maybe he ought to watch out himself.

The cab stopped a block short of Tommy's town house. The street was deserted, although it was only six in the evening. The light was gone and the orange anticrime lights were peeking through the bare branches of trees in the parkway.

If there was an FBI guy, he might be watching the town house. Shit.

Bart Brixton went into the Four Farthings tavern on the corner of Cleveland and Dickens and dropped a quarter in the pay phone. The place was too loud for Tuesday and brittle bits of conversation fell here and there.

"Yeah?"

"Tommy? It's me. I'm at the Farthings."

"Okay. I'm coming down."

Click.

Bart wiped his forehead. To his surprise, he was sweating though the evening was cool. It wasn't the same thing as a shooting gallery, of course. A shooting gallery wasn't flesh and bones and blood.

He stepped outside and felt relief as the breeze kissed him.

A shooting gallery.

Why was he sweating? Well, that was just adrenaline. This thing had gone too far not to carry through. He would have to carry it through. Besides, there would be, what, five or six million coming back to him alone? He had all of Tommy's markers, all the bets put down in Tommy's name.

Shit. If he killed Tommy, the books would refuse to pay. They don't give money to widows or good friends like Bart Brixton. He hadn't thought of that.

Tommy Sain came across Lincoln Avenue, dodging a CTA bus in the process. The tavern was full of nurses from the hospital down the street as well as people like Bart Brixton. It was Tommy's local.

"I didn't expect to see you," Tommy said. "Is there anything wrong?"

Yes. Everything in the world, you shitless wonder, Bart Brixton thought. I got to deal with dummies like you and Frances Downes, no wonder the Japanese are beating us. His briefcase weighed seventy-five pounds at least. That gun was rattling around in the papers and it couldn't go off. Not for three weeks at least, until the game was over and they had collected. Tommy Sain was a lucky son of a bitch and he didn't even know it in that moment.

"Nothing's wrong," Bart said, and gave him a con man's smile. "Nothing could be righter than two bachelors batching it on a good night to get laid." And he slapped his old buddy on the back as they went inside.

CHAPTER 37

DROVER CALLED FOX. They were rarely more than six hours apart when Drover was really working for him.

"I got a call from O'Malley at NFL Security. He wants to talk to you. I got a number." He gave it to Drover.

"I got Lenny. I'm at Stapleton. I'm flying back to Chicago."

"This is really costing me."

"You want me to stop?"

"What did Lenny say?"

"I sent you some cereal by Federal Express."

"I don't want any cereal."

"There's a woman named Frances Downes, a model in Chicago, who was a friend of Deanna Gascon when the Gascons were a couple. Naturally, Len wanted to hit on her. After the divorce, Frances let herself be hit on. I thought that was appropriate. Anyway, Len says she's a health nut down to bringing in her own cereal. Her own cereal, she takes it to a guy's apartment where he's going to screw her."

"Odd. I've heard of odder things. There was that woman who had a baby and didn't even know she was pregnant. How can you not know you're pregnant?"

"Ignorance. Something lacking in her sex education courses. Maybe she had the measles when they were being told about that. Maybe the teacher didn't know. To get back to this: I want you to get a lab to tell me what the stuff is. It is not what is on the label on the box. I think it's the source of Lenny's steroids.''

"In cereal?''

"You can put the stuff in anything. Go test it and call me in Chicago.''

"When do I get it?''

"Fed Ex tomorrow morning.''

"All right.''

"At this rate, no one is going to ever make another football bet.''

"You know much about hockey?''

"It involves street fighting on figure skates, I think,'' Drover said.

"Later.''

Kelly said, "Nancy is taking a nap. She's getting on okay. She's funny, I like her, we bet the lottery together. She's says I'm lucky.''

"You're something, all right. Don't bother her, I'll call you later. I'll be in Chicago tonight, staying at the Raphael Hotel.'' He gave Kelly a number. "I got names, I need faces, I think this thing can be over by Thursday.''

"She was counting on Wednesday night,'' Kelly said.

Drover paused.

"She told you that?''

"Not in words. In my years as a fire fighter, I learned about people.''

"I trust your judgment. Any bad signs around?''

"I haven't seen anything. I've got my people keeping their eyes open.''

"Give my whatever to Nancy.''

"Love,'' Kelly said. "That's what we call it.''

CHAPTER 38

FRANCES DOWNES HAD her own place, a condo on East Lake Shore Drive, and it wasn't all that usual for her to show up at Bart's apartment, especially late on a weekday evening. She was shaking bad when Bart opened the door.

He took her inside and she wanted to be hugged.

"Why are you shaking, honey?"

He led her into the white-on-black living room. She wore jeans from Gloria and no perfume. She was on the verge of something and Bart thought she was coming down off a high and needed a boost to get back on the roller coaster. But it wasn't that.

"A man named Drover," she said. "He said he was from a sports betting service in Las Vegas and he scared me, Bart, he really scared me. He came to my place at nine. He said he was from the FBI. That's when I flushed the stuff down the toilet."

"I gave you two bags."

"What was I going to do? If he was from the FBI, what was I going to do? He could have sent me to prison."

"He said he was from the FBI?"

"He showed me a card. There was a crazy name on it."

"Cleaver," Bart Brixton said.

Her eyes went wide. "You know him. He's talked to you, too?"

"I know about him. You said he isn't from the FBI."

"He said his real name was Drover and he said he worked for the Fox Vernon Sports Service in Las Vegas. He said I gave steroids to Len. To Lenny. He knows, for God's sake, he knows."

"Honey, honey, you're just a little up. Let me get you something."

He got her a drink and two small green pills. The drink and the pills went down and in a little while she wasn't shaking but her eyes still looked haunted.

"You told me to take that cereal."

"I knew he didn't eat cereal, he'd eat cereal with you. He said in an interview he ate eggs every day for breakfast. So you gave him some muscle builders. Not much. Won't hurt him. But it stays in your system a long time."

"You said it wouldn't hurt him," she repeated.

"What did I just say? He isn't hurt. In four weeks, he'll be back good as new. I think Denver is going to win the Super Bowl. But they're gonna lose their ass to the Saints."

"We fixed a football game."

"So what? You just realized that?"

She had realized it before but it was clearer now with a man named Cleaver or Drover saying she was part of a conspiracy and there were a lot of people who were going to get hurt.

"You didn't tell him about me?"

"I didn't tell him about anything. You think I was going to admit I gave Len Gascon some tainted cereal?"

"It wasn't tainted, it had steroids in it. Not the same thing."

"What could he do to me?"

"Did he threaten you?"

"Yes."

"What did he say?"

"He said there were bad people who did not like to get taken, not even by a pretty girl."

"Then what did you say?"

"I said I didn't know what he was talking about. Then he said, did I know Tom Sain. Just like that. I didn't know what to say. I said I didn't know him. He said that was funny, that Tom Sain said he knew me. Then I said I had met him. Met him at a party. I said he was a married man. He said he knew that, said that he had talked to Maggie Sain and that Tom Sain was out drinking with his buddy Bart Brixton."

"Shit. Double shit."

"He said this, I didn't say anything."

"You stupid cunt."

"I didn't say anything to him."

"You just sat there and let him do the talking. He say anything else?"

"He said there were laws about conspiracy."

"He said that?"

"He said the real FBI might be calling some day and that they wouldn't be polite."

"He said that?" Bart was saying it over and over and he couldn't help it.

"I was scared. He scared me bad, especially when he talked about the bad people."

"He talked about the bad people a lot?"

"Just a little."

"He doesn't have any standing. Whoever he is, he isn't a G-man."

"I'm scared."

"I know you are. Here, let me get you something."

She did it in the bathroom. She came out glittering, a million-dollar baby, her eyes gleaming. She felt a lot better.

Bart sat there, deciding. The guy was working on his

own, he was trying to set something up but what could he set up?

On the other hand, there might very well be Outfit guys who would be out to get him if they knew about the fix. And he was stuck being nursemaid to Tommy Sain because all the bet slips were in Sain's hand.

And now Frances was about to come undone. That would not do at all.

"Honey, I feel a lot better."

Yeah. And that will last until the next time you come down.

"A lot better. Thanks."

"You could thank me."

She slipped off her jeans. She wasn't wearing underwear. This must be a date.

Later, she said, "I got a six o'clock wake-up."

"You want to sleep here?"

"No. I got my clothes and everything."

"You want some candy to take with you?"

"Yes, please."

"Only don't shoot it down the toilet every time you get jumpy. Put it in a safe place."

"I'm sorry, honey," she said. "You know I'm sorry."

"Sure, Frances."

She caught a cab and he stood at the window, watching the yellow car drive away, waiting to understand something. Frances was second-rate, so was Tommy, they'd end up putting him in a box. If he could see some way, but there might be no way at all.

And then he thought of something and it made him smile.

Drover. He connected all these loose cannons rolling around. If there was no Drover, there was no comeback to Bart Brixton. Frances could stop being scared and so could Tommy Sain. All he had to do was take care of one problem.

It was dead perfect, absolutely, positively. Dead. Certain.

CHAPTER 39

NANCY HARRINGTON WASHED glasses left over from lunch. Kelly was at the far end of the bar, writing checks on a sheaf of bills. The place was empty and quiet; it was the middle of Wednesday afternoon on another routinely, boringly perfect day in Santa Cruz.

"You want anything, Kelly?"

"Just a glass of soda, Nancy."

She brought it down to him and stood next to him for a moment. "I really appreciate all this, Kelly, I really do."

Kelly looked up with mild, puzzled eyes. "You mean a job? Nancy, the hardest part of running a joint is finding anyone who wants to work. And after you find someone who wants to work, you gotta teach them to wash their hands before they make hamburgers and basic things like you pour into a glass at the open end."

"I mean, when I called Drover last week and you answered—"

"Wouldn't you do the same thing?"

"I just mean . . . it's hard to say thanks if you haven't learned how."

Kelly said, "If you keep embarrassing me, I might have to have a drink. Make it V.O. and soda, a child's portion."

She smiled and started down the bar to the bottles.

And saw him.

He had opened the door and shoved it behind him. They heard the bolt slide home.

"You bastard," she said in a very quiet voice, and Kelly stared at the apparition. It was Slim Dingo and he held a .45 Colt automatic in his left hand. Kelly pushed his stool back and stood up. "This a stickup?"

"No. More in the nature of taking back my property. You are my property, Nancy, I thought we had that all worked out last week."

She stood absolutely still in the middle of the bar. Her face was white with rage and fear.

"It's Wednesday and I been waiting for your boyfriend but I got things to do. I figure it was best to take the bull by the horns. You comin', Nancy."

"You the guy did that to her?"

"Your name is Kelly, ain't it? She's stickin' closer to you than bees to honey. I figure you been pokin' her on the side. She likes gettin' poked, all kinds of things. Come on here, Nancy, we got a long trip ahead of us."

"Stay right there, Nancy."

Slim Dingo stared right through Kelly. "You think I won't shoot you? Shit, I done worse. Besides, I got a federal immunity and I can do just about what I want, so don't think I won't shoot you if that's the way it's gotta be."

"Stay right there, Nancy."

She turned then and looked at Black Kelly. She saw his hand disappear under the bar and she knew what he was going to do.

"He'll shoot you, Kelly, don't do anything."

"I seen guys like him all my life. He shoots me with that thing and it'll be the last thing he ever does in his life." This was as flat as a desert skyline. Kelly's voice hadn't changed, nothing had changed, but there was something behind the voice and the eyes turned cold blue that commanded the room. He brought up the bar. It was a regular fire department crowbar, called a Halligan bar, used to smash windows in burning buildings and pull down smoldering siding from houses. They had given it to him in mock ceremonies after he took his medical retirement from the Chicago Fire Department. It was plated in fourteen-karat gold.

"You wanna shoot me?" Kelly said. He got around the bar now and stood ten feet from Slim Dingo. "You got the guts for it? You turn around and walk and don't ever come near this lady again. I should just brain you on principle. Didn't your mama ever teach you not to strike a lady? Or didn't you have a mama?"

Slim Dingo said, "You want to bluff it out? I been playing poker for a living for a long time."

"Put the gun down."

"I think you're bluff."

Kelly took another step.

Slim held the gun higher.

And Nancy threw the bottle of V.O. across the bar. It struck his arm.

Slim turned and Kelly took two more steps and slapped his shoulder with the crowbar, breaking the collarbone in one blow.

Slim Dingo was not bluffing.

The horse killer discharged and the slug caught Kelly high in the chest, spinning him around against the bar. The shock of the gunshot filled the place and they all could smell the smoke.

Kelly never said a word. He brought the crowbar around and smashed Slim Dingo's good left hand, the one that held the pistol. The gun clattered on the wooden floor and Slim Dingo had to cry out, either from the pain of a moment before or because he knew what was going to happen next.

Blood covered Kelly's massive chest and streaked his face but the eyes were part of another machine, absolutely inhuman.

Kelly hit Slim Dingo in the face with the crowbar and broke his nose and jaw and hit him again across the head and Slim was suddenly on his knees, barely conscious, not understanding where all the pain was coming from.

"Kelly, Kelly, don't—"

She might have been talking to the ocean.

Kelly was over him and the next crowbar blow fell on the top of his head, splitting the skull. Slim's eyes rolled up and he crashed forward, smashing his nose on the floorboards. Kelly wanted to hit him again but he felt very weak in that moment, the rage gone and there was a bullet hole in his body. That was it. Someone had shot him exactly like Davey McCarthy got shot by a sniper on the North Side that time while they were fighting a two-eleven in a rooming house. Davey went down and didn't even know he'd been shot until the cops told him. Exactly like that.

"Kelly," she cried.

He turned to look at her. A dreamy smile came over his face. He was still standing but not for long.

"You wasted a whole bottle of V.O.," he said, trying to make a joke that would explain to her that he didn't feel a thing. But she didn't laugh and it was time for him to go to sleep, so he dropped the crowbar and started to explain something, something about Davey McCarthy or someone, and then it was time to go to bed because they might be called out to fight a big one because . . .

CHAPTER 40

O'MALLEY SAID THE League was buying and Drover said he always wanted to be corrupted by an official from the NFL. They had known each other for three years and strictly on an informational basis.

O'Malley had a cop's faint sense of superiority when dealing with a civilian who was probably a known associate of people in the criminal element. But if the NFL was buying, Drover was taking. It amused him for some reason. Drover amused him. Given a different scene, where he was a real cop still, he would have laughed putting scum like Drover in the chair.

It was noon Wednesday. O'Malley ordered the famous clam chowder in the Coq d'Or room of the Drake and Drover followed suit, adding a bacon, lettuce, and tomato sandwich to go with the bottle of Heineken's.

"You suddenly develop an appetite?"

"When you've come to the end of a case, it hits you like that." He was smiling because O'Malley didn't quite get it all yet and because he was seeing his way clear to do a good thing. He knew O'Malley, knew all of those cops in all of the alleys, watching him on the roof of the movie house.

O'Malley said, for the second time, "There's no way the commissioner could have anything to do with that."

"There's a first time for everything."

"Gascon tested positive for steroids."

"Because he was given them."

"So you say."

"As of twenty minutes ago, so I know. Fox has got the evidence."

O'Malley frowned some more. "I like your conspiracy but it has holes all over it."

"Talk to the ladies. Talk to Tommy Sain's wife. I did. She confirmed a lot of stuff I was getting from more suspicious types. She's a good lady. And she's not involved in this thing. Talk to Frances Downes. That's the commissioner's old girlfriend. She also likes to fuck quarterbacks and she gave the steroids to Gascon. You like that connection? Commissioner's girlfriend fixed football game. Headline news. The commissioner didn't do anything but he wouldn't last ten minutes in office after that one."

"You're trying to blackmail the NFL."

"Sure."

"Why?"

"Don't be an asshole, O'Malley."

"If you know something and we know, then that's two too many know."

"They were trying to fix the New Orleans game."

"Sure, but what you're proposing goes back on every principle the league set down."

"The league's principles are important to me," Drover said. "I pray for the commissioner before I go to bed every night. But in this case, a kid named Gascon got sidewindered. And a lot of books are holding a lot of bets that shouldn't be there."

"That's what you care about."

"Don't say it with that cop sneer. I don't need it. I don't even need you, O'Malley, I'm trying to do you a favor.

You drop a dime on your commissioner and tell him the reality of the world.''

''And who's gonna know?''

''Me. Fox.''

''We can't make deals with gamblers.''

''I don't gamble. I watch sport. That's the fun of my job.''

''This is real bad stuff you're asking me.''

''I didn't fix anything, O'Malley. I did your work for you. I gave you names. The commish was used, you were used, the league was used, and that quarterback was used. If I got to call Dusty Baumann at the *Rocky Mountain News* or Kyle Coleman at *The Denver Post,* I'll give them a sports story that would cover page one even if Russia started World War Three the same day.''

''I gotta have time to talk to him.''

''You want another beer?'' the waiter said.

Drover smiled. ''Yes. He's buying.''

O'Malley said, ''You know I got no authority. The league can't back down on a drug test, it would send out the wrong kind of message—''

''Okay, let's cut this deal then. You suspend him this week and the commish calls him into Four-ten Park Avenue to have a heart-to-heart. After the publicized chat, the commish says that though the test results were confirmed, Gascon was the victim of something or other, to do with getting his back straightened out in the off-season and that the commish is convinced that Len Gascon never, ever intentionally took steroids and the suspension has been lifted. Give him a lie test, he'll pass it. See how it works?''

''That can't happen.''

''Look, stranger things have happened. Remember the birthday cake for the ayatollah? Life in these Unites States is constantly being hilarious and this is just another anecdote.''

"What about this conspiracy? This guy Bart Brixton?"

"Who am I going to report him to? The FBI? Bart Brixton gets away with it along with his girlfriend Frances and his boyfriend Tommy Sain. Don't worry, the integrity of the great game remains unchanged. You have to trust me on that. I hate to let this Bart Brixton guy go but, what the hell, he's going to lose his shirt at the books when Gascon is told he can play in the New Orleans game."

O'Malley thought about it.

"I gotta drop a dime," O'Malley conceded. "I don't know if it'll fly."

The soup arrived.

CHAPTER 41

"CALL THE NUMBER."

"Maggie called him."

"I want you to call the number and don't tell me about your fucking wife."

"So I'll call. Don't call Maggie my fucking wife."

"I didn't mean that. I meant, don't bring your wife into this. You were crazy to make her call him."

"I didn't make her do anything. She called him."

"Because you gave her a number."

"You had me hanging out there. The threat is against me, not against you."

"There isn't any threat. This is a two-bit operator for a sports book. He wants to scare you."

"So he scared me."

"Look at me, Tommy." Tom looked. "Be scared."

After three rings, a girl answered. "This is Patricia."

"This is Tom Sain. I got to talk to the man."

"You can reach him at area three-one-two," and then she recited the number of the Raphael.

Tom hung up. Bart dialed the number. After two rings, he heard, "Raphael Hotel, good afternoon."

"I want to talk to Mr. Drover."

"Just a moment."

There were three rings.

"Yeah?"

"This is Bart Brixton."

Pause. Brixton smiled at that. The bastard never expected a call.

"What can I do for you?"

"Let's get together."

"That sounds like fun. Do I have to bring a date?"

"No. Just you and me."

"That sounds kinky."

Bart smiled. He liked the cool voice. It matched his own.

"You've been bad-mouthing me around the city, I was wondering why?"

"Everything connects to you. Mrs. Sain told me about you and your dating Frances Downes and it just looks so good about you. By the way, I like the way you set up the commissioner at that charity party in New York. That was a neat touch."

"Listen, phones have listeners. Let's chat, shall we?"

"Sure."

"You like to meet me?"

"I'd like nothing better. I'm waiting for a call."

"You meet me tonight down by Cafe Brauer. We can take a walk, look at the water."

"I know the café. In Lincoln Park. They reopened it?"

"Oh sure."

"They did, huh?"

"Oh sure."

"Seven."

"That suits me. Sooner the better."

Bart Brixton replaced the receiver. "I'm going to meet him."

"Why are you going to do that?"

Bart looked at Tommy. "I'm gonna waste him."

"You're what?"

"Tommy. This is five or six million. This is world war. I don't have time for weak sisters."

"You can't just kill someone."

Bart thought about that. "Yes I can."

"You're going to kill him in Lincoln Park?"

"Not the first time things like this happen."

"Bart, I've known you ten years."

"So what? I put you in a deal and you put me in the wringer. I'm not going to let it go down the toilet."

"I didn't mean to do anything—"

"You're a piece of shit, you know that? Your wife knows that. She has to do your laundry."

"Don't talk about Maggie."

"This is money. You fixed a football game in the NFL."

"I made bets."

"I want the slips."

"Why?"

"Because I want them. I don't want you running to the G about this. You're pussy, they put you in prison and you'd wear a dress. How'd you like to wear a dress for some big nigger?"

"I don't have to take this."

Bart hit him. In the belly and low. Tommy wanted to throw up but then he didn't. Bart hit him again.

"What do you think this is about?"

"That hurt."

Bart hit him again.

This time Tommy Sain threw up on Bart's rug.

"Now clean it up."

He moaned.

Bart hit him again.

"Don't hit me again."

"Then stop being a smart boy. Start doing what I tell you. Get me the slips."

Tommy said, "What if I don't?"

"Then I whack you, that's what if you don't."

"You're my friend."

"I'm my friend, Tommy. You can go along but you can't take it when it turns. You're a fucking gambler junkie. I took you along for a payoff and you don't have the guts."

"I don't want to kill anyone. Not over anything."

"You get me those slips by six. Right in my hand. All of them. And then I take care of this shit from Vegas and you and I can be friends again. You understand how it is?"

"I didn't think—"

"No, you didn't. Did not think. You are shit to me, friend. You get those slips and you and I can be buddies again and we'll have a few pops and see some secretaries and screw around. This is over in three weeks, Tommy." Softer. "Can't you stand prosperity? We got money coming."

"Not over money, not to kill someone."

"You really want to go to prison? You really got a secret wish to be a white boy in prison? You know what they would make you do?"

"How can you talk about killing someone?"

Bart grinned. It was easy.

"What d'ya want to do? Buy him off? You think this guy would buy off if we split with him?"

Tommy stared. "All right, Bart, you said it. You want to kill someone over a bet."

"Happens all the time."

"What is this macho shit? You been seeing too many movies or something? You don't go around killing people over a bet. Over some money."

"This is millions; millions of dollars is more than some money. What do we do every day of our lives? In our straight jobs? Straight jobs? We buy and sell on someone else's miseries. When farmers lose their hogs to swine fever or some such shit, we go a new crop of bellies, and the greedy hayseeds see they can make more money in the next market by raising more pork. And we know their hayseed minds so we short out on the next crop of pork bellies and the farmers sit around in their Grange halls or whatever and say, 'Duh, the assholes in Chicago took us again and we got too many pigs that got to be slaughtered and we won't get our price.'

"It's the way of the world, Tommy, I got to explain it to you at this late date? One man's misery is another man's fortune. We took the chumps in your book and we take the mob in their books. We win, Tommy. We drive Mercedeses and we have car phones and snow candy and girls to go down on us. That's how you count the winners."

"It isn't enough to kill for."

This was hopeless. Bart thought about hitting him again. Tommy's streak of sudden morality was taking too much time. Bart decided. Tommy was shaking inside and it showed in his scared eyes. Imagine running to his bitch wife to help him. That was weak, real weak. The con came over those dull green eyes and he nodded slowly, as though he had been thinking about it.

"All right. Maybe you're right."

Pause. They could both hear Tommy breathing.

"Maybe we can buy him with chump change. Maybe give him twenty-five thousand to forget it."

"Why wouldn't he? I mean, that's a lot of money and I never saw a bookie yet wouldn't screw his own mother for the juice," Tommy said. He felt better. Not good but better.

"I got to meet him at the Cafe Brauer."

"Okay, why don't I come along?"

Bart stared at him. Yeah. Why not? He saw all the sides of it in that moment and he thought it was just as well.

Too bad about Tommy but maybe it had to be this way, maybe it had to be this way from the beginning of things. When he killed this guy Drover, Tommy'd be scared right back into line.

CHAPTER 42

O'MALLEY SAID, "HE'LL go for it. He doesn't like it but he'll go for it."

"You call Gascon?"

"We talked to his agent. His agent was right there in the commissioner's office. He was going to sue, he was going to go on television and denounce the NFL, I forget whether he was going to do that before or after he sued. He sues and Gascon just pays. That's the way it works, huh?"

Drover said, "Then I can get out of here. I'm sick of hotel rooms."

"Yeah, I know. I travel too much. I wish I could be in Florida all winter instead of places we play most of our football. I mean, Chicago, Minneapolis, fucking Cleveland. Cleveland is colder than a witch's tit, I can't even imagine summer there."

"So you call Gascon for a chitchat and Gascon says blah-blah and he gets to play after Sunday's game which means he goes against New Orleans. I did what I was supposed to do." It amazed Drover at that moment, to think it was over.

"Your medal will be in the mail."

"Okay, cop. You did your cop thing. Now go back to New York and beat your wife or roll a drunk or whatever it is you do best."

"If we weren't sitting in this lobby, I might just show you what I do best."

"Isn't that usually handled in the men's room? In the stalls? I don't know but I'm sure you do."

"A wise asshole. You need a favor, you can whistle Dixie next time."

"As long as I don't have to whistle you. The trouble is, everything is a big favor with you, O'Malley. You take and take. A book, a guy in business, legit, like Fox, he's scum to you because he makes more money than you do and he doesn't have to pay you off to do it. The next time I need a favor, I'll know right where to come. Because you owe me, O'Malley, now and forever, for saving your precious fucking football league from a scandal. And don't threaten me, not ever. I haven't been scared since the first time I saw *Frankenstein*. And that only lasted until I figured out anyone who couldn't outrun the monster deserved to get strangled."

"Buy your own beer next time."

"I will."

Lori Gibbons.

He was packed and ready to check out. A stroll in Lincoln Park and then he was flying home to Santa Cruz. It was just three there now. He might surprise Nancy Harrington with flowers. Or something.

And there was Lori Gibbons.

She wore her attendant's uniform, the one with the striped blouse and striped skirt that must have been designed by the same guy who makes prison matron's wear. Still, she looked quite edible to Drover.

"You're leaving—"

"It's over. Did you see Len Gascon?"

"It's over?"

"Gascon did have steroids but it was a mistake, someone else's mistake. He was set up. The NFL is going to make it right. Why did you come here?''

''To see you.''

''Why?''

''I thought about it.''

''About what?''

''About one smart ass in my life being enough. I thought about it when I called Len and he was drunk. Do you drink?''

''Every goddamned day, as Patton might say.''

''Do you drink to excess? Len was drunk, he was so sorry for himself.''

''I don't get sorry for myself.''

''That's a lie. Men are always sorry for themselves.''

''And women are always there to laugh at their hurties.''

''You like this all the time?''

''So you thought there might be just an itsy-bitsy inch of room for a second smart ass?'' Drover said.

''You always do that? Jump ahead in conversation? Don't you give a girl a chance? I had a speech in my head.''

''Will this be platonic or the other kind?''

''Are you married?''

''No.''

''Why?''

''I was a bum for a long time, living the newspaper life. I saw too many guys who were married, except it was their wives who were married. I didn't want that. I don't need a wifey at home and my mom was the only mom I ever wanted.''

''You probably think I'm a nut.''

''Only about health.''

''How many sit-ups a day did you promise me?''

''What do you want? A hundred? Two? Name the price.''

"Two hundred."

"Are you worth it?"

"I'm flying to Denver tonight."

"I have to fly to Santa Cruz. There's a friend there who's hurt."

"Oh, I'm sorry." Lori said, "A woman?"

"Yes."

"How did she get hurt?"

"A man beat her up."

"That's terrible. What are you going to do?"

"Find the man, I guess. And beat him up for a change."

"Do you always do this? I mean, are you a rent-a-knight?"

"Money can't buy me, Lori. Only soft words from pretty women."

"What about not-so-pretty women?"

"I never saw one I didn't like."

She smiled that nice overbite smile at that. And kissed him. "I've got to go, my taxi is waiting."

"You do things like this? On the spur of the moment?"

"What better time?" she said, and kissed him again and let him feel the weight of her against him and make him realize that inside that prison matron's uniform was a real, live woman.

CHAPTER 43

NANCY WAS BEYOND tears. She had been beyond tears when Johno killed himself. Tragedy that strikes again and again does more than numb the heart; it makes the pain seem a permanent condition of being.

The cops came first and then the federal men and they were talking to her and she was saying things but she didn't know what she was doing. She wanted to call Drover but there was no time at first.

The ambulance raced up the hill to the little hospital and the helicopter came a half hour later all the way down from San Francisco. It was very serious.

But it wasn't fatal yet.

When she had thrown the bottle, Slim Dingo was on the verge of firing. The shot was just that much off. It had struck Kelly's massive chest above the heart and pierced the lung. This was going to be a serious operation.

She wanted to go to him but the federal agents had detained her and said they would take her to San Francisco later, that they wanted to know about her and her relationship with Slim Dingo. One of the federal men was named Goran. He was obnoxious. He kept asking her about her old life, singing in the Vegas saloons, and how she was part of the environment and how Johno was into the mob and the mob killed him and why she slept around.

And this Goran finally asked her about sleeping with

Slim Dingo on that weekend long ago, the weekend she had given herself to save Johno from his gambling debt. That's when the numb went out of her and was replaced with something else.

"You bastards, you fucking cops are all the same, you're all assholes," Nancy said. "That man saved my life, he stepped in front of a gun. That . . . Dingo . . . that bastard. He beat me, he beat me bad last week and he told me he was going to keep doing it and Kelly and Drover took me in. Dingo raped me."

Goran said, "You can tell the difference between rape and ordinary screwing still, Nancy?"

"You are really scum."

"No, that's you, Nancy. The scum that knows itself. You and your husband, Johno Harrington. And your friend Drover, how many did you give him? And Kelly? All of you and you put the whack on Slim Dingo so he couldn't testify against you and your great pals in the mob. Well, we got a lot out of Slim Dingo and that will go a long way and you're not going to be very popular with us from now on, you and this Drover and your friend Kelly, if your friend makes it which I seriously doubt anyway. If it was up to me, we would have left that face on the barroom floor."

"You don't get it, I was beaten and raped by Slim Dingo."

"And you had to give him back the money you stole from him."

Nancy stared at Goran. And then she began to memorize him. She stared with her mouth open and her swollen eyes were a haunted testimonial to the pain and outrage suddenly filling the numb places.

"You. You. The FBI. Drover said it. He said he couldn't figure out how Slim knew about the money. You told him. You picked Drover up in Chicago and you wanted the money. To give to your snitch, Slim Dingo. He was wired for you and working for you. You let Slim Dingo know where I lived and you let him come to my house and nearly beat me to death and rape me and you didn't care because Slim was more important to you than people.''

"People like you, Nancy, a slut saloon singer.''

"I had a voice. You got no right—''

"You wanna sing for us now, Nancy? You can sing for us and we'll listen. About your friends and about what really went down today, how you set up the hit on Dingo.''

"Slim Dingo walked into Kelly's and said I had to go with him, he said he would kill Kelly if he tried to stop him. He was crazy, you could see his eyes, the way he talked slow. And Kelly came around the bar with that crowbar, I didn't even know it was there. Kelly told him to get out and Slim Dingo shot him and before he went down, Kelly hit him. I wish to God you'd have been there too and Kelly could have whacked you, a real bastard like you.''

"Okay, Nancy, you want to play it tough, play it tough. We could make it easy on you or not so easy.''

"I want to make call.''

"You want to call your lawyer?''

"None of your business who I want to call.''

"Is it long distance?''

"Listen in. That's all you guys know how to do is listen to other people's conversations.''

"Sure.'' Goran got up, suddenly tiring of it. "Give her a phone, Reilly. We gotta respect her rights at least until we slam the gate on her.''

And Nancy dialed the 800 number.

CHAPTER 44

"MR. DROVER? TELEPHONE."

He had just checked out. He picked up the phone on the side of the lobby.

"Shit on fans time," Fox Vernon said. "Your friend Kelly whacked a guy."

"Kelly doesn't even carry a gun."

"He used a crowbar."

Sometimes your mind goes black, just for a second. When the picture was restored, the colors were gone. Just black and white now.

"Nancy."

"Nancy made the call to our special number. I'm sending down a lawyer from San Francisco, you remember Chappie?"

"What's going on?"

"Kelly was shot. By Slim Dingo. He's in surgery and Nancy is under arrest for conspiracy to commit murder. It seems the G suggested that Kelly and Nancy lured Slim Dingo into that place by the sea and whacked him on behalf of the crime syndicate. It couldn't happen that way, could it?"

"Kelly? Are you serious? With a crowbar? In his own place in the middle of the afternoon? What's got into the G out there, they've been reading comic books?"

"That's what I thought," Fox said. "Is the matter in Chicago resolved?"

"Gascon is going to be reinstated after Sunday. The other thing, well, there's not that much I can do. I'm not going to turn in a gambling book on the stock exchange, I have my principles. And Gascon is going to beat shit out of the Saints so you ought to be able to get your lines evened out, you've got over two weeks."

"What about Tony Rolls?"

"I'll take care of it."

"You were going to tell him about the book on the exchange."

"I thought about it. But Tony is temperamental. This doesn't involve killing. I've got to work something else out."

"What can you work out?"

"I'm like Lord Byron, waiting for Chillon to inspire me."

"I don't read poetry. It doesn't go anyplace."

"What about Kelly? Is Kelly going to make it?"

"They say he's fairly strong. I got this from a friend of mine at the hospital. I don't know."

"I've got the eight o'clock to SFX. I was going to surprise them."

Fox Vernon said, "I guess you resolved this, Drover, in a half-ass way."

"Everything is half-ass," Drover said. "I thought Slim Dingo was a remote chance. Just remote. I told Black to watch her and he watched her too good. Slim Dingo was a one-hundred-to-one shot coming there. I mean, where did he know where to go? I mean, it's like going to Nancy's house in Anaheim in the first place—"

"Hundred-to-ones win. Especially when they have help."

Again, it all went black. And then it came up on the screen and this time the picture was back in color.

"The G."

"Nancy said they told her that Slim was wired."

"And those clowns in Chicago wanted Slim's money back for him to keep him happy. When I sent it to Kelly instead, the G put a watch on me. On me going to Nancy's house. On the whole thing. Only now they let Slim get his own money and Slim went out and beat her and Slim knew she had gone with us . . . Christ, I did this to Nancy. And Kelly. I put them in this with my cute idea to steal this asshole's money and give her a stake."

"Is that all this was?"

"Favor for a favor."

"That was very foolish, Jimmy."

"I act the fool now and then."

"My man should get Nancy sprung in the morning. If not, you know where she is." He gave Drover telephone numbers and the name of the hospital.

"Drover."

"What?"

"You saved a game. If the fix had worked this time, there would have been a next time. Count on it. If the Outfit wanted to know about the stock exchange book, it probably was that they wanted to know how it would work, a good fix, and put it in themselves."

"That occurred to me."

"Watch yourself until you get on the plane. Chicago. Bang-bang, Al Capone."

"Good night, Foxer. Thanks about helping Nancy."

CHAPTER 45

LINCOLN PARK WAS full of bare trees and patches of brown grass. The park is along the North Side lakefront of Chicago and it is wet on one side and contained by high rises on the other. It was early in the evening but it was dark. Kids skateboarded on the concrete along the North Avenue beach boathouse. There was the usual mix of lovers and muggers and cops who rested their behinds on three-wheel motorcycles. The Brauer was an old café, recently restored, and there were enough people around it to make it unlonely.

Drover didn't care. He had his gym bag in hand and Nancy in his thoughts. And his friend Kelly. When you know someone for only five years, and you meet closer toward the middle of your life, you count it for more. Kelly was in critical condition because of something Drover asked him to do. And Nancy, poor unlucky Nancy Harrington, was in jail because of all the men she had ever known in her life.

The only good thing was Slim Dingo. He wouldn't be squeezing juice out of rocks anymore. In a way, despite what happened afterward, Drover felt good about hitting him that way in Tony Rolls's palace in River Forest.

He knew Bart Brixton without knowing before what he would look like. They both wore trench coats because of the wind off the lake. Tommy Sain and Bart Brixton, but you could have told a Bart Brixton in any crowd. The arrogance was barely in check.

"Let's walk and talk."

"Sure. I left my raincoat home, I forgot how early winter can come."

"Yeah," Tommy said. He was being agreeable and seemed just as nervous as he had that day on the exchange.

Bart said, "The thing is, we got a good deal set up."

"I know. You used that model, Frances Downes, to set up Gascon with steroids. And you used Tommy here to lay off the bets. The problem is, you bet on the wrong team, Bart. You bet on New Orleans. New Orleans doesn't stand a chance."

Bart stopped. "That's where you're wrong."

"The Saints can lick the Broncs because they don't have a quarterback," Tommy Sain explained.

Drover smiled in the dark. The trees filtered the streetlamps and here it was light and here it was dark. They all listened to the sound of the lake. It was gentle now but it filled their ears. They were north of the café. Across the way, a lion in the old zoo roared and it transformed the shadows and made them menacing. Imagine a lion roaring in a city park.

"We want to offer you twenty-five dimes in cash for you to say nothing."

"You got the money?"

"I got the money."

"On you?"

"On me."

"How do you carry around that much money in a park like this? I could whistle up a mugger like that if I told him you were that set up."

"You don't believe me?"

"I don't believe you," Drover said.

Bart took out the small pistol. "I guess I can't fool you."

"Bart," Tommy said.

"Shut the fuck up." Very quietly. "The trouble is, Drover, Mr. Drover, Mr. Stick My Fucking Nose in Business Drover, is that you are an even bigger pain in the ass than Tommy and we are going to have a hemorrhoid cure right now."

Drover thought about Kelly. What would Kelly do? But now they both knew what Kelly would do and that would always be a thing that they knew about each other, the time Kelly did the knight errant without knowing about it and beat a bad man to death. Drover knew he wasn't a hero because he had been in Vietnam and been scared shitless in the jungle for thirteen months. Guns scared him. Like now.

They were standing in a dark thicket and they could hear the lion roaring again and the sound of the heaving lake and smell the breeze and feel the cold on their cheeks.

Drover said, "I already spilled it. To the NFL. They're going to reinstate Gascon after Sunday. He's going to play in the Saints game after all. And you guys put it all on the Saints. I hope you have big savings accounts to pay off your customers in Tommy's book."

"You're lying," Bart said.

"Look at me, Bart. You know lies when you read them. That makes you a good trader. I know lies too. O'Malley with NFL security. You put steroids in the cereal that Frances brought along in her health nut bullshit to Gascon. And Gascon shared. Gascon's fingerprints are on the cereal box. Also Frances's. We got a lab in Vegas to analyze the wheat flakes. Steroids can be disguised and there were steroids in there, amidst the Wheaties."

"You got the box?" Bart was truly amazed. "You son of a bitch, you got the fucking box?"

"And I win the prize, right?"

"What are we going to do, Bart. There're millions we're going to have to pay off—"

Bart looked at him.

"You. You're going to have to pay off, Tommy. You ran the book, not me."

"Bart—"

"You made the bets, not me. You wanted to keep the fucking bets slips, well, I got them in my pocket and you can have them back. I'll just drop them on you when we get finished."

"Finished with what?" Drover said.

"What do you think? You screwed me, buddy, but now your screwing days are over. And poor Tommy, he made all those bets and he won't be able to cover his own customers when Denver makes mincemeat out of the Saints in two weeks. I'm sorry, Tommy. I'm sorry you killed yourself. It happens. But we still kill this guy."

Bart meant it. Drover saw he meant it. He thought of a prayer he used to say in Vietnam when the fight was full of death and the night was full of fire, in the time when you could not think at all;

God help me stand it.

"You don't kill no one," Vin said.

"Who are you?"

"The fuck is asking? The fuck you are? Put that pea-shooter down and your hands behind your fucking head."

"The fuck you saying?"

Vin put a Colt Python .357 Magnum in Bart's right ear. "You fuckin' can hear with one ear, can't you?"

Bart dropped the pistol on the brown grass and stood very still.

Vin lowered the piece. "You, asshole, and you, ass-hole, and you, asshole, come over here."

The three assholes did as they were told.

The van was parked at the curb and Tony Rolls sat like an ominous Buddha in his wheelchair in the back of it. There was a driver with no name and sunglasses.

"Get in," Vin said to Drover.

Drover climbed inside and Vin closed the sliding door.

There was a pencil's worth of light in the darkness and that was all.

"You wasn't gonna tell me."

"I wasn't gonna tell you," Drover said.

"We had a bargain."

"It wasn't worth dying over."

"You think it's better you die?"

"I took care of the thing."

"I hear that Gascon is coming back."

"How'd you hear that?"

"They got phones in Vegas. The commissioner's office doesn't fart in the toilet room that we don't know."

"That was the fix."

"And it was those two assholes?"

"Those two assholes, as you put it so well. Tell Vin to stop calling me an asshole, I'm not in the same category."

"So we gotta whack you, Drover."

"That's the second time tonight someone has talked whack to me. The word is overused in our society. How about just beat up."

"Slim Dingo, that cocksucker, he was a government wire."

"Someone was."

"You were right about that. That is one I owe you."

"Then let's call it square and go home."

"You disappoint me. You were letting those guys off, is that it?"

"They bet against the Broncs because they fixed the game. I unfixed it. They stole the money from their customers. They are not only going to lose at the books where

they placed their bets but they are going to have to come
up with an awful lot of money to cover their own customers. Money is a good punisher, especially to guys like
them.''

"How'd they do the fix?''

"So I tell you and you try it out some time.''

"I told you that day in California, I believe in letting
well enough alone. The game works, people bet on it, we
don't try to fix something that ain't broke.''

"So don't fix something that ain't broke," Drover said.
Tony Rolls thought about it.

"I'd like to whack them anyway," he said.

"They've whacked themselves.''

A long silence.

And then the El train chuckle of Tony Rolls.

"Yeah. I like that. They outfoxed themselves.''

"That's it.''

"You're all right, Drover, it's too bad you stayed
straight. You could of been made in Chicago.''

"I'm not Sicilian.''

"Hey, we had guys wasn't Sicilian. That dago shit is
for New York, Chicago is an open town. We had Murray
the Hump, lots of guys.''

"Okay, equal opportunity employer, I understand. But
the thing is, I don't go that way.''

"No.'' A long pause in the darkness of the van. "You
go a lost way. Your friend, this guy Kelly, this was a stand-
up guy.''

"Was?''

"Oh no, I mean, is. He's out of the surgery. We were
watching the action. My cousin in San Francisco tole me
all about it.''

"You got a big family.''

"The biggest.''

"Don't whack nobody, Tony. Go home and think kind thoughts."

"What are you going to do about getting Dingo's money?"

"I guess I can't."

"So you did all this for nothing?"

"It happens."

"Okay. I'll let the chumps go and tell them they stop playing around with things they don't understand. Put the fear on them. Is that okay by you?"

"Tony, put the fear on them."

"Get out then. Vin, tell those bright boys to get their ass in here."

"What about him?"

Vin looked at Drover.

Drover looked at Vin.

Tony Rolls rumbled it out.

"He wants you to stop calling him an asshole, so stop doing it. You call him Mr. Drover, like he was a friend of mine."

CHAPTER 46

IT TURNED OUT that Maggie Sain and Nancy Harrington ended up with something in common, even though they would never know each other. They both found their husbands in the same room of their homes in the same condition. Tommy Sain had figured and figured and the numbers weren't there. He had committed the ultimate sin of a bookie: He had held the bets instead of laying them off and settling for 10 percent juice. He had used the money from his illegal "football futures" pool to bet it all on a dead certain long shot—New Orleans over Denver. Now he would have to pay it back out of his own hide and he had figured that he could do it if he stripped his savings, sold Maggie's Miata as well as the town house on Cleveland Street and lived on Maggie's salary—and charity—for the next three years. And lived with Maggie's contempt because, no matter what, she would never have left him.

So he had to leave her.

Not that he didn't try. He went to Bart just before and asked for a big loan to cover the upcoming losses and Bart had smiled that con man's smile and said, "You know about dangling in the wind? You are the danglee, Tommy. It was your book, it was you who collected, it is you who are paying off." And Tommy knew it was true and that Bart had won again, made him the chump again.

He mailed the long letter detailing the scheme to the

local office of the Federal Bureau of Investigation and included Bart's name many times and enclosed betting slips. If he had to leave Maggie, he'd make Bart Brixton the danglee designate.

He thought about it for a glazed moment before pulling the trigger. He had handled all the bets and the bet slips were in his name. Bookies only paid to the man who put down the bet and the name on all the slips was Tommy Sain. Win, lose, or draw, Bart had been out of it until the moment Tommy mailed the letter to the FBI. How would Bart get out of it? Tommy Sain had been found with a smile on his shattered face because the last thought he had was that—no matter what—Bart Brixton would have to hold the bag. It was dead certain and it would break Bart into little pieces.

CHAPTER 47

THE USUALS AT Kelly's emporium put up paper sham-
rocks on the bar mirror and called it Saint Patrick's Day,
even though it was early November. Kelly came back in
a wheelchair, which was supposed to be temporary. He
had dropped forty pounds in the hospital and looked better for it. His face was pale but his eyes were burning
and that meant he was really alive, not just faking it.

Drover pushed the chair down the pier, exactly as he
had done for Tony Rolls. Fox Vernon said the lines all
over the Vegas books were clear of suspicion. In New
York City, Gascon and the commissioner did a press
conference of profound blather that puzzled sportswriters for days.

Deep gloom set in in New Orleans. Belle Fontaine
said to Drover on the phone, "Y'all might wear out
your welcome if folks was to know that you had anything to do with getting Gascon off the tin roof."

"Belle, I thought Gascon was a coonass good ole boy
from Loosiana."

"Shit, could of waited til New Orleans kicked the Broncos' ass."

Nancy was behind the bar, serving green beer, and
Charlie was slicing corned beef in the kitchen. "Welcome
home," Nancy said to Kelly.

"My dear," he said. "V.O. and soda, child's portion."

It was a good time because friendship is so precious in a lonely world that such parties transcend mere partying and become part of religion or philosophy or something in that range.

Charges against Kelly and Nancy were all dropped because they were so ridiculous. Something else ridiculous happened. Nancy said she would keep on working for Kelly if that was all right. It certainly was. Nancy and Kelly shared silences on some slow afternoons that made Drover turn his eyes away. Nancy didn't move in with Kelly but she got a place in the town and they could talk to each other as if they had known each other all their lives.

The best friend, Drover decided with a smile, was getting the girl.

The cash came by Federal Express three weeks later, even after the New Orleans game. The amount was exactly the amount that Drover had cheated from Slim Dingo in that card game. He never figured out how they had gotten it—although it wasn't so hard to figure. One of the Texas boys had simply driven over to the ranch, picked the lock, rifled the safe, and driven away. The FBI didn't arrive at the ranch until two days after Slim was killed. They had no reason to.

The FBI was reasonably satisfied.

Slim Dingo had been pushing it too much and he might have been an embarrassment to SOG, as the FBI headquarters on Pennsylvania Avenue in Washington is called. Embarrassment to the agency (Seat of Government) is considered slightly more serious than World War III inside the FBI.

Besides, there had been two wired men in that poker game.

Joe Camp was still making music for Jose Jiminez and Gordon Hathaway.

CHAPTER 48

THEIR SEATS IN the Louisiana Superdome on Poydras
Street just north of downtown could not be considered
flashy. They were up high in the immense chamber but
there are just about no bad sight lines in this "weird ware-
house of sports memorabilia," as one of the *Times-
Picayune* writers had put it.

Put it nicely.

Len Gascon and the Orange Invincibles proved the Rozelle rule that Sunday afternoon and Drover and Lori Gibbons saw it all from the roof of the arena. Sixty thousand
stunned spectators saw Lenny Gascon not know how to
throw the football.

He threw it so often to the men wearing the gold fleur-
de-lis that someone suggested he was color blind or trying
to get good seats for the Mardi Gras.

The amazement washed across the country; the best
team in the country was getting beat. No, hell, it was
beating itself.

Gascon looked across the line at Chambers, the Stickum
man with the hands the size of baseball mitts, and said
hello to him and asked him if he had a nice day and wasn't
New Orleans a fun party town and, excuse me, Chambers,
I have to throw this ball away over by the sidelines where
New Orleans players like to congregate.

At the half, the Broncos were down, 21–6, and the Saints' locker room was as stunned as the Broncos'.

"What's wrong with Len?" Lori said.

"I thought you were going to be concerned with me from now on," Drover said, "I bought you the popcorn."

"But you put salt on it. Salt is bad for you."

"Salt is good for you. Saltpeter is bad for you."

She gave him that smile, the one they use on train engines to light up the way through tunnels.

"I can't believe he's doing this badly."

"Any given Sunday. The mighty do fall. It couldn't happen to a nicer guy."

"I know you don't like Len but you—"

"He'll grow up. Today is a learning experience. That's what we call it when shit hits the fan."

"Don't say shit."

"If you weren't a terrific you-know-what, I would tell you what to do with your advice."

"But I am. A terrific you-know-what."

"Never seen better."

She studied his profile in the third quarter. He watched the spots of the game the way some people watch pool. It was angles mixed with brawn, muscles mixed with mathematics. Len came back but now the team was dispirited. It happens, especially when a sure thing comes up.

"You're frowning."

"Chambers is thrown off. He's running the wrong patterns because he can't trust Gascon. When you start losing faith, you start dropping the ball."

"What happened?"

"Gascon threw the team off and now they're panicking."

"Don't you wish you were doing what you did? Writing about it?"

Then he looked at her. The eyes were blank places in his face and Lori bit her under lip.

They watched the game until the Forgotten Quarterback was brought in in the fourth quarter to complete Gascon's humiliation.

They made love in the long, slow time of Sunday afternoon, in a bed so soft they felt like babies in it. Lori was beautiful through and through and smelled like a woman who had lived her whole life drinking buttermilk and chewing buttercups. Drover chewed on her and licked her and when he lay in her lap, feeling her against his belly and between his legs, and when she moaned—when he could get that moan of satisfaction and feel her lips and the edge of her teeth on his neck—it was the most beautiful time in the world and it wouldn't last forever, the way it was supposed to.

And long after, she said, "Write me a story."

"What story?"

"About the game."

"I don't write stories anymore."

"Write me a story, just for me."

"I don't have a typewriter."

"Just tell me."

She stared into his soul and she was naked next to him. He saw the good thing coming out of her eyes and pouring into him.

He lay back on the sheets and closed his eyes.

He saw the words.

They came from left to right.

He saw the words and opened his mouth.

"Immortality comes from God and the Broncos come from Denver."

She giggled.

He smiled.

"All right: Because Len Gascon became confused over who his friends are—he is a Loosiana boy, after all—his Denver buddies, especially Charles Chambers, decided to turn their backs on him."

She giggled again.

"All right, all right: Len Gascon confuses the offense in the first half with erratic pass play and that caused the second half as the New Orleans Saints surprised the Denver Broncos, thirty-one to nine. Sunday."

And then he went on in a slow voice that saw words in his head, exactly as he once saw them at a typewriter in a press box. The words were simple and the sentences were direct and they were not mocking of the effort of the athletes but tried to explain the failure of the Broncos and the success of the Saints that particular afternoon. When he was done, his eyes were still closed and she bent over him and kissed him.

And then she saw his eyes were probably wet.

AUTHOR'S NOTE

Sports and gambling are mixed up with each other. Sometimes it is illegal, like the fix of the 1919 World Series by a bunch of White Sox players. Sometimes it is as legal as a sports book in Las Vegas where hundreds of thousands in wagers go down every Sunday in football season. This novel reflects both sides of the coin toss.

In betting parlance, a "dollar" is $100. A "couple of dollars" is $200. A "nickel" is $500. A "dime" is $1,000 (in an older parlance, $1,000 is also a "grand").

Sports gambling is legal only in Nevada. Sports gambling here refers to such games as football, basketball, and baseball. Horse and dog racing are not sports in this parlance. Dissemination of sports gambling information is not illegal, however; that is why daily newspapers carry the Las Vegas "line" on football and basketball games, to make betting easier, even if it is illegal to use the information. Freedom of speech is a wonderful thing and it helps to sell newspapers and TV commercials—in case you thought those point spreads articulated on the NFL *Today* pregame show were filler.

Oregon was the first state outside Nevada to make a version of sports gambling legal by the introduction of a "lottery" on pro football games based on the Las Vegas line. It is a straight rip-off of the wildly illegal "parlay card" that kids have sold in city saloons for decades.

Reference is also made to a common method of betting on state lottery numbers—reference to alleged codes found in newspaper comic strips, "dream books" (which numerically interpret dreams), and crossword puzzle clues. This is the voodoo side of gambling and has its adherents. If it didn't, states wouldn't be in the lottery business. I don't do lotteries but I watch people who do them every day with the glazed amazement I have for veteran bingo players and people who relax by throwing heavy balls in bowling alleys.

Bookie, book, and bookmaker all refer to a person who keeps "book" on illegal bets and accepts them. His profit is called "juice" or "vig" or "vigorish" and is typically 10 percent of a bet. The best books are not gamblers but they lay off the bets with other books or syndicates of books so that the winners and losers on a given game bet are roughly equal—the difference being the 10 percent profit that accrues to the bookie.

Organized crime—the loose amalgam of "families" or "outfits" that grew out of illegal gangs first formed to import and make illegal booze during Prohibition—is deeply involved in sports gambling. This does not mean that every book, legal and illegal, is part of a national crime conspiracy. It merely means that the "outfit" is a fact of gambling life.

The Internal Revenue Service estimates that more than $25 billion is bet illegally every year and that none of this money is taxed. Legally, around $2 billion taxed dollars are bet on sports events. The most popular betting event is the NCAA "Final Four" each spring; the second most popular event is the Super Bowl. The popularity of these events in the gambling environment reflects the general popularity of them among people who merely watch sports for the fun of it.

Finally, the National Football League has always kept up informal contacts with the sports betting community to watch for unusual gambling actions that might mean a game is fixed. And, starting in 1989, the NFL has instituted a routine policy of testing ten to twenty players per team at random for drugs and steroids.

These facts are reflected in *Drover*.

Bill Granger

GRITTY, SUSPENSEFUL NOVELS
BY MASTER STORYTELLERS
FROM AVON BOOKS

OUT ON THE CUTTING EDGE
by Lawrence Block
70993-7/$4.95 US/$5.95 Can
"Exceptional...A whale of a knockout punch to the solar plexus."
New York Daily News

FORCE OF NATURE
by Stephen Solomita
70949-X/$4.95 US/$5.95 Can
"Powerful and relentlessly engaging...Tension at a riveting peak" *Publishers Weekly*

A TWIST OF THE KNIFE
by Stephen Solomita
70997-X/$4.95 US/$5.95 Can
"A sizzler...Wambaugh and Caunitz had better look out"
Associated Press

BLACK CHERRY BLUES
by James Lee Burke
71204-0/$4.95 US/$5.95 Can
"Remarkable...A terrific story...The plot crackles with events and suspense...Not to be missed!"
Los Angeles Times Book Review